The Summer House

Center Point
Large Print

Also by Hannah McKinnon and available from Center Point Large Print:

Mystic Summer

This Large Print Book carries the Seal of Approval of N.A.V.H.

The *Summer House*

Hannah McKinnon

CENTER POINT LARGE PRINT
THORNDIKE, MAINE

This Center Point Large Print edition
is published in the year 2017 by arrangement with
Atria Books, a division of Simon & Schuster, Inc.

The text of this Large Print edition is unabridged.
In other aspects, this book may vary
from the original edition.
Printed in the United States of America
on permanent paper.
Set in 16-point Times New Roman type.

ISBN: 978-1-68324-480-6

Library of Congress Cataloging-in-Publication Data

Names: McKinnon, Hannah Roberts, author.
Title: The summer house / Hannah McKinnon.
Description: Center Point Large Print edition. | Thorndike, Maine :
    Center Point Large Print, 2017.
Identifiers: LCCN 2017019755 | ISBN 9781683244806
    (hardcover : alk. paper)
Subjects: LCSH: Life change events—Fiction. | Family secrets—
    Fiction. | Adult children—Fiction. | Domestic fiction. | Large type
    books. | BISAC: FICTION / Contemporary Women. | FICTION /
    Family Life. | FICTION / Literary.
Classification: LCC PS3613.C5638 S86 2017b | DDC 813/.6—dc23
LC record available at https://lccn.loc.gov/2017019755

For my grandparents,
Marjorie Varcoe and Seth Coughlin,
who lived the good stories
and also lived to tell them.

To family,
both the ones you're born into
and the ones you make.

In all their visceral, love worn,
patched-up glory.
As my grandmother liked to say,
"We're all survivors."

Clem

Something was not right. Throughout the night, driving spring rains had battered against the windowpanes, and flashes of lightning illuminated their bedroom in tumultuous bursts. But now the house was eerily silent. Turning over, she reached for the alarm clock on her bedside table: 7:15. She'd never get the kids ready for the school bus on time. Groaning, she slid back beneath the warmth of the down comforter.

Outside, the morning light was gauzy. The storm, having dissipated, had given way to slender fingertips of sunlight that stretched across the hardwood floors of her bedroom. Clem turned and pressed her palm to Ben's empty pillow, still creased from where his head had lain. He must've risen early and gone for a run, which surprised her. The Darby case, which had consumed him for the last several weeks, was finally going to trial next week. They'd barely held a conversation outside of household business and the kids because when Ben arrived home, which was almost always late, he was depleted—something Clem understood. This was the way things were before a big trial, but she still missed him—the simple rituals of filling him in on George and Maddy's days while he stood at the bathroom sink brushing his teeth before bed, or curling up on the couch together with Thai takeout on a Friday night. Ben seemed just beyond her reach. Which was why she was both taken aback and suddenly aroused when he'd crawled into bed sometime after midnight and pulled her up against him. They'd made love hungrily, like they had not done in some time, and it had filled her limbs with a loose, sweet relief that had led to a dreamless sleep so deep she hadn't heard the remnants of the storm. Or Ben when he'd apparently risen that morning. She pressed her nose to the cool surface of his pillowcase and inhaled contentedly.

From the hall came the sudden patter of footsteps, and Maddy peeked around the door. "Morning, baby," Clem said, pulling the covers aside. George would be in his own bed down the hall, still blanketed in slumber. But not Maddy. She scuttled across the toile duvet like a little animal, all tangled hair and elbows and kneecaps as she tumbled up and over Clem until they were nose to nose.

"Pancakes?" she whispered.

Downstairs, the new coffeemaker burped and spit. It was a hulking stainless-steel contraption, and Clem was in love with it. The newly renovated kitchen of their Cambridge house positively hummed, and Clem would not apologize for the contentment she found in the cool stainless-steel glint of her Viking range and the marble countertops. It was not about the quantifiable substance of the chef-grade haven. Rather, it was the familial refuge she made there: rolling out pastry dough with the kids or plucking a bottle of wine from the rack to pour into her grandmother's Old Galway Claret glasses when friends gathered for one of her casual, leisurely dinners. In this kitchen, she nourished the people she loved most, and from that, she fed herself.

Clem had known this was *their house* since that windy autumn day they'd driven by on the way to a doctor's appointment when she was newly pregnant with George. They were lost and late, and she was annoyed with Ben for taking what he had promised her was a shortcut through Cambridge's perplexing street network. She'd squealed at first sight of the old Victorian row house, causing Ben to stomp the brakes and pull over, after which she dragged him up the front stoop to peer into the empty first-floor windows.

"This is it," she'd breathed. Ben had shaken his head, but she'd felt it just as certainly she would soon feel that unborn baby shifting inside her womb. Eight years and another child later, it was finally renovated. The warm honey-hued hardwoods complemented the understated gray-and-white palette she'd chosen alongside their

Newton designer, with whom Ben had joked about the kitchen, "As long as Clem's happy . . . and saves me whatever she whips up in here when I finally limp home from the office." He'd been right; it was the heart of their home, in the heart of their tiny Boston neighborhood. And Clem had never been happier.

Now she stood at the churning coffeemaker, mug poised in midair. "Slower than a wet week," she mused.

"But it stopped raining," Maddy replied around a mouthful of pancake. The kids sat at the kitchen island, in differing stages of school-readiness. A glob of syrup dropped onto Maddy's purple skirt. George grimaced and handed her a napkin.

"I know, baby. It's just an expression."

The empty lunchboxes gaped at her from the countertop like two hungry mouths. She riffled through the fridge, grabbing American cheese, bread, and two apples. They were out of yogurt.

"Can you pack me some chips?" George asked, coming to inspect her progress. His breath smelled like toothpaste. Clem planted a kiss on his neatly combed hair.

"Sure, but eat the fruit first."

Maddy considered this. "I like to save my fruit for later."

"You mean for the squirrels," George said.

"Not true!" Maddy protested. Then, emphatically, "I save it for the birds."

"Fruit first," Clem repeated to both of them as she tossed a small bag of chips into each lunchbox. She glanced at the wall clock. Five minutes until the bus. "Maddy, finish your pancake. And go brush your teeth!" She grabbed George's sticky plate and set it in the sink.

The smell of Ethiopian Yirgacheffe filled the kitchen. Clem quickly filled her coffee mug and then filled one for Ben, setting it aside on the island. He was late, and she silently willed him to make it home before the bus came. Maddy didn't like to leave for school without saying good-bye to her daddy first. And Clem hadn't had enough coffee to navigate a tantrum this early in the day.

"Shoes!" she called, filling their thermoses. What was she forgetting? She checked the calendar over the small kitchen desk that Ben had dubbed her "command center." It was strewn with bills and school projects. She squinted at the calendar. *George—Home Game: 4:00.* And there, in red pen below it: *Kids—Dentist: 4:15.*

"Shit," she muttered under her breath. She'd have to reschedule. Again. She was one reschedule away from having to change dentists all together. Hell, they were probably hoping she would. But she hadn't known that he'd have a game when she'd made the appointment, and Ben was one of the coaches. Coaching George's team was about the only thing Ben managed to leave the office early for.

"George," she called into the foyer. "I'm picking you up after school for soccer. It's a game day."

"Okay, Mom. But I'll need a note. And my uniform."

"Shit," she muttered under her breath again, as she recalled seeing his blue-and-white uniform rolled up in the back of the SUV. "Maddy, did you put on shoes?"

Maddy appeared in the doorway in a pair of strappy yellow wedge sandals, a hand-me-down pair from a neighbor that Clem had deemed the "ankle breakers."

"No, sorry. Not for school," Clem said.

Maddy crossed her arms.

Clem tossed back her coffee. This was a battle she'd have to wage, and win, in the next three minutes. "Come on, your Mary Janes are in your cubby." She grabbed the lunchboxes and thermoses from the counter. "I'll help you."

"Mary Jane is ugly," Maddy mumbled.

Clem tried to stifle her laugh. "Come sit."

Maddy plopped obediently on the antique hall bench but tucked her feet beneath her where Clem could not reach them. Clem wrestled one foot out and pried a scuffed wedge off. By now Ben should not only have come home from his run but be showered and downstairs to help her ferry everyone out to the bus stop. Where *was* he?

Outside, she heard the crunch of tires in the pea-gravel drive. It couldn't be the bus, which pulled up to the curb. But she didn't have time to look to see who it was.

"Hey, Mom," George said, peering out the front door, "is Mrs. Cleary okay?"

Mrs. Cleary, their elderly neighbor, was known to knock on the door at the most inopportune times, like when one of the kids was spiraling into full-blown meltdown. Or, like now, as she was trying to shepherd everyone out the door and running late. Clem groaned. "Is Mrs. Cleary here?"

George shook his head. "No, but there's a police car in her driveway."

Clem finished buckling Maddy's shoes and hopped to her feet. Sure enough, a cruiser was parked in the driveway next door.

"There's no siren or lights," George noted solemnly, echoing Clem's thoughts.

"She probably called them about Rufus again." Mrs. Cleary's terrier, nearly as ancient as she, was prone to wandering out of her yard and up the sidewalk—something that sent them all outside: the kids on the hunt for Rufus, and Clem to prevent Mrs. Cleary from falling down on the uneven sidewalk as she tried to catch him. "I'm sure he's fine. Now quick: coats! Backpacks!"

She hurried into the kitchen, jotted a note for George on the school's monogrammed notepad, and scooped up Maddy's coat as she raced back through the foyer.

Outside, she was relieved to see the bus rolling up to their mailbox. They'd made it! She tucked the note hastily into George's backpack and kissed each of her children good-bye. *"Love you!"* she called.

Halfway up the bus steps, George stopped and pointed past her. "Look."

Clem turned, thinking it must be Ben jogging up the sidewalk toward them. But it wasn't her husband.

The police car was pulling into their driveway now. Clem blinked. Mrs. Cleary stood on her front porch in her bathrobe. Rufus, she was relieved to see, stood at her feet.

The car stopped and an older officer stepped out from behind the driver's seat.

"Mom?"

Behind her the bus engine hummed impatiently. "I'm sure it's nothing," Clem said, turning back to George. "I'll pick you up after school. Have fun today!" She waved at the bus driver for good measure and stepped back as the yellow doors slapped shut and the bus moaned, heaving itself back onto the road. Maddy made a silly face from the window, making Clem smile and momentarily forget the squad car parked behind her.

When she turned, there were two of them. A petite female officer with her hair pulled back in a ponytail had joined the older officer, who now stepped toward her.

"Excuse us, ma'am. I'm Lieutenant Esposito." He flashed his badge and gestured to the young female officer beside him. "And this is Officer DeLuca."

Clem met them in the middle of the grassy yard, extending her hand to each. "Good morning. Can I help you?"

Lieutenant Esposito paused. "Do you know Benjamin Edward Dwight?"

Clem squinted at them in the early morning light. "My husband? He went for a run, but I'm expecting him home any second." She paused. "Is everything all right?"

Officer DeLuca glanced up at the house, but Lieutenant Esposito met Clem's questioning gaze. His own was gray and watery. "Perhaps we could go inside, ma'am?"

Mrs. Cleary was still watching them from her porch next door. Clem felt a flutter of panic in her chest. What was happening?

Officer DeLuca placed a gentle hand on her arm. "Mrs. Dwight? We'd really like to talk to you inside." And then she understood.

Clem's knees buckled. When she put out her hands to signal *stop, please stop,* the female officer stepped forward and grasped them. "It's all right, Mrs. Dwight."

But it was not. It was her Ben. Found half an

hour ago on the leaf-strewn shoulder of Brattle Street. An ambulance had been called, and he'd been transported to Auburn Hospital. They would take her there now. Was there anyone she wanted to call first?

An hour later, standing in her sweatpants and the same T-shirt she'd slept in, Clem was met by an attending ER doctor in the fluorescent-lit waiting room. She noticed the gold wedding band on his finger, the reassuring sprinkle of gray hair behind his ears. "Mrs. Dwight? I'm Doctor Sanford."

Clem rushed toward him. "How is he?"

"Please, come with me." The doctor invited her back through the swinging doors to the long hallway of examination rooms. Clem peered nervously into each sterile doorway they passed. They continued past the first room, then another, until they stopped at a small alcove at the end of the hall, where Dr. Sanford, clipboard in hand, indicated one of several upholstered chairs and asked her to have a seat. She could not.

So he stood with her and cleared his throat.

"I'm so sorry, Mrs. Dwight."

Ben was gone. The EMTs had tried, to no avail, to resuscitate him on the ambulance ride in. It appeared he'd died from a traumatic brain injury incurred by the impact of the car that had struck him on the road that morning. An autopsy would be done to confirm those findings, but

Dr. Sanford wanted to reassure her that it was his medical opinion Ben had not suffered.

Clem sat down hard. Her first thought was: *But he's coaching George's team at four o'clock.*

And then the waiting room went dark.

Paige

She never should have let Ned talk her into staying late for his team's lacrosse game. It was a Friday night—she knew what summer traffic was like on a Friday. Weekenders, renters, and wash-ashores, like her family, knew that once you hit the Westerly Bypass, the brief-but-eternal four-mile connector that delivered you from Stonington, Connecticut, to Westerly, Rhode Island, you were pretty much screwed. She reached across to the passenger side and rested her hand on Arthur's cinnamon fur. The terrier barely stirred in his old-dog sleep.

"How much longer, Mom?" Ned asked loudly. His earbuds were in. As far as she could tell, he hadn't looked up from his iPad since Old Saybrook. Which was about where she'd given up trying to engage her two teens in conversation, the only other exchange occurring when she'd swerved into a rest stop and begged Ned to throw his lacrosse bag in the trunk. Little good that did—the sour smell of athletic shoes was still ripe in the Volvo. Paige rolled down her window.

"Hopefully we won't be sitting here much

longer." What she really wanted to say was, *If only you'd listened to me earlier . . .*

In the rearview mirror, she watched Emma sweep back her long red hair as she pulled her gaze slowly from her book. The fourteen-year-old tipped her nose up to the breeze; Paige knew she was trying to detect salt air. But they weren't close enough to the summer house yet.

"How's Huck?" Paige asked.

Emma had only just plucked her summer reading list out of the mailbox days earlier, and already she was more than halfway through it. She dog-eared her page and met Paige's gaze in the mirror. "Huck and Jim are on the Ohio River, and the fog is rolling in. Huck is trying to decide whether to go ahead without Jim or stay on the raft."

Beside Emma, Ned groaned. "The raft. Do they ever get off that damn raft?"

"Ned," Paige warned.

Emma rolled her eyes. "If you'd actually read the book, you'd know that they do. Besides, Huck is about to go ahead in the canoe."

Ned threw up his hands. "See? Now they'll be stuck in a canoe."

Paige adjusted the mirror and smiled at them. Her children, separated only by a year, were so different. Ned, her easygoing firstborn, who jogged headlong into life like it was a giant game to be won and who was now a full head taller than his mother. Why had no one ever warned her how disconcerting it would be to stand on tiptoe to hug the very son you had nestled in your arms what felt like only yesterday? Ah, *yesterday:* the day she'd found a bottle of vodka in Ned's closet. Paige winced. She still hadn't told David. She'd stumbled over it while packing for the trip, stuffed in the corner beneath his tennis shoes. When she'd grasped the bottle in her hand, the clear liquid sloshed around inside, just as her stomach had. Paige knew he'd been to high school parties where kids drank, so she and David made a point to talk to both of their kids about it regularly. *We'd rather you didn't, but if you do . . . Don't get in the car with anyone who's been drinking . . . Call us, no matter what time.* But until now she'd never caught Ned with any evidence. It came like a kick in the teeth.

But it was also the day before David's big interview at the university, and Paige was elbow deep at work before leaving for vacation, so she'd put it off. Though, truthfully, she'd hoped in the meantime Ned would come clean when he discovered the bottle missing. Unlike Emma, who would never do such a thing to begin with, Ned would react when he discovered the alcohol missing: either with outrage that she'd "invaded his privacy" or with a rehearsed hangdog expression accompanied by a lame excuse. *Something.* But at the end of the day when he'd come home from lacrosse camp, wolfed down dinner, and later put away the clean laundry she'd strategically left by his closet without so much as a guilty glance, Paige was stunned. She studied him now in the rearview mirror.

David would be coming up tomorrow. They'd confront Ned together, as privately as they could without the rest of the family sticking their beaks in. Christ. Wouldn't his uncle Sam get a kick out of it.

The long line of cars in front of her crept along, and she shifted impatiently in her seat. Her back ached. She needed to use the bathroom. She couldn't help but wonder about the Wheelers' spaniel, whose broken pelvis she'd operated on that morning. As soon as they got to the house she would call Janie, her head vet tech, to check in.

The Jeep in front of them stopped short again. Paige stomped the brakes. Behind her, Ned's iPad crashed to the floor.

"Mom! Geez," he cried, retrieving it from under her seat.

"I know, I know," Paige snapped irritably. This stretch was the part of the trip she hated most. She cursed David silently, then felt bad. Hopefully the interview would go well. He needed the work, and it wasn't just about the money.

What they needed was to get to the summer house. The house—a gray, cedar-shingled two-story tucked back along the bluffs of Weekapaug Beach—had been in the Merrill family since Richard's parents had had the foresight to buy it from a retired fisherman during a summer visit in the early 1920s. Originally a rustic two-room fishing cottage, it had since survived not only the Great New England Hurricane of 1938 but also two restorations and three subsequent decades of the Merrill family. Although its improvements over the years, including a second-story addition and gambrel roof, had allowed it a somewhat more stately façade, Flossy insisted that the house maintain its original carriage, akin to what she referred to as an "aged sea captain": weathered but wise.

At the house, Paige knew her mother would already be stationed at the kitchen window watching the driveway. Florence, or Flossy, as all three of her children called her, would have been up since sunrise washing linens, straightening rooms, and ordering their enduring father, Richard, to the overgrown shrubs with hedge trimmers or into the depths of the garage to locate the ancient blue-and-white enamel lobster pot. It was the same routine every summer. The dust covers would have been plucked from the sofas and the scuffed, sloping hardwood floors swept clean of every granule of beach sand. It was nearing six o'clock now; Paige shuddered at the thought of all those bustling, efficient hours.

Clem would probably roll in first with the kids. It would be good to finally set eyes on her. Clem was a terrible liar. She couldn't possibly be faring as well as she insisted she was. As for her brother, Sam, Paige wasn't sure she had the energy today. It didn't matter that she was forty-five and he was forty-two; he still knew exactly how to get under her skin. He and Evan had arrived the night before, and she would bet on finding them settled on the back porch with cocktails, cool and crisp in their insufferable Nanny Reds, while she and the kids unfolded themselves from the sticky, messy car in their standard family-vacation dishevelment. Just thinking about it, she tucked a stray hair back into her ponytail. For Sam, a vacation at the summer house seemed to Paige like just a continuation of his life—business travel, car services, and long lunch meetings (plated lunches in real restaurants, unlike the brown-bag tuna sandwiches she threw together each morning). Work weeks that ended lingering over romantic dinners with Evan in dark Georgetown bistros or weekend jaunts to Rehoboth Beach. Sam could wax poetic all he wanted about the tortures of his sixty-hour week; she was pretty sure he never drove home covered in pet hair and reeking of cat urine.

Eventually they edged their way to the traffic light that marked the end of the Westerly Bypass, and moments later—magically—they were swooping past the Westerly Airport and turning left toward town. As was tradition, they'd drive through Watch Hill village first. Salt ponds and marinas cropped up along the road, and the shingled New England houses grew more stately as they approached the historic resort village. Moments later they coasted down Bay Street into the charming heart of the village, and Paige was finally able to let the air out of her lungs. To her right, Little Narragansett Bay sparkled, its pristine boats nearly glittering on their lines, and just beyond it at the edge of the cove, the venerable Watch Hill Yacht Club. To her left, the three-tiered, crisp-white porches of the Watch Hill Inn echoed the white masts and sails of the harbor it overlooked. The decks were already teeming with diners. She drove past Bay Street's charming storefronts, slowing to peek at her favorite, the 1916 Olympia Tea Room, where she, Flossy, and Clem would occasionally escape for a lunch free of men and children. Tourists strolled the sidewalk in their summer pastels, some armed with ice cream cones from St. Clair Annex. Up ahead, at the northern point of the street, the famed antique carousel loomed.

"Look guys, the horses are flying!" she said. Even as teens, both kids perked up in the backseat. Tucked on the corner beside the East Beach entrance, the Watch Hill carousel was the oldest in North America. Paige rolled down her window to hear the old-fashioned music. The hand-carved wooden horses still sported manes and tails of real horsehair, their saddles and bridles repainted in the same primary colors they had been when Paige was small enough to swing her leg over the saddle and try her hand at catching the brass ring. Past the carousel, Bay Street forked left and continued uphill along the ocean bluff, giving way to a strip of imposing Victorian mansions behind stone walls and private gates, perched along the bluff so that the Atlantic surf merged with blue sky into one shimmering backdrop. Paige felt her breath escape her. At the crest of the hill, they rolled up to the titanic façade of the historic Ocean House hotel. Its canary-yellow clapboards and sweeping white porches were the most eminent harbingers of summer in the seaside village. She slowed as a rush of childhood memories filled her: sitting on the grand porch among the resort guests as they sipped gimlets and watched the sun set over Narragansett Bay; the scrape of the heavy wooden chairs along the deck as she stood up to lean over the railing and gaze at the crashing surf below; the squeals of laughter when she and Clem hid beneath the billiards table in the giant hall rec room as Sam and the other young guests scratched the flannel surface with their pool cues, while at the front of the hotel's first floor, in the paneled main dining room, her parents and grandparents lingered over diminutive glasses of brandy. Each Ocean House memory was as gilded as the seaside hamlet it overlooked.

"Welcome home," she whispered to herself.

Minutes later, when they finally pulled into her parents' crushed-shell driveway and came to a stop at the cedar-shingled cottage, Ned removed his earbuds and rolled down his window. And Emma, without looking up from her book, closed her eyes dreamily. "Yep, I can smell the salt. We're here."

Flossy

The lobsters clicked and clambered over one another in the old farmhouse sink. Flossy tried not to look at them. Best not to make eye contact before the water was at full boil. Overhead, the ceiling thumped and thudded as the first two of her grandchildren dragged their suitcases down the upstairs hall. Ned and Emma would be settling into the nautical depths of the red-and-blue great room, the cavernous sleeping space over the garage, lined military style with bunk beds where all the grandkids could be tucked safely beneath the eaves and crisp whale motif blankets. Paige would be settling into the yellow gingham room with the queen bed overlooking the back lawns and the beach below the bluff. Flossy let out a long breath. There was just one more carload to go before all of her offspring were accounted for.

Paige had looked road-worn to Flossy upon her arrival. Her curly hair, despite being pulled back in a childish elastic, had escaped and sprung out at curious angles around her head, not unlike that of her wirehaired dog, Arthur. And her eyes—

there was tiredness behind the determined blue glint she'd inherited from her mother. On the one hand, Paige was the one Flossy probably worried least about. She'd graduated from Vassar, where she'd gotten her degree in fine arts. She then marched straight into the veterinary sciences school at Cornell, ignoring her family's raised eyebrows, and without so much as an explanation as to how her years spent in campus studios painting colonial-era farmyard animals had suddenly translated into the study of veterinary medicine. It was a move that relieved Flossy as much as it had saddened her husband, Richard. She supposed she'd liked those paintings about as much as a person could be expected to, but really, how many bovine portraits did Richard expect their eldest child to sell? Paige had been a headstrong child, moving quietly but stubbornly down paths of her own choosing, thankfully not derailed by the need to people-please, as her younger sister, Clem, had been. Or be the life of the party, as Samuel had proved exceedingly skilled at. Paige ran a solid domestic-animal veterinary practice in the village of Litchfield, Connecticut, where she also raised two bright children, and somehow also carried on a marriage to a man Flossy could not quite put her thumb on, but who seemed agreeable enough to roll along in the efficient wake that followed her daughter. No, Flossy had not spent a single sleepless night on Paige. But still—those deep circles under her eyes were unusual.

Sam had arrived the night before with Evan. Their arrival was always so civilized compared to the others'. Sam had stood on the front step and called out boyishly, "Flossy, Pop . . . we're home!" It got her every time. He'd picked her up and spun her around the living room while Evan stood patiently to the side, flowers in one hand and chilled wine in the other. Evan fussed over her new linen capris, which she'd purchased in one of the Watch Hill boutiques just that morning after fretting over the tangerine color. It had seemed so bright, but she'd decided that *bright* was exactly what they needed this summer. There was no discussion of the disappointments the boys had suffered earlier that spring, as suggested, strongly, by Richard the night before their arrival. Flossy was desperate to know more of what had transpired on what was to be the last of many trips to Austin, Texas.

"Give them time to settle," Richard had advised. "Let's focus on welcoming them back."

So welcome them she did. There had been gin and tonics on the back porch and grilled salmon for supper. Later, they'd taken the sandy trail that awaited them at the far end of the yard, where the beach grass grew scraggly and dense, scraping against their bare legs as they made their way down its steep, winding path to the shore. They'd watched the sun go down from the dunes, enjoying the quiet of the empty beach and joking about how loud tomorrow would be when the grandkids all rolled in. Flossy had kept her promise, biting her tongue when the subject of grandchildren arose, trying not to search their expressions too obviously. And if disappointment had flickered within her when neither Evan nor Sam broached the topic, she was certain to keep it cloaked. Flossy always kept her word.

That morning, before the others arrived, Evan had risen early and brewed espresso, setting out the small Lenox cups he knew Flossy liked. How she loved that man! Ever since, he'd trailed her quietly through her lengthy to-do list: making beds and putting fresh towels in the bathrooms, stubbornly ignoring her hints to go join Samuel on the beach, and smart enough to steer clear of her monogrammed heirloom linens with the iron. Those she saved only for the downstairs powder room. They'd been her grandmother's, and she kept them tucked away in acid-free tissue paper in the antique highboy in the upstairs hall. Everyone in the family knew not to use them to dry their hands. But although Evan's polite assistance sometimes flustered her—couldn't he just join the others down on the beach and leave her to set the table the way *she* liked?—she couldn't help but notice how he grabbed the broom when

Samuel eventually traipsed through the back screen door late that afternoon, newly freckled, smelling of sunscreen, and tracking beach sand across her ancient hardwoods. He'd slapped Samuel playfully on the rear end and proceeded to sweep every last grain into the dustpan. Yes, Evan was a roll-up-your-sleeves kind of guy. A giver. He'd make a wonderful father. If only.

Now, Clem was the only one still on the road. Alone, with two small children. She was the one who had kept Flossy awake the night before. Oh, who was she kidding? She'd been keeping Flossy awake since that day when everything changed.

The call had come just over a year ago, in the spring. It had been an ordinary day in the way most days seemed ordinary to Flossy since she had retired the year before as the public high school librarian. She'd been in the garden, bent over a patch of dandelion weed that had rooted itself precariously close to her tender toad lilies; how she'd not seen this offensive patch against the cultivated backdrop of her yard was beyond her. She was on her knees with a trowel when Richard had opened the back door and called out to her.

Flossy could not remember what he'd said exactly. Something about Clem. What she did remember was momentarily turning her attention back to the obstinate weed, determined to remove it before trudging up to the patio where she would take a break on the lounge and take her youngest daughter's call. She hadn't heard from Clem all week, and it was an oddly warm day; she could use an iced tea and a chat.

But then Richard came up behind her, his tall frame shading the garden bed for a dark instant. And in that moment, as she stood and turned to face his wet eyes behind his reading glasses, she knew that whatever he had to say would alter her forever.

"Tell me!"

Richard, never one to be without words, could only shake his head. She'd hesitated, fumbling to remove her dirt-caked garden gloves before taking the phone. Before putting it to her ear and saying Clem's name.

That had been fifteen months ago—fifteen months and a funeral and countless visits ago. Months of worrying and praying and waiting for the easy laugh, which had once rolled so regularly out of her youngest child's mouth, to return. A laugh that usually came so easily to her third child that Flossy had often wondered at the source of such happiness, and if she had been somehow cheated out of it. A constant flow of cheer had seemed to surround Clem and her tidy Boston-based family, where handsome, affable Ben worked as a partner at Howell and Mansfield Law Firm, and Clem had found her greatest joy staying home to raise her young family.

In the weeks after Ben's accident, Flossy and Richard moved in with Clem and the children in an attempt to keep things as normal as their new normal allowed: putting dinner on the table, running baths, turning the pages of bedtime stories. During those moments Clem would appear from her bedroom like a ghost, coaxing broccoli into George's mouth at dinner. Tucking her children onto her lap as they recited the words to *Goodnight Moon.* Running a brush through Maddy's baby-fine hair after a warm bath. But then she'd fade away from them, returning to the dark recesses of her room the moment the children were tucked into their beds. She was always just beyond Flossy's reach.

Richard had wondered aloud if it would be prudent to call in a nanny or bring a grief counselor to the house, leaving Flossy outraged. No, they did not need outside help. Clem just needed time. And them! But she knew he did not believe her, even if he allowed her to think that he did. Clem's loss had paralyzed them all. Flossy was her mother. She had always figured things out. But this grief—it was something even she could not wrap her arms around.

But after that first endless month, when the funeral services had been arranged and endured, when the neighbors' food deliveries eventually ebbed and the phone stopped ringing, settling into the gray solitude that blanketed them all in the aftermath, Clementine seemed to shed her grief. Well, maybe *shed* wasn't the correct term, Flossy thought. Not like a snake undergoing a natural process. *Discarded.* A decision Clem seemed to have made. Whether conscious or reactive, Flossy couldn't say. But she could pinpoint the day it happened: Flossy had tiptoed down the steep craftsman staircase to begin what had become her morning routine of pouring orange juice into plastic sippy cups and whisking eggs, when she came upon a kitchen already lit and humming with activity. There was Clem, not in her rumpled blue bathrobe but dressed and showered, standing at the kitchen stove watching pancakes bubble in the skillet. Coffee was percolating. The table was set. She turned to look at her mother. "We need to get a Christmas tree," she said.

It had brought Flossy both relief and sadness. Finally they could pack their suitcases and bid the torturous pull-out couch good-bye. But there was something else: right before Clem had sensed her mother standing in the doorway that morning, Flossy noticed something that caused her heart to heave. She caught it in the split second before Clem looked up and rearranged her expression, before she stretched her lips into an almost-convincing smile and greeted her mother, as if it were any other day *before*. They would survive, but it was still with them. It would always be with them.

The *after*—as Flossy had named it, causing Richard to shake his head and mumble that it was like the bad title of an even more badly written book—had introduced them to a Clem none of them quite recognized, despite the fact that she appeared mostly the same. She kept her house in the same manner; toys were strewn across area rugs and picked up for company before being strewn again. The children's backpacks were organized for school each morning, and their teeth were brushed. Maddy suddenly refused to wear any shirt except a button-down, just like her daddy. George returned to the town soccer field that his father used to coach him on. Clem attended parent-teacher conferences and PTA meetings with consistency, if not zeal. Dinners were made and served with the same practiced regularity as her Sunday phone calls home, during which Flossy would inquire, "How are you, sweetheart?"

And Clem would reply, breezily, "Mom. I'm fine."

Fine. Flossy had never met a more useless word.

But maybe Clem was telling a version of the truth. After all, they had not only survived that first Christmas without Ben, they had almost enjoyed it. Even if it was fueled by that splendid case of port that Samuel had brought and promptly opened, though it was barely eight o'clock in the morning. There had been laughter as presents were passed and torn into, despite the lone gift box labeled DAD, in red crayon, which remained unopened beneath the tree. Flossy could never bring herself to ask what was in that box. But she admired the measures Clem took to keep Ben present for the children: recalling silly stories about their father and tucking photos of him in every corner of the house. Even going the extra step to sign his name on their birthday cards that spring, though that one had given Flossy some pause.

Now, two Julys later, Clem was returning to the summer house. It would not be the same, but they would make new memories this year. Happy memories! If only she could get this house in shape to do it. There was so much work to be done, and although some of it was indeed for Richard's upcoming seventy-fifth birthday, there was the *other* reason—the reason she and Richard had agreed not to tell the children until after vacation.

For as many years as Flossy had known her husband, they'd spent part or most of their summers in this house on Sea Spray Road. Initially, she'd been a guest of Richard's when his parents were still alive, and she'd come up to spend a few nights with his family at the shore. Later, when they married and began to have little ones of their own, the house was handed down to them. For the Merrill family, it had provided a summer haven and escape akin to something in a Norman Rockwell painting. How many watermelons had been consumed on the back deck, whose railing the kids leaned over to see who could spit their seeds the farthest? How many bottles of sunscreen had been spilled and applied on that deck? Some of the beach towels in the pantry closet off the kitchen were as old as their memories of summering at the shingled cottage. Flossy couldn't bear to throw them out, so she washed and folded them at the end of each season and tucked them away, each year a little more faded than the last. They'd lived in this house. They'd loved in this house.

Which is why it was such a difficult decision to sell it. Richard had posed the idea a few years before, when the kids had started coming up less and less. There were summer camps and athletic camps. They went away with other families. They were too busy, too far away, or, in Flossy's opinion, too disinterested in the house that had once kept them all together. The one who did keep popping by was their neighbor, who'd made polite inquiries to show his interest in the home and his wish to buy it if and when they were ever ready. They'd declined, of course. They had children and grandchildren. There were summers to be shared. But the house needed some work; and each winter it became more of a hassle to winterize and more of a worry, with storms like Hurricane Sandy. They were getting older, wanting to take care of themselves, and they were finding the house was yet another thing to look after and fret over.

They put out feelers to the kids: did they have any interest in taking over the house? Initially, Flossy was sure they'd fight over it. How surprised, and taken aback, she'd been when Sam commented matter-of-factly that he and Evan were just too far away in DC for it to be of any real use for them. Paige was too entrenched in her new practice, and then David lost his job; it wasn't realistic for them. And Clem—well, none of them wanted to burden her with anything else after the year she'd endured. Flossy was still wondering if Clem would truly be able to keep her own house in Boston. Another was simply out of the question. To her dismay, the kids had seemed flippant about the whole matter, and the final straw was when Sam suggested they lease it out to summer tourists. As if it were just any other vacation rental and not their great-grandparents' seaside cottage that had seen several generations of Merrills happily through salty, sun-drenched summers.

So, last summer, after she and Richard had found themselves sitting alone in the Adirondack chairs for the whole of August, Maurice had popped by for a glass of wine with his annual inquiry about the house, and they finally admitted that maybe . . . perhaps . . . they were ready to sell—as hard as it would be. But they would not tell the kids until after their week together. Finally, they would all be here, under one roof, and Flossy was determined that they'd make the most of this last precious vacation at the shore.

The clock in the sitting room chimed, and it was then Flossy noticed Joe, the painter, standing in the kitchen doorway, as if waiting for her to finish her worries. "Mrs. Merrill? I have the White Dove sample ready, if you want to take a look."

"Joe." She set down her *Frugal Gourmet* cookbook. "You've been painting for us through three children and four grandkids. I wish you would just call me Flossy."

Joe Collins had been a mere boy the first time Flossy and Richard had hired his father to freshen up the summer house. Now, since Joe Sr. had passed, Joe Jr. owned the family business. He was handsome in the rugged way of his father, and possessed the same unassuming nature that left his expression neutral no matter what chaos was taking place beneath the rungs of his metal ladder. Flossy often wondered at the things he must have seen and heard over the years.

She followed him into the living room. "I love

it," she said, pausing in front of the bay window to inspect the trim.

"Very well."

"It's not a bright white. Or a winter white. More of an ocean-cap white, if you know what I mean." She pressed her hands together. "Perfect for the coast."

Joe let out a breath. This was his third trip here to sample whites. She hadn't believed him when he told her there were more than a thousand different shades of it.

"So I'll order eight cans of the Dove?" he asked, pulling out a small notepad from his back pocket. His pencil waited above the paper, and it gave Flossy pause.

"Eight?"

Joe raised one eyebrow, but his tone remained level. "Yes, for the upstairs and downstairs—windows, doors, baseboards, and moldings. Two coats each."

"Huh." Eight sounded like a lot of White Dove. Flossy took a step back and squinted at the sample. Did she detect a little gray in it?

Joe cleared his throat, pencil still poised. "Mrs. Merrill?"

Just then the phone rang. "I'm sorry, Joe. Can I think about this one more day?"

"You can think about it as many days as you want, but each day means I order the paint a day later."

The phone rang again.

"Which delays the job another day."

Flossy studied the trim again. Yes, she definitely saw gray. But she really needed Joe to get started. The party was only a week away. This was the last summer the family had in the house!

The phone kept ringing. Someone needed to answer the phone. Where was Richard? It could be Vesta bakery; she'd left them a detailed message about the lemon tarts. "I'm sorry, I must get that!"

Joe tucked the notepad back in his pocket. "Another day, then."

By the time she reached the phone, it was silent. Whoever it had been did not leave a message. No matter. Just another missed call, just another missed day of paint. Honestly, why wasn't Clem there yet?

Flossy stood at the kitchen counter, her arms crossed. She watched Joe's white truck roll out of the driveway and wondered what shade of white *that* was. On the stovetop the lobster pot's lid clattered noisily, announcing full boil. She glared at the now empty drive outside the window, then at the useless clock on the wall. She flipped off the stove's burner and left the lobsters clicking senselessly in the sink.

Sam

No doubt about it, Paige looked like shit. She had never been one to fuss about looks, but that was largely because, like the rest of the Merrill clan, she'd been blessed in that department and didn't have to. Flaxen-haired and blue-eyed, except for Clem, who had somehow inherited flecks of sea-glass green in hers, the Merrill children had been both bright and pleasing to look at, thanks to the long-limbed and fair-complexioned Scandinavian ancestry on Richard's side. The particular twinkle in Sam's eyes went beyond the humorless Swedes, however.

"What do you think is going on with Paige?" he asked Evan as he stood in front of the dresser mirror. It was only eight o'clock in the morning, and he wanted to squeeze in a run before the family started herding everyone together for their traditional first day at the beach. "She seems more tightly wound than usual, if that's possible. And did you see the look she gave me when I asked where David was?"

"Be nice." Evan was propped up in bed, reading a novel Flossy had left on his pillow—something

42

Sam could never remember her doing for him. His dark limbs stretched out against the ivory bedding only highlighted the ropes and curves of his muscled physique. Sam grinned in the mirror at his husband's reflection. How had he gotten so lucky?

Evan lowered his book. "Why don't you just ask her?" Then, seeing the exasperated look on Sam's face, he said, "First day of vacation tradition: Paige wants us to go to East Beach with the kids."

Paige wants was all Sam heard. He was used to his older sister's silent direction of family plans; he supposed her commandeering nature served her well in her veterinary practice. Last night after she'd arrived, she'd regaled them with accounts of her OR schedule, from lineups of canine femoral surgeries and soft tissue repairs to commonplace spays: all told over full plates of dinner, no less. Followed by a full report of Ned's lacrosse camp and Emma's summer enrichment classes. *All triumphs!*—as confirmed by Richard's beatific expression at the far end of the dinner table. At one point Paige asked Emma to recount a debate she'd participated in at school. Shyly, his niece had offered a few scant details about the topic, her focus remaining on her dinner.

"Go on," Paige had said, her eyes lighting up. "Tell them your closing argument!" Sam had recognized the pained flicker in the teen's averted gaze.

"Did you see the way Em slunk off before dessert was even served? Paige is smothering the kid."

Evan cocked his head thoughtfully. "She's a teenager, Sam. How comfortable were you around your parents at that age? Though I'd have killed for that child's complexion."

But Sam wasn't listening. He checked his phone once more before turning it off. There had already been two messages from Adya, his assistant, that morning. He'd returned her call from the bathroom with the shower running, so Evan wouldn't hear. "Unplugging" was a pledge he was trying to keep this week. He was initially relieved to hear that Adya just needed his approval on a schedule change for an overseas call. Until he realized it would be at eleven o'clock that night.

"I'm going down for breakfast," he said, slipping the phone into his pocket. "Want anything?"

Evan shook his head, not glancing up from his book this time. "Flossy set out fruit and bagels. I think she's waiting for everyone else to wake up before she gets the bacon and eggs going."

Sam sighed. He'd have to make it a long run. The menu at their annual summer gathering ranked high on the list of indulgences he and

Evan rarely allowed themselves: lobster, buttered corn, and greasy, stick-to-your-ribs breakfasts. If they were at home, in their airy DuPont Circle apartment, they would be juicing.

He rummaged through his duffel bag in search of his running shoes. Damn it, had he forgotten his sneakers? He'd have to borrow Evan's, which were a half size too big. He found Evan's Brooks in his suitcase. It was then that he noticed the checkered gift bag from the trendy baby store on Wisconsin Avenue, where they'd registered. He glanced over at Evan, who was still reading. When he reached inside, he knew already that it was the pair of baby slippers: fluffy pink, with tiny bunny ears and whiskers sewn across each toe. The very slippers he'd given Evan when they found out that Tania, the doe-eyed sixteen-year-old with the lizard tattoo from Austin, Texas, had chosen them. And that the baby was a girl.

Sam rolled the bag up and tucked it gently back in Evan's suitcase, his heart heavy in his chest.

Downstairs, the house was quiet. Richard sat outside at the picnic table with the morning paper. There was no sign of Clem, or, surprisingly, of her little ones, by whom he was used to being awakened at some ungodly predawn hour. They'd arrived late last night, Clem sailing wordlessly through the front door with Maddy tucked neatly against her shoulder, already fast asleep. Sam had barely had a chance to ruffle George's hair before they'd all made a beeline upstairs for the night. He'd have to corner her later.

"What's cooking?"

The screen door jerked open. It was Paige, her cheeks flushed and her skin dewy with sweat. Sam eyed her running shorts. "Cup of coffee?" he asked.

She shook her head. "No, thanks, already had two. Before my five miles." She stopped in the middle of the kitchen and bent, stretching her hamstrings. "I forgot how much harder it is to run in the sand. You still running?" she asked, peering up at him.

Sam moved around her and went to the fridge in search of the fruit platter Evan had mentioned. "Left my sneakers in DC."

Paige grunted, balancing on one leg and pulling the other up behind her. "What's your time these days?"

Sam nodded at the clock. "It's eight thirty, Paige."

She narrowed her eyes, saying nothing. Then, "I'm down to a sub seven. In case you find your sneakers." Before he could respond she was already trotting up the stairs.

"Go shower," he called after her. "You stink."

Outside, the morning was blindingly bright in the way that only a seaside morning could be, the sun already shimmering off the sandy bluff at the backyard's edge. Sam squinted, lowering himself into one of the teak chairs beside his father. He scanned the yard where they had played as kids; the spot where they'd held epic whiffle ball games and barbecues. Now all he could wonder was: who mowed the grass? Richard was in decent shape for a man his age, but surely he wasn't up to maneuvering the ancient push mower kept in the shed.

"How'd you sleep?" Sam asked his father.

Richard Merrill lowered his paper and appraised his middle child over his glasses lovingly. It was good to have them all under one roof again. Each year he became more aware of how uncertain time was—this past year most of all.

"I slept like a man of the sea." It was his father's standard reply when at the cottage. No matter everyone's age or ailments, the brisk salt air wafting up over the dunes was a legendary inducer of slumber. Even as restive infants, Sam's nieces and nephews had been lulled to sleep through the nights whenever they visited the summer house. Sam recalled David remarking with marvel that they should consider moving to the coast when they'd visited the first summer after Ned was born. Richard had smiled knowingly then, too.

"So, are you ready to celebrate the big seven-five next weekend?" Sam asked.

Richard lifted his hand. "Your mother's idea. God knows who's coming or what she's got planned. I'm just going to show up when I'm told. At my age, any birthday is worth celebrating."

"Oh, come on, Pops." His father, who they all agreed did not seem to age at the same pace as other men of his decade, had always looked strong as an oak. But this summer, Sam couldn't help but notice his thinning hair, and that its distinguished salt-and-pepper color had surrendered entirely to salt. Still, his father was robust—a man who filled door frames, unlike Sam's lithe runner's build. They were similar only in height. Richard Merrill was a man whose stature allowed you to believe that he'd played football, back in his day, as compared to Sam's years of varsity cross country. "An individual sport," his father had mused, when Sam told him he'd joined the team. And that had been all.

Sam regarded his father's hands still clutching the paper. This they also shared: large, strong hands. Hands that Evan had called capable when he and Sam were first dating.

"How's work treating you these days?" Richard asked, turning to face him. It was a relief; Sam half feared he'd ask about the baby. It was too soon.

But work he could talk about all day. Currently an associate with Interim Bank, Sam was climbing, and quickly, to managing director. In his early days with the bank, he'd worked his way up handling their European clients. Sam was a deal junkie: his colleagues nicknamed him Maverick. High on espresso and hunched over his desk in the open office floor, he'd slide on his noise-canceling Bose headphones and work on financial models for hours, until either his Excel spreadsheets blurred or Adya slipped a bag of takeout between his face and his monitor. But it didn't matter to him how many companies he acquired, or what kind of numbers he brought in each quarter. In the end it was his father's recognition he sought most feverishly. A man who took his brown-bag lunch on Fairfield University's green quad and never had a taste for the acrid pace or posturing of his son's corporate world.

"Even with the volatility in recent months, my team identified a target market in China, and now that the financials are in place, we're working on a time frame to merge."

Richard nodded thoughtfully. "Impressive. I know you've been working toward this for some time. Are you enjoying it?"

Sam flinched. Had his father not heard what he'd just told him? The notion of *joy* had not been something he'd considered. "Well, yeah the firm's pretty stoked. It's our first venture into the Asian market, and so far things are running on time."

Richard glanced up at a gull circling overhead, and Sam waited. "How about Evan? I know it's been a rough spring for you two. If there's anything your mother and I can do, just say the word."

Sam closed his eyes at his father's words and nodded. The thing was, there was nothing any of them could do.

They'd been warned in the first meeting with their adoption agent, Malayka, that the process itself was as shifting as the emotions that came with each step. In the end, domestic adoption had seemed like the best fit, and after they'd familiarized themselves with the options and risks, they landed on a private, open adoption. Evan was elated. But to Sam, it was the inverse of finding a needle in a haystack.

"We're the needle," he'd tried to explain to Evan. "It's the birth parents who are going to be looking for *us*."

"It goes both ways," Evan had tried to reassure him.

"But think of the hoops," Sam continued. They were in the kitchen making dinner, fresh from the adoption agency. Sam had just finished chopping vegetables for a stir-fry; he went to the fridge and pulled out two beers. Evan stood at the range, swirling hot oil in a pan, listening quietly. "We complete the applications, the interviews, take the classes, and then we still have to get through the home studies. And don't forget the profile we have to make for prospective parents. I'm sorry, but I can't help but feel like we're selling ourselves."

Evan shrugged. "We are."

"And then what? We sit back and wait? I don't know if I can handle that." He walked around the island and sank onto one of the Calvin barstools that Evan had insisted on when they'd redesigned. Despite the protest Sam had made when he'd seen the price, Evan had been right about the leather-and-hide seats: they were as comfortable to sit on as they were pleasing to look at. And now, with such important things to worry about, Sam regretted ever having complained about them to begin with. Chairs could be bought, returned, exchanged. Just like his deals at work, they were exchanges between people. Currency. Products demanded were products supplied. Sam understood these things; he weighed the risks involved and exercised his control accordingly. Not so when it came to the role of adoptees. He ran his hands through his cropped hair. "Our role just seems so passive. So damned helpless."

Evan pulled the wok off the burner and turned to him. "I know, babe. It's not in your nature to sit back. But you have to have faith that some mother out there is going to look at our profile and say, 'That's them! That's the couple I want for my baby.'" He took a sip of the beer Sam had handed him, his demeanor as composed as it had been two hours earlier sitting in Malayka's overheated office.

Now, in the cool, stainless-steel safety of his kitchen, Sam scoffed. "What if no one wants us?" There. He'd said it.

"Sam, look where we live in this city. We have so much love and opportunity to give a child. We're young, we're educated, and we're professionals."

"We're gay."

Evan shook his head. "They will want us." He leaned back against the granite countertop and crossed his arms, but his expression remained soft. "You want to know how I look at it? There is a mother out there who is carrying our child." He paused. "That's her time. But one day that baby will decide it's ready, and she'll give birth. And that's when it will become *our* time. You hear me, Sam? Our baby is out there."

Sam couldn't help it. A tear spilled from his eye. The certainty with which Evan spoke of them and of their baby moved him immeasurably. "What if it takes a year? Or two?"

Evan didn't flinch. "Then we nest. We work on our nest and we wait." His voice was as steady as his gaze. Sam rose from his seat and went to him.

He let Evan pull him in tight, and as Sam rested his head on the expanse of his husband's chest, he imagined a tree—an oak tree, stalwart and irreverent against a gray haze. Its branches turned up toward heaven, the crook of each shadowy limb beckoning all the troubled birds from the sky.

"Okay," Sam whispered, pressing his eyelids closed. "We'll nest."

Nested they had. Thirteen months later, they had received a call from their attorney. The facts followed like ticker tape: Tania was sixteen and lived in Austin with her mother. She was six months along in a healthy pregnancy, her first one, and the baby girl was due in mid-April. Tania was seeking an open adoption. She'd sifted through the haystack, and she'd chosen them.

From then on, things read more like a story-book. They'd flown down to Austin to meet. They'd connected. Contracts had been drafted, and hopes ran high. The jubilance that followed in the months until the birth manifested in giddy late-night conversations, setting up a nursery, and sharing their news with friends and family. If the story had ended like the fairy tale it began as, Sam and Evan would be at the summer house with their baby now.

Now, Sam looked away from his father's expectant gaze and out over the haze that was rising over the water. "Don't worry, Dad. Evan and I are doing fine," he lied.

Clem

Clem awoke to the veritable thrum of family vacation: the vibrato of kitchen conversation below, children's laughter, and the repetitive slap of the screen door. Neither of the kids had crawled into bed with her last night. Curious, she rose and padded down the hall to the bunkroom to check on them. All four beds were empty, the sheets tossed aside.

The most prominent feature of the shared room was the sweeping sailcloth curtain, fashioned from an old headsail Flossy had picked up years ago at a boating yard auction, rigged down the middle on mainsheet roping. It was used as a divider between the girls' side and the boys'. On one side of the sail were the blue-and-white-striped beds of the boys. On the other, the pastel-whale-printed duvets of the girls. Of the four, she noted that only George's bed was made.

She headed back down the hall, wondering if the kids had eaten. Then she panicked. Would they have gone down to the beach without her? It was a longstanding house rule instituted in her own childhood by Richard: no beach without an adult. But now that Ned and Emma were older, she doubted it applied to them, and if the older two went, her own would surely try to follow. She tugged one of Ben's old Columbia sweatshirts over her head and hurried downstairs.

There, spread across the family room couches in various states of repose, were all four kids. Ned glanced up from his phone. "Hey, Aunt Clem."

Maddy and George were nestled on either side of Emma, watching cartoons on the new TV. They'd never had a TV in the summer house growing up; Flossy wouldn't hear of it. Now, Clem couldn't help but wonder at the timing of its arrival.

She perched on the arm of the couch and scrutinized their expressions. "Morning, guys. You sleep okay?"

"I had a bagel," Maddy told her, scooching up onto her mother's lap. Clem pulled her in for a hug.

"Good girl. George?"

He shrugged, eyes fixed on the TV screen. "I ate."

"Eggs, fruit, and bacon," Flossy added from the kitchen. Of course. Her mother would have seen to it. "Now, how about you? There's plenty left."

Clem flashed her a tired smile. "Just coffee, thanks."

"No eggs?"

She ignored Flossy's furrowed brow. No

different than the one she'd given her last night when Clem had managed only a few bits of the elaborate lobster dinner her mother had laid out. "I'll grab a bite later," she said for good measure.

Paige had apparently risen early to go for a run and was already back upstairs showering. Sam and Evan were outside on the deck with Richard, sharing bits of the newspaper and chatting. Clem intended to join them all, to make some effort at "integrating," as Dr. Weston called it, but as soon as she'd stirred milk and sugar into her mug, she found herself heading away from the noisy family room and toward the front door. Outside, the air was already thick with humidity and the scent of salt. She leaned over the front porch railing and inhaled. She'd made it.

In the weeks leading up to this trip, Clem hadn't been so sure she would. Flossy had told her not to worry about *anything:* she'd stocked the summer house with new towels, bedding, even beach toys for the kids. *Just bring yourselves!* she'd insisted, in a voice so full of hope and longing that Clem already felt suffocated. It was then that her second thoughts had crept in.

Theoretically, Clem had known it would be hard returning to the house without Ben. But one thing she'd learned in the last year was that she couldn't predict the *ways* in which it would be hard. Grief was like an omnipresent bird of prey, always circling. She felt its shadow, but she couldn't tell when it would strike. Whether it was induced by the logistics of navigating clogged interstate highways with two hungry, exhausted children, or by the smooth, cool surface of a seashell pressed in the palm of her hand by her youngest child, the grief always found her.

So she'd focused instead on what she did know. Weeks before their departure she'd made lists, bought swimsuits, and plucked suitcases from the recesses of the attic. (They'd traveled exactly nowhere since Ben had left them.) Clem wasn't sure if she'd packed too much or too little. She agonized over how the kids would react, walking through the front door without their father. For them, memories of Ben were everywhere in this house and along these beaches. Would Maddy set foot on East Beach and recall her father trotting headlong into the waves with her shrieking atop his shoulders? Would George lay eyes on the tattered Trivial Pursuit box tucked on the living room shelf that Ben had reigned over on many a late summer evening and become undone at the memory? Would she?

And yet, here they were. One uneventful, uninterrupted night of sleep behind them, and two bellies already filled with breakfast. Today, they would go to East Beach, just as they did each summer on the first day of vacation. She took a sip of coffee and forced out a long breath. What had Dr. Weston said to her about focusing on images of comfort? Clem tried to conjure the waves, the relaxed downtown energy of Watch Hill, and the carousel. What she pictured instead was the orange bottle of Xanax upstairs in her purse. The bottle she kept close by. Just in case.

Two hours later, the narrow East Beach entrance by the carousel was already clogged with beachgoers. Situated at the north end of busy Bay Street, adjacent to the historic carousel, the tiny, sandy parking lot was almost full by the time they arrived, crammed together in Clem's Suburban. Which meant they had to circle around the village center until they found a place to park. Sam nearly had a fit. "I told you guys we should just grab a quick bagel at St. Clair for breakfast," he said.

"Flossy would never have allowed it," Evan reminded him.

Luckily, Paige spotted an elderly woman backing out of a space. She, Evan, and the older kids loaded themselves up with their gear and headed through the beach entrance to stake out their encampment of beach chairs, coolers, and sand toys. Clem and Sam were left in charge of buying the traditional strawberry lemonades from St. Clair Annex, just up the street. It was a first-day-at-the-shore custom, the same one Richard and Flossy had instituted when they were kids:

lemonades, beach, carousel. Clem ushered her kids down the village sidewalk to the takeout window at St. Clair. Sam placed the order.

It was the first time they'd been alone, and he draped an arm over her shoulders and looked at her over the top of his Ray-Bans. "How are we? Really."

Clem smiled, leaning into her big brother. It had been a long time since she'd rested her head on anyone's shoulder. "So far, so good."

He raised one eyebrow. "Then tell me what you're on, because I want some."

She smacked him on the chest. "Nothing. And no, you don't."

"You lie."

She glanced over at Maddy and George, who were standing at the old-fashioned popcorn cart watching the woman pass out red-and-white-striped bags of the buttery snack. "The doctor gave me a script if I need it. But I'm fine."

Sam cocked his head. "Ah, there's the *fine* Mom keeps talking about."

"What's that supposed to mean?"

Sam tipped the girl at the takeout window and balanced the two trays of lemonades between them.

"First sip of the summer," he said, offering one to her.

Clem plucked one of the tall paper cups out of a tray. It was icy cold, and she could see the dark-red shade of fresh strawberries muddled at the bottom.

"I forgot how good these are," Clem said, taking a deep sip of the sweet, lemony drink.

Sam licked his lips and clucked his tongue. "All it needs is vodka."

At their beach plot, Clem slathered the kids with sunscreen and eyed the waves. To her relief, the tide was out.

"Maddy. *Please* stand still," she groaned. George had already slipped through her white, greasy fingers twice.

"Mommy," Maddy whined, "you're making me all sandy." It was true. She'd dropped the sunscreen bottle in the sand at least twice. Now, she was pretty sure she was giving the poor kid more of a microdermabrasion treatment than shielding her fair, freckled skin.

"Okay, go on." But Maddy didn't budge. She stood, arms sticking out from her sides like a scarecrow, and inspected her pasty, streaked belly. Clem realized with a sigh that she'd dumped at least half the bottle on her, along with the sand.

Sam smirked. "I think you missed a spot."

"What? Where?" But Maddy took off toward the waves with her brother and cousins.

"Stop," Paige warned, throwing Sam a look. "He's only teasing," she told Clem. "Now, please, sit down and relax. You're making me tired just watching you."

"Oh. Right." Clem flopped down into a beach chair. It was the first time she'd stopped moving all morning.

Paige held up the sunscreen bottle. "Your kids are probably good until at least next Tuesday, but did you put any lotion on?"

Had she? Clem, who'd just closed her eyes behind her oversized sunglasses, ran a finger down the curve of her nose, which was sticky—from sweat or sunscreen, she couldn't say. "I don't know," she said with a sigh. "But can someone please watch the kids? I just need five."

Evan, who had been stretched out on a towel with his face shielded by a smart straw cowboy hat, leaned over and plopped the hat over her curly hair. "Take ten." Then he ambled down to the water's edge toward the children.

"I need an Evan," Paige mused.

Which struck Clem, because as far as she could tell, Paige already had one.

"Um, hello?" she said, raising her hand. "Widowed mother of two over here."

Despite the humid breeze rolling in off the water, she felt her siblings freeze on either side of her.

"Oh, Clem. I didn't mean . . ."

"Stop," Clem said, before Paige could finish. Enough people back home in Boston felt sorry for her. She couldn't stand it if her family did as well. "I was joking. Speaking of needing to relax."

To her right, Sam let out a nervous chuckle and stretched out with his lemonade. Even he seemed to be reining himself in around her, which was disappointing. She'd been counting on his barefaced humor to ferry her through the first day—at least until cocktail hour. She could certainly count on him to get that going.

Emma, who'd been sitting quietly to the side, watching the swimmers, suddenly stood. "I'm going for a walk."

Emma's long, red hair was pulled back in a ponytail, her Merrill-blue eyes shaded by oversized sunglasses. She was no longer the preteen from recent summers past, whose angular frame and knobby knees Clem had empathized with.

"That sounds good. Maybe we can collect some shells," Paige said, hopping up.

Emma paused. "Mom, I was kind of hoping for some alone time."

"Oh, okay. Sure." Paige sat back down.

Clem felt bad for her sister as she watched her niece head purposefully down the beach without looking back. Just two summers ago she'd been stretched beside Clem on a beach towel reading aloud from a copy of *American Girl.*

"Is she okay?" Clem asked.

"She's a teenager," Paige said with a shrug. "Ned's the one I'm keeping an eye on this year."

Clem's gaze swung to her nephew, who was poised on his boogie board beside George in the water. Ned had always been the more playful one, sometimes mischievously so. Two summers ago they'd caught him driving Richard's red vintage VW Bug up the driveway with the top down. But Clem loved that Ned was spending so much time with George, who idolized his older cousin. They were both good kids—Paige was lucky.

"When does David get here?" Sam asked.

Clem had been wondering the same thing. Paige's family usually arrived in one painfully ordered unit: Paige at the wheel, Thule attachment packed to survive a week in traffic, and David in tow like one of the kids. Ben had once wondered aloud if David found it emasculating to be relegated to the passenger's seat all the time. Flossy had been quick to point out that the other men in the family should take note: David got to drink coffee or sleep the whole way up. Perhaps he had it all figured out.

Paige checked her watch. "He'll be here for dinner." She remained propped up on her elbows, eyes trained on the kids in the water. The open spots on the small beach had filled in with beachgoers already. In moments like this, Clem wouldn't argue her older sister's efficiency. Let her play lifeguard. She couldn't recall the last time someone else had been beside her to be on duty. Even just ten minutes of shut-eye seemed like heaven.

The sun had moved high overhead, swathing the beach in a sleep-inducing heat. Clem sighed contentedly. Behind her, the old-fashioned organ music wafted over from the carousel, and she felt her mind drift lazily. For the last six months in Boston, a sense of normalcy had begun to ebb back. They'd gotten through the first year of birthdays, the first Thanksgiving, the first Christmas, even the anniversary of Ben's accident. Each one was like a small circling back to that day, a wound reopened. Sometimes, in the early months, those days invited a fit of panic that crushed her chest and made her prop herself up against a wall just to breathe. But eventually, even those subsided. Her therapist noted her progress aloud, spreading out her weekly appointments to twice monthly. She began sleeping through the night—a milestone so simple and exempting.

In that same vein, this trip was another milestone to be endured. Returning to the summer house for the first time since Ben had left them. She still liked to think of it as his *leaving*. Which was ridiculous; he couldn't come back. But there was something about the image of him lacing up his sneakers and heading purposefully out their front door that wet spring morning that somehow freed her from the horrific thoughts that had haunted her those first nights alone in their bed. Back then, she'd spent her days wandering the house shrouded in grief, consumed with how to ferry the children and herself from one moment to the next. There had been the immediate details of the service, and later details of Ben's estate. Always the details of daily life to uphold—so many details that propelled her through the hours and ultimately the weeks. But at night, alone in their king-sized bed with nothing for her hands to do, Clem's brain shifted into hyper-focus on details of a different kind. She imagined Ben running along the foggy bend on Brattle Street, his muscled legs pumping methodically, the shimmering stretch of gray asphalt ahead of him. Had there been a screech of brakes or slip of tires? Had Ben sensed the car listing over the white line? Worst of all: had he jerked to look over his shoulder in that static unit of time and space before impact and known?

Reflexively, her legs jerked in the sand. "Stop!" Clem cried, bolting upright. Around her, the beach started to spin.

"Clem?" Her sister and brother sat up alongside her, staring.

It had happened again. She'd fallen asleep for mere seconds, and it had happened. She stood unsteadily and lurched toward the water. "I've got to check on the kids."

Paige pointed in their direction. "They're fine. I've been watching them the whole time."

"No!" Clem snapped, spinning around to face her siblings. The startled look on Sam's face said it all. She tried to take a deep breath. "I need to check."

Why was this happening here? This was vacation. Rhode Island was her haven. She needed the orange bottle of pills on her nightstand. She needed to get the kids out of the water.

The sand was already hot beneath her bare feet as she stalked down to the water's edge. The waves looked bigger down here. Clem felt like she might throw up as she halted at the shore. "George? Maddy? Come out. Come out and play in the sand now."

Evan was standing waist deep in the water, holding onto Maddy's hands and spinning her around. Up and down she undulated like the waves, shrieking in joy each time her belly skimmed the surface—the surface the gray shade of asphalt. Clem's stomach turned. "Evan, please," Clem managed, "bring her back in."

Evan obliged, confused. "You look pale. Everything okay?"

Clem ignored the question, reaching for Maddy's hands. "Come on, let's go build sand castles."

But Maddy did not want to. "No, Mommy!

Uncle Evan is spinning me." She tugged her hand free from her mother's. "Come watch."

Clem reached for daughter again, her tiny wrist cold and slippery in her hand. She needed them out of the waves. "Madeleine, it's time for sand castles." She was aware that a couple with small children next to them was watching her curiously. Her heart quickened. "Now!"

Maddy shook her head, a spray of salt water whisking off her curls. "Later. I'm spinning now."

George rode in on a wave behind Ned, the two boys laughing and wobbling as they struggled against the tide with their boogie boards. Clem held up her free hand.

"George, let's go," she barked.

Reluctantly, he waded over. "Go where?"

Maddy was whimpering now, twisting away from her mother's grip and back toward the waves. Clem turned to glare at the woman behind her, who was now staring openly.

Thankfully, Evan stepped in, though for whose benefit Clem wasn't sure. "Come on, Maddy," he said softly. "I'll make castles with you and Mommy, too."

But Maddy sat down in the sand. "I won't."

Clem's vision blurred. The din of carousel music and children's laughter rose up around her like the bile in her throat. The roaring in her ears crested into a screech of tires.

"Now!" she screamed. She tugged Maddy's hand and pulled her up the beach. Maddy howled. Parents parted as she plowed through.

George trotted worriedly alongside her. "Mom, what's going on?" But he knew. He knew to come and do what she was asking, even if he didn't understand why.

Clem tried to adjust her grasp and her voice accordingly. "It's okay, Maddy. We'll have fun. You'll see." But Maddy had already been having fun in the waves with the boys. And Clem had gone and ruined it. Again.

Clem gritted her teeth against the chattering that had set in.

Ahead, Sam and Paige rose from their beach chairs. As she surged up the beach toward them, they halted uncertainly. How many times in the last year had Clem seen people hesitate when they saw her coming? In grocery store aisles. In school hallways. People would freeze, a flush of concern coloring their faces before they asked how she was. Clem wanted to be invisible.

Emma materialized at Clem's shoulder. "Aunt Clem?"

"Grab the buckets and shovels," Clem said, forcing her voice into a bright falsetto. "We're going to make a castle."

Clem sank to her knees in the sand, her hands shaking. Buckets magically appeared. Ned joined in, cajoling George to follow. Eventually, Maddy stopped fussing and reached for a pink shovel. The adults followed suit, if with too much enthusiasm, their gazes fixed on the sand.

Sam cleared his throat. "That's a great tower, Maddy. Want some more water?"

"I'll find some seashells for windows," Emma offered. She hurried down to the water's edge with a pail, and Clem sank back on her haunches with relief. The spinning beach began to slow.

As the sound of wet sand being scooped filled the small space at the center of their huddle, the roaring in her ears diminished. Clem took a ragged breath and looked out over the wet heads of her babies to the foaming gray stretch of water, fighting the tears that had begun to spill. No one dared look at her.

Clem closed her eyes. If no one ever looked at her again, that would be okay. It would be fucking wonderful.

Paige

Her sense of relief when David's car pulled in was physical. "Dad's here!" she shouted to the kids, who were outside on the deck stacking a tower of Jenga blocks with their little cousins. She hurried out to meet him. David looked rumpled. His eyes were glassy, as if he had not slept, an affliction he'd been suffering from for some time. Something that usually perplexed Paige, but given her own afflictions here at the summer house, she felt a sudden wave of empathy. "You're here!" She grabbed both sides of his face and kissed his unshaven cheek. David stepped back, looking unnerved.

"What?" she asked, feeling suddenly self-conscious.

He shook his head. "Nothing." He retrieved his duffel bag from the backseat.

"So, how'd the interview go?"

"Pretty well, but I likely won't hear anything until the end of the week. The department is interviewing two more candidates."

Paige felt her insides deflate as she followed him up the shell driveway. "Two more?"

"So, how is everyone?"

Paige jammed her hands into her back pockets. How were they? "I don't know. Emma suddenly wants nothing to do with me. Evan and Sam seem tense." She paused. "And Clem—well, she kind of had an episode at East Beach this morning. I'm worried about her." She hadn't even gotten to the vodka bottle in Ned's closet.

David paused on the walkway and looked over his shoulder at her. "So, in other words, it's been normal."

His looseness, which she was trying hard lately to appreciate, exasperated her most at times like this. "You know what I mean, David. I just want everyone to spend some quality family time together. I think they all need this."

He chuckled. "They need this, or you do?"

Paige gave him a look. "We all do." By day two of any other vacation, they would have rounded up the family for the traditional much-celebrated and hard-fought game of Trivial Pursuit and made the first of many bonfires down by the water, where they'd count shooting stars as the younger ones fell asleep on one of Flossy's frayed quilts. To her mother's dismay, they hadn't even managed to get through the traditional welcome-back lobster dinner the night before. Clem had taken one bite and disappeared upstairs. Sam and Evan, usually the chatterboxes, had eaten mostly in silence. Even Richard had seemed more contemplative than usual.

But all of that would hopefully change now that David was here. He was so much better at navigating this kind of stuff than she was. "So, you have a good feeling about how the interview went, right?"

David stopped at the porch steps and turned to face her. "Paige. Will you just let me take off my shoes and grab a cold beer? Maybe say hi to my kids?" He sighed. "I told you everything I know. You need to be patient."

She followed him inside. She had been patient. It had been six months since Trinity had let David go. And though she would never tell him this, could never tell him, she'd seen it coming at the faculty holiday party that past winter. David had long been a popular professor among the undergrads, but Paige had wondered if Marcy Shrine, his department head, shared the same buffed affection of the freshman class. Paige had inferred the opposite that night at the president's house, where she'd found herself standing across the room from her husband but alongside Marcy. Paige had observed Marcy's eyes narrow to mere slits as the room listened to David, who was holding court by the parlor fireplace, a tumbler of whisky in hand. It was a sight that had caused Paige to whisk yet another glass of champagne off a passing server's tray and promptly tip it back, while at the other end of the Persian rug David's cheeks grew rosier and his anecdotes more vivid as glasses emptied and the evening wore on. Paige had tried to raise these concerns with David, softly, across the pillow that night. It wasn't the first staff gathering at which she'd gleaned these tensions. But David had laughed and rolled over, telling her not to worry, Marcy was loathed by nearly everyone in the department. Besides, rumor had it she was being courted by Smith for a writer-in-residence sabbatical. Yes, it was his tenth year at the university, and he still hadn't received tenure, but she shouldn't worry about his teaching trajectory—it was stable, if staid. And his semester calendar allowed him to be home with the kids for holidays and summers. It was a win-win situation for all of them, he reminded her, with a trace of irritation. Why couldn't she understand that?

But in the last year, Paige couldn't ignore the fact that there were things David did not seem to see. While he'd been the one who'd initially chosen their renovated historic farmhouse, quick to point out the merits of the competitive school system and wholesome neighborhoods in the rural western hills of Connecticut, he had recently come to seem disenchanted with it. He complained about the long commute "from the country" to Hartford. The home was too drafty, the acreage too laborious. When the rows of heirloom apple trees he'd once been thrilled to inherit with the farm—and for which he'd

73

spent the entire first winter reading about the intricacies of hand pruning—became overgrown, she wondered if their neglected crop would even be viable for picking that fall. It wasn't just the property he neglected. She'd noticed that he'd stopped staying up late in the den, which they'd converted from a butler's pantry, pounding away on the vintage Underwood typewriter that he insisted on working from, choosing instead to flop alongside Ned on the couch in front of ESPN. Or sometimes climbing the stairs and turning in for the night, hours before even the kids had. It worried Paige. But so, too, did the bills. And the kids' school schedules, and Ned's travel lacrosse team, and Emma's ACT prep courses. David was in a funk. He would come around. She was taking care of enough people and pets and details, so David would have to fix this himself.

Now, she followed him inside the summer house. Ned had come in from the deck, and when he saw his dad, he threw his long arms around David, clapping him on the back in the way that men did to one another, leaving Paige struck by how grown-up their son looked.

"For you, Flossy." He extended a robust bundle of sunflowers, their woody green stalks tied with grosgrain ribbon. She hadn't even noticed he'd been carrying them, but of course he had stopped at the rustic little farm stand he knew

Flossy liked at the north end of Airport Road. Paige wanted to reach for his hand and squeeze it. But he would only look at her in the same way he'd looked at her moments earlier when she'd hugged and kissed him by the car, because Paige was not prone to such demonstrations. But why?

It was something she was aware of, something she'd been meaning to address somehow. She knew her husband needed things from her, things she wanted to give, meant to give, but there was always so much to do. Like now: the kids were coming back inside asking about dinner. Sam and Evan appeared—who wanted to head down to the beach to throw the football around? Suddenly the house shuddered to life. *This!* This was what she'd wanted from her family since arriving.

But Paige found herself frozen in the center f the kitchen as beers were plucked from the fridge and towels thrown over shoulders.

"Mom, aren't you coming?" Ned asked, breezing past her.

Even Richard seemed to be moving purposefully, hunting down the cooler from the pantry and handing it over to Flossy, who tossed snacks inside: grapes, a hunk of Camembert, pita chips. Grilled steak sandwiches were pulled from the fridge—when had her mother made those?

Arthur rose from his dog bed and scrabbled across the hardwood floors to stand beside her as the screen door slapped open and shut, again and again, until the house was empty. She watched them all traipse across the yard and down the beach path, until the last head disappeared in the dune grass. Paige paused, barefoot, in the doorway. She wanted to follow them. Behind her the ancient Westinghouse refrigerator hummed, the only sound in the house. The sunflowers lay prostrate on the kitchen island. She went to find a vase.

Flossy

Joe was back, with eight cans of White Dove paint. After poring over new samples and holding them up to the light in various rooms, Flossy had given up. She'd enlisted the help of all the kids. Paige and Clem had both picked a color called bone, which had made Sam smirk, "Ever the orthopedist." Though he'd been no help, declaring them all the same. Richard frowned through his bifocals and asked what was wrong with the trim color they had now. Evan had lasted the longest, helping her narrow it down to two new whites. But when Joe had called back, she couldn't find the strip, couldn't remember the names, and suddenly remembered that she'd never called the bakery back. "White Dove!" she'd barked into the phone. She hadn't been in to check his work since he had arrived. At this point, she hardly cared if the dove turned out to be purple.

She had talked to the caterer, and the menu was almost finalized. She'd made a beverage list that someone would have to go pick up at the liquor store. And she'd checked the tracking information on the gorgeous teak serving table she'd ordered for the backyard, but it was two days late on delivery. Two days! She'd made frantic calls to the furniture store, who assured her it would arrive on time. The table was a last-minute splurge—something Richard did not need to know about. He would've asked why they needed outdoor furniture when they were selling the house. Or why they couldn't just rent one from the tent company, which was already delivering things for serving and guest seating. But Flossy had stumbled across this gorgeous piece on Pinterest a few weeks earlier, and as soon as she set eyes on the advertisement, showing a man and a woman dressed all in white toasting each other at an ocean-side soiree, something just happened, causing her to then click ADD TO CART before she could think twice. Flossy had pictured the evening of the party as sunset drenched, the flash of crystal goblets and splashes of summer pastels of their smartly dressed guests. The new table was a narrow pedestal design, perfect for setting up beneath the arbor just in front of the ocean view. She might even ask the tent company to arrange for paper lanterns to be strung overhead. Oh! Flossy could just picture the bartender standing behind the serving table, pouring sparkling amber glasses of champagne. If only the table would get there in time.

She'd admit it: the birthday party was an

excuse to get all her kids and grandkids back to the cottage—a feat that seemed increasingly impossible each year. Flossy reached into the depths of the refrigerator for her latest weapons: cold lobster from the night before, chilled chicken breasts, two sprigs of the Asian citrus rosemary that unbearable Judy Broadbent, from her library book club, had recommended she plant. Judy couldn't pick a decent book to throw at someone, but she knew herbs. Flossy infused her vinaigrette with it and poured it over sliced summer melons. She assembled all the cheerful ingredients on the stainless-steel-topped kitchen island, stepped back, and sighed. Why didn't her kids want to come home?

The excuses: Paige was short one vet in the clinic. Sam was traveling (a man who frequented the far corners of Asia couldn't manage a drive three states north?). Clem, well—Clem was the only one who had a good reason. But even before Ben had died, there had been an endless stretch when either one or both of the kids were sick. Take your pick: stomach bug, croup, the dreadfully named hand-foot-and-mouth disease. As if Flossy had not ferried her own three children through decades of flu seasons— vaccine-free, mind you.

Christmas was the pits. Every holiday season Flossy loathed those insufferable commercials by Audi and Pottery Barn and the like—beaming families outfitted in fisherman sweaters spilling out of shiny cars at the grandparents' Adirondack chalet. Who were those people? It didn't matter. Flossy wished those very people would pull up in front of her house in their infuriating matching red scarves. Hell, Flossy wanted her family to *be* those people.

Her grandkids were already growing up so fast that in her more bitter moments she found herself wondering if she even still knew them. For Thanksgiving, Paige always ended up going to her in-laws'. Clem used to host, but Flossy and Richard had shared that day with Ben's parents from Saratoga Springs, which wasn't quite the same. That tasteless cornbread stuffing his mother insisted on serving? In the center of the table, no less, while Flossy's own chestnut recipe had never once made it onto the menu. As for Samuel and Evan, they kept a social schedule that none of them, combined, could rival. They had promised to come home this past Thanksgiving, but Sam had given his regrets at the last minute, citing work commitments. Flossy shook her head. Young people let their careers rule their lives. And worse: all that nonsense about friends substituting as family!

Judy Broadbent seemed immune to such troubles. Her daughter, Caroline, had not only returned home the summer she graduated college to teach in the local preschool, but had also seen fit to marry a lovely doctor, who'd been only too happy to pack his bags and move into the house directly across the street from Judy's stately saltbox in the historic district, where they rapidly produced three towheaded grandchildren in unjust succession. Judy had since canceled more tennis matches than she kept, never failing to regale Flossy with the details of how she spent her grandchild-rich afternoons: the intricate popsicle-stick sculptures they glued, the apples they'd picked in the local orchard, or the home-made pie they'd made together afterward in her newly remodeled kitchen. Judy never made a good pie.

How could Flossy compete with that? Her own children were more concerned with careers and friends. Flossy did not like this generation who shucked their parents like withered husks and turned their attention to sleek granite islands and hulking SUVs in order to better entertain their neighbors. She'd witnessed this sad trend among Clem's friends when she and Richard had driven up to Boston for the kids' birthday parties. There had been more adults than kids loitering around the yard, and since when did people serve signature cocktails at a child's birthday? (Clem had gently reminded Flossy of the family album evidence of her smoking Virginia Slims in the background of her childhood birthday pictures. But *everyone* did back then.) And where were all the grandparents and elderly aunts and uncles? The family? Not watching from the comforts of a wingback chair in the corner, no! That spot was reserved for the hired entertainment. Let's not even get her started on *that* racket. Three hundred dollars for a pot-bellied man in a safari suit toting a tarantula?

As for Paige, Flossy wasn't sure if her eldest even had any real friends—a thought that gave her pause over her fruit bowl. But no matter, because family was flesh and bone. Family was *everything*.

At that moment one of her favorite family members, Emma, strolled in, her lovely face concealed by another book. Flossy should be glad it wasn't some iDevice, she supposed, but the child had barely made conversation since arriving. At least Emma remained predictable and steadfast. Nothing like little Maddy, whose exuberant hug could melt you in the same beat that her fierce look could wilt you. Or Ned, who swept through the house like a Labrador retriever, all arms and legs and tongue-lolling energy that could knock you over as quickly as it sailed out. And George: sweet, serious George, with that freckled nose always wrinkled in consternation at his sister's antics. Oh, how glad she was she'd managed to lure them all home this summer!

"Why don't you help me make dinner? I want

to hear all about the new classes you'll be taking next fall," Flossy told Emma. Tonight, she was making Clem's summer favorite—chilled chicken and avocado salad—since last night's lobster dinner had basically been a disaster.

Tonight would be different. Tonight she would get everyone to the table to eat, to talk, to laugh. Just as they'd done at the beach all afternoon. They had all dispersed the second they'd gotten back from the beach, but no matter. She'd get them all back for dinner.

Emma took her place beside Flossy at the island. She selected two avocados from the bowl and deftly sliced and pitted each, leaving the green flesh smooth.

"You're a natural," Flossy murmured.

"Thanks, Grammy. I do this at home all the time."

Flossy wondered for a worried beat if this was because Paige was always working late. As for David, she still had no idea what was happening with his job search. She'd tried to inquire delicately, but that Paige was like a vault.

As Emma sliced and talked about a Mr. Fischer's Spanish class (did no public school appreciate those melodious rolling r's of the French language?), Flossy stole a peek at Ned, George, and Maddy outside on the deck. They'd gotten the SORRY! game off the living room shelf again, and she watched now as George unceremoniously dumped the contents of the game box. Pieces bounced and rolled across the deck boards. She wondered if this had anything to do with missing his father. "Boys, why don't you locate your grandfather?" she called out to them. "He'd love a game of SORRY!"

Richard hated board games, especially SORRY!, but it would do him good. Where was he, anyway? She craned her neck to see out the kitchen window, searching the yard, but there was only Sam—on yet another maddening call—pacing the far edge of the yard near the beach path, which she'd seen Clem head down moments earlier.

She handed her granddaughter a lemon to squeeze. Emma frowned, hesitating before setting it down on the counter.

"What's wrong?"

"Grammy, is it true what Uncle Sam said about this counter?"

Flossy eyed Sam, who was still on his phone, pacing the yard like a fenced-in thoroughbred. "What did Uncle Sam say?"

"He said this counter used to be an examination table from the county morgue"—she lowered her voice—"and that bodies were embalmed on it."

Flossy's knife slid through the honeydew melon she was slicing, nearly taking off the tip of her thumb. "Good Lord!"

In the next room, Joe cleared his throat.

Flossy glared out the window at Sam. *What was the matter with him?* "This countertop is a piece of local Watch Hill history. Your great grandfather salvaged it from the back kitchen of the old Snuffy's restaurant. *Not* the coroner."

Emma let out a breath. "Good. Because that would be pretty gross."

Flossy could feel her eyelid begin to twitch. *What if Clem had heard that nonsense?* "When exactly did your uncle share that little tidbit with you?"

Emma shrugged. "Last summer." Then she caught herself. "No, sorry. It would've been the summer before . . . " she corrected.

"Of course." Flossy nodded sharply. Because none of them had come last summer, despite Flossy's pleas.

Flossy set down her knife, strode to the deck, and pushed the screen door aside with a slap. "Samuel! Come take out the trash!" she barked.

Behind her, Emma ducked her chin and tried to contain her laugh.

Honestly. These children of hers.

The front door opened, and she was relieved to see Evan was back from the bakery, where he'd delivered the deposit for the party desserts. He held up a paper bag. "Blueberry muffins. Couldn't resist."

Flossy tried to contain her enthusiasm. "What a treat!" She'd been waiting for a private moment with Evan since everyone had arrived. With dinner preparations done and everyone else off entertaining themselves without so much as a thought as to who was making dinner, she had no qualms about stealing that moment. It was certainly due her.

"Emma, why don't you go help the boys wrap up their board game? It's almost dinner time." Flossy handed her the bag of muffins. "Here, take these outside for you and the boys to split. Let us know what you think."

"But aren't we eating dinner soon?"

Shoot. She wasn't about to ruin another dinner. Oh, what the hell. "Just sample them," she instructed.

Emma shrugged. "Okay, Gram."

She turned to Evan. "Darling, help me pour drinks?"

Flossy pretended to toss the salad as Evan pulled dinner glasses from the cupboard. Such a striking young man he was. But there was a sadness that pulled on his spine that she could see from across the room. "I made chicken salad for dinner. I was going to serve it over lettuce, but I just remembered I have this gorgeous loaf of sourdough. Want to try a bite?" She stopped when she looked up and saw the expression on Evan's face.

"Oh, honey. What can I do for you? It's not a sandwich, is it?"

He shook his head wistfully. "I'm not hungry. But maybe Sam is."

Flossy went over and patted his cheek. "Samuel is a grown man; he can get his own damn sandwich. Come sit a minute. My knee hurts."

It didn't, but since it seemed to be the only topic all three of her kids could agree on since arriving, she may as well get some mileage out of it.

"Why didn't you say so?" he said, taking her arm and guiding her into the living room. "I would've made dinner."

"Which is why I said nothing." She lowered herself onto the once vanilla-colored couch, which was now more a shade of wet sand. "Look at this furniture. Why on earth did I let Clem talk us into decorating the summer house in these pale blues and whites?" The colors conjured the sky and sea that rolled just a few hundred feet below the bluff in their backyard, but over the years the cotton had frayed and the children had spilled, and Flossy had begun to fantasize about having all of it reupholstered in a utilitarian color called something like "Swamp." But that would only put Richard over the edge. Just like their youngest, he loathed change. "So, what do you think?"

Evan sat across from her on the couch, meeting her gaze. "About the upholstery?"

She smiled sadly. Flossy could lie to her own children, but not to Evan.

"What're you up to, Flo?" He was the only one she allowed to call her that.

She leaned in. "I didn't want to say anything in front of the children, but I wanted to tell you face-to-face how sorry Richard and I are about Texas." Texas. A place, not a name that could begin to sum up all that her boys had endured down there.

Evan looked down at his bare feet.

"What happened?" she asked.

"It just wasn't our baby," he said softly.

Flossy felt the tears pricking her eyes, and she willed them away. All any of them knew, from the short group message that Samuel had sent over Memorial Day weekend, was that they'd come home from Texas with an empty baby carrier. The young mother had changed her mind.

Flossy wasted no time in imagining the worst: that this naïve teen had done so because Evan and Samuel were gay—a thought that drew ire up inside her as thick and viscous as crude oil. But Richard had cautioned her not to jump to such conclusions. Wasn't it commonplace for a mother to decide to keep the child after giving birth? Could they really blame her if that were the case? These were questions Richard had raised with his usual maddening logic. Flossy didn't care what questions he posed. She wanted answers.

Flossy reached out to Evan. His upper arm was strong and thick, like ship rope, through his linen shirt. "Your baby is still out there—of that I am sure."

Evan smiled sadly. "I hope so. There's another mother, Mara. She's in the process of considering prospective families, but she called us back to meet with her again last week. We're hoping to hear a decision from her very soon."

Flossy sat back, stunned and relieved. "Why didn't you boys tell me? That's wonderful!"

"We didn't want to get everyone's hopes up, after what happened the last time. Besides, Mara hasn't made a decision yet."

This was the best news Flossy had heard in a long time. "I'm going to pray for you."

Evan raised his eyebrows. "You going to church somewhere I don't know about, Flo?"

It was a family joke. The family had long belonged to the local Protestant church at home in Connecticut, and attended sporadically, usually when they gathered for the holidays. But even then, on Easter or Christmas, Flossy remained home, stationed at the stove. "I don't need anyone to tell me what to be thankful for or how many sins have been forgiven on my behalf," she'd say. "We've got enough blessings and sinners under this roof already, and I am intimately acquainted with each and every one."

Now, Flossy waved her hand at him. "Pray, meditate, kick sand. Just know I'm on you boys' side."

The screen door jerked open, and Emma poked her head in. "Grammy? The little kids are hungry."

Together they rifled through cabinets for plates and napkins. Emma retrieved silverware from the drawer. Richard appeared from his mysterious jaunt with a bag from the market. What would he say when she told him what Evan had said? She didn't dare get her hopes up too much; Evan was right. But oh! This Mara! She'd be a fool not to pick these two boys—a damned fool.

"Just in time for dinner!" Richard mused cheerily, pulling out a bottle of chardonnay.

Just in time, she thought to herself as she put the finishing touches on the food. How like them all to appear whenever a meal was about to be dropped on the table. As if on cue, David came through the front door.

"Good bike ride?" Evan asked. Flossy was pleased to see the color in David's cheeks when he smiled. The visit was already agreeing with him.

"Smells good in here," David said. "Need a hand?"

Richard handed him the bottle of wine to uncork.

Flossy watched out of the corner of her eye as Evan went out to the deck and sat down with the kids. He ruffled George's hair gently, and the little boy leaned in to his uncle without taking his eyes off the game board. She glanced away.

"Here, Richard, take these glasses outside, will you?" Obligingly, he carried the tray of drinks outside, leaving her to collect herself as she surveyed the landscape of her family. Samuel, still on his call, began making his way across the yard. They were here, all of them together at the summer house, just as she'd wanted. And yet a sense of unrest still fluttered within.

Beyond them, the row of brown hedges stirred in the ocean breeze. Just looking at them made the base of Flossy's head throb. Once small and manicured, they'd created a natural border around the deck, when the kids were young. But since then, they'd filled out in all the wrong places, despite her attempts to shear them every spring. One was dying, smack dab in the middle, and its brown skeletal frame was a blight directly in her line of vision to the edge of her yard and the stretch of ocean beyond. She'd only asked Richard a hundred times to remove them that summer, but first he couldn't find the trimmers, and when he did they weren't sharp enough, which led to a trip to the hardware store. They'd since realized the hedge was dying, and she'd decided he should just go ahead and dig it out, roots and all. But then his back was acting up, and she didn't want him injuring himself, especially before his birthday party. So Sam had agreed to trim them when he arrived. But still, there they were. Those *goddamned* hedges.

Clem

Sunday was the kind of beach day one spent the long winter months daydreaming about, and the whole family was parked across the sand in various states of repose. Evan was buried in sand up to his neck, as George and Maddy raced back and forth to the water's edge with buckets of water. Only his hands stuck out, at an awkward angle where one imagined his waist must be under all that sand. He kept wrinkling his nose and asking George to wipe the sand off it for him.

"Cement him in good!" Maddy ordered. Paige stood off to the side, making calls to her office to check on some dog or other who was recovering from one surgery or another. Richard dozed in a beach chair, an open book slipping off his lap. Even Sam seemed less edgy, stretched across a towel, well out of the way of the kids' and Evan's sand-flinging activity. Flossy was the only one on high alert, having parked her beach chair so close Clem could practically hear her breathing in her ear.

"Are you sure you aren't getting too much sun?" Flossy asked, leaning closer. "We've been down here for a long time. I think everyone's getting ready to head back up to the house."

Clem wordlessly pointed at her floppy straw hat and the kids' hats, and then held up a bottle of sunscreen for good measure. "You guys can go ahead. The kids and I will be up soon." She just wanted fifteen minutes to herself.

Yesterday at East Beach had been a disaster, no thanks to her siblings, who couldn't refrain from offering their two cents on every decision she made. Even Evan, who usually stepped aside to let Sam and his sisters navigate the rough road of ancient childhood battle wounds that they inevitably seemed to revisit during reunions. *Has this happened before? Do you want to take a nap? Have you been in touch with your doctor lately?* She cringed at the memory. What was wrong with everybody? She knew what was wrong with her. She just needed more time. She needed everyone to leave her alone.

It had been a while since one of her episodes. Still, she knew it had been a bad one, and today she was determined to make it up to the kids. So she'd risen early and stolen away to town as soon as the storefronts on Main Street opened. The new sand toys she'd found now littered the beach in front of her, the bright plastic landscape interrupted only by a lopsided sand castle whose watery moat was now home to several hermit crabs who hadn't dug fast enough to escape

Maddy's deft fingers. The entire family had helped to make an afternoon of it, and as much as she'd enjoyed the distraction and the extra sets of hands and eyes, now she was happy to see them packing up their beach chairs and shaking the sand off their towels.

"You sure you don't want company?" Evan asked. "Sam and I can stay down here and keep an eye on the kids if you want to take a snooze."

Clem lifted the brim of her hat and squinted up at him; how she loved this man! His concern was the only one that somehow didn't grate her nerves. "Thanks, sweetie. But we're fine. We'll see you back up at the house."

Sam, loaded up with beach bags, stood over her casting a shadow. "Okay, but no griping when you get the cold shower," he half teased.

Clem closed her eyes and smiled. Let them go shower and change for dinner. She didn't care if the last of the hot water was all used up by the time she got back; she'd happily use the cold outdoor shower in the side yard, as long as she could steal a few minutes' peace.

Now, at Clem's feet, Maddy knelt over her new bucket adoringly. "Hello, Sebastian," she whispered into the watery recess.

George trotted up from the water's edge, listing sideways with the weight of his bucket, water sloshing against his legs. "Here," he puffed, crashing onto the sand beside his sister. He dumped the contents of the pail into the moat. "Maddy, you've gotta keep it full, or they'll crawl away." He counted the hermit crabs aloud. "One, two, three, four . . . hey, we're missing one!"

Maddy covered her bucket protectively with both hands and scowled.

Clem smiled and leaned back in her beach chair. Yes, this was what they all needed—hermit crabs and sand toys. And the glorious stretch of empty sand before them. She would languish the rest of the day on the beach if the kids wanted to.

With her loud, boisterous family gone, they had the beach all to themselves, which wasn't unusual. Save for a couple of beach paths that wound down to the water off their private road, there was neither easy access nor a place for visitors to park. Unlike the state beaches with their giant parking lots in Westerly and Charlestown, this stretch of shore was dotted with cottages and private driveways. Throughout the day, neighbors would emerge to set up beach chairs and lay out towels, still leaving plenty of space and quiet. This beach had long been a slice of heaven that the Merrill children did not take for granted.

So it was with some curiosity that Clem noticed, out of the corner of her right eye, the figure striding across the sand. She sat up. It was a young man in red swim trunks. He seemed to have come from the Weitzman's place next door.

She watched as he tossed his towel on the sand by the high-tide mark before trotting toward the surf. He was fit and tawny-skinned, the muscles of his back tensing as he jogged straight into the waves. Clem watched as he dove into the white froth. His arms sliced through the choppy water as he swam away from her. After last night's rainfall, it had to be cold. Directly in his path, she noted the large metal buoy bobbing gently on the gray ocean surface. Without breaking his pace, he circled the buoy and turned back for shore. It was then that she realized she was matching the breath in her chest with his stroke. As he returned to the beach, Clem sat up straight. She plucked the novel she'd brought out of her beach bag and cracked it open, glancing over the page as he emerged from the water. Was he one of the three Weitzman kids she'd grown up with? But no—Andrew Weitzman was in his mid-forties, married with kids. Clem had been closest to Suzy, the middle sister. They were inseparable in the way that only summer friendships allowed: endless sandy days interrupted only by dinner back at their own houses, before racing back down the beach path to play in the dune grass and watch the sun set before someone initiated a game of flashlight tag. The last Clem had heard, Suzy had moved to Los Angeles with her husband and had had a baby. The only other member of the Weitzman family was the baby, Fritz. Fritzy, as they had all called him, had been what his father, Ray, had once referred to as an "oopsy" baby, after more than a few bottles of wine had been opened at one of the family's bonfires. The men had all laughed, Richard included, but Clem remembered the scowl Flossy had thrown her father's way across the flames. Fritzy had been an infant the summer Clem was in the fourth grade. Watching this young man over the top of her book as he strode across the sand, she was pretty sure this was not Fritz. He'd be—what?—recently graduated from college? The shaggy-haired man in front of her looked too young. He must be a summer renter.

To her delight, he stopped by his towel and shook his head like a dog. Something inside her stirred. She watched as he toweled off, put his sunglasses back on, and turned her way.

"Beautiful," he said, smiling. She flushed, and then realized he was talking about the water. "Best time of day to swim."

She nodded, and before she could recover to reply, he was trotting up the path toward the house. Clem let her breath out as he disappeared between the dunes.

As if sensing his mother's attention had strayed, George followed her gaze across the beach. "Who's that?" he asked.

"I don't know," Clem said, swiveling back to her offspring. But it occurred to her that she was suddenly determined to find out.

Clem

She made sure she was at the beach by four thirty the next day. If he was disciplined about his solo swim at the end of each day, then so would she be about showing up to witness it.

They'd spent the day in Watch Hill, shopping on Bay Street, and now it was just Clem and the kids. She told herself (and Flossy) that they were catching a quick swim before dinner. By four forty-five, when he still hadn't show up, Clem realized she'd been clenching her teeth—something she'd apparently been doing for the past year, her dentist had pointed out at her last appointment. She'd come to think of the accompanying headaches as another added physiological manifestation of grief. And of widowhood. Her dentist prescribed a bite plate that she was to sleep in, a cumbersome piece of plastic that previously she likely would have shoved into the recesses of her bedside table drawer without a thought. But now she wore it without complaint. What was one more small annoyance against the backdrop of her new life?

Now, she flexed her jaw and reminded herself to relax. He was just a stranger in red swim trunks who had happened to share her beach yesterday afternoon. What did it matter to her if he showed up or not? She was here with her kids. To relax. To let go of worries, the least of which would be whether or not some kid in the house next door crossed her line of vision as he peeled off his shirt and dove headfirst into the surf. But that suntan line at the base of his back above his red board shorts. And the way he shook his slick head when he emerged from the surf. Something inside her stirred again.

"Mom, I'm hot." Maddy raced over, spraying Clem with sand.

"Maddy." She rummaged through the beach bag. "Put your sun hat on. Or better yet, hop in the water." She pointed to the surf coming in, and just as she did, he walked past her index finger. He turned, just in time to see her pointing directly at him. She thrust the sun hat at Maddy. "Here. Put it on. Now."

Maddy grumbled and tugged the hat over her head, and Clem tried to focus her attention on the tie. She peered over her daughter's shoulder. He was standing at the shore, hands on his hips. Good Lord, he was fit.

"When's snack?" Maddy asked. "I'm starving." She had positioned herself directly in her mother's line of vision. But Clem would not peer around her daughter to better see him. She would not.

"Check the cooler. There's cheese and crackers," she said. As Maddy trudged away, Clem sat back and let her breath out. He was in the water now, already halfway to the buoy. Something about the sure way his arms sliced through the water soothed her. She followed his stroke, her breath evening out with his smooth rhythm. The day was clear and bright, the sun reflecting sharply off the water so she had to squint, but she kept her eyes trained on his progress, lulled by memories.

Every spring, Ben's law firm sponsored an adult soccer league. Like many of the younger men and women at the firm, he'd joined the team, and Clem used to bring the kids down to Battery Park to watch their Saturday games. There was something about Ben on the field that had always filled her with a sense of peace. Ben was an athlete in the truest sense—a lithe, agile player. But it was his gait that distinguished him on the field. No matter how often she arrived late at the game, she could always pick Ben out on the field: sprinting, purposeful, his arms pumping methodically at his sides, Greek-like in form. But it was the way he ran when not chasing the ball that hit her right in the soft spot of her middle. In the exuberant moment after scoring a goal, Ben would throw his head back in the wind, his stride loose and leggy, like a child's. It was joy in motion. And it never failed to fill her with the same.

There were so many things Clem missed about Ben. If someone had asked her shortly after he had died, there were the obvious things: his arm thrown over her side in the middle of the night; the look in his eye when he knelt down to listen to his children— *really* listen—as they descended upon him shouting and talking over each other the second he walked in the door from work. But watching his body move through space on the soccer field—the grace in that reckless abandonment— was one thing that never would have occurred to her. And how her insides had ached when she'd seen it that spring in young George as he'd sprinted down the sideline during one of his soccer matches. She'd had to leave the bleachers and go to her car, where she'd heaved over the steering wheel until her eyes were dry. It was something she had never known she would miss until that moment.

Now, sitting on the beach at her family's summer house, something inside Clem was triggered. Unlike the wash of emotions that had shadowed her in the past year, this feeling was anchored very much in the present. There was no connection to those fall afternoons watching Ben in Battery Park that roused her memory. Not for this beach. Certainly not for this boy, barely a man, emerging from the water. Whatever it was, it stilled her insides and elongated her breath in a way she suddenly recognized, in a way she realized she'd stopped feeling for some time. It was yearning. So she decided to allow herself these stolen moments each afternoon. This voyeurism, or whatever it was she could call it. She was only human. And as far as she was concerned, a grieving widow and young mother was just about as raw a human as one could get.

Her children were kneeling in the sand by the water, shrieking and feverishly digging holes as quickly as the incoming waves filled them. Behind them, the young man was emerging from the surf. Suddenly he stopped, bent down, and retrieved something from an incoming wave. She couldn't see what it was, but he studied it before turning toward her children. When he said something to them, she straightened. Maddy and George looked up. She leaned forward, straining to hear over the rush of waves.

"Mommy!" Maddy shouted up to her, waving her arms. "Come look."

Clem stood, and he looked up and smiled.

"Coming." Clem adjusted her sarong and hurried down the beach. The sand burned the soles of her feet, causing her to take quick, hopping steps. She probably looked like a stork approaching.

"Look!" Maddy shrieked. "It's a sea orchard."

"Urchin," Clem and the young man said

together. She tried to focus on the small, shiny urchin balanced in his upturned palm, but she snuck a sideways glance at his face. His eyes were green, lighter than her own. His lashes were thick and dark.

"I don't think I've ever seen a live one here," she said.

He thrust his hand in her direction, and she involuntarily stepped back. "It won't sting," he said, eyes twinkling. He rolled the prickly ball of sea life gently into her open hand, which she hadn't realized she'd extended.

"It's beautiful," she managed.

The kids sprang into action, gathering buckets and water. "Let's make it a house!" George shouted. The man laughed. There was something so familiar about him, she thought.

As the kids set up the bucket, he turned to her. "I hope that was okay, showing them the urchin," he said.

Clem allowed her eyes to travel across his face. Friendly. Handsome. The eyes again. She nodded. "Of course, thank you. They love stuff like this."

"Can we keep it?" Maddy crowed. "Please! Ooh, let's take it home to show the uncles!"

But George was already reaching for it. "No," he said, firmly. "It belongs to the ocean. We're letting it go."

"That's right," Clem said, kneeling down, level

with Maddy's disappointed scowl. "He's wild, honey. But you can enjoy him for a few minutes before we put him back."

Maddy's brow unfurrowed slightly. "But I want to keep him."

"No!" George insisted, reaching for the bucket.

Maddy grasped the plastic handle with both hands and sat down hard. "He's mine!" she hollered.

Clem closed her eyes. Here they were, in typical sibling fashion, about to thrash it out. In front of this perfectly nice stranger, no less.

"Maddy, listen to Mommy. We can catch critters and study them, but then we have to let them go."

She leaned in until she was nose to nose with her daughter's consternation. Maddy was so stubborn, so fierce. Just like Clem had been, according to Flossy. Her blue eyes sparkled with hot tears, and the sadness behind them was as familiar as it was heartbreaking for Clem. "I'll miss him," she whispered.

Clem wrapped her arms around her sandy, wet toddler and pulled her in. As it always did, Maddy's heartache made her forget everything else around them. Until she felt the sand shift beside her. It was him.

He kneeled behind Clem and waited until Maddy peeked up at him.

"You know, I'm pretty sure I saw that urchin yesterday."

Maddy buried her face in her mother's hair, but he went on.

"I think he came to the beach with his family, just like you did today with your family."

Clem could feel Maddy's head turn. "He has a brother?" she asked in a small voice.

The young man cocked his head. "I think maybe it was a sister. She was pretty sparkly. And prickly!" He wiggled his fingers playfully, imitating little spikes.

Maddy laughed.

"His parents are probably wondering where he is," he added, gathering his towel and standing. "Imagine how worried your mom would be if she took you to the beach, but then she couldn't find you."

Maddy thought this over, and after an excruciatingly long moment she placed the urchin gently back in the bucket. "Okay. I'll put him back in a few minutes."

"Good girl. Five minutes," Clem said.

Maddy turned to regard her mother. "Six," she mouthed.

Beside her, the young man covered his laugh. Clem stood and turned to him, feeling a sudden rush of gratitude for this stranger.

"Thank you," she said. "Not just for showing them the urchin, but for what you said to her." She paused. "Maddy has trouble letting go of things."

He held her gaze, unblinking. Did he find her familiar, too? "It's okay. Beautiful things are hard to let go of."

Clem felt her face flush beneath the brim of her hat. There was nothing she could think of to say. "Well, thanks."

"You bet." He waved good-bye to the kids and then turned toward the dunes. Wordlessly, she watched him go.

Now the kids were arguing about where to let the urchin go, and she sensed they were one spilled bucket of water away from a meltdown. But Clem couldn't steal her gaze away, even when the young man disappeared up the path through the dunes.

Adjacent, from her family's own beach path, came the sound of voices. Flossy's straw hat emerged above the beach grass, and the soft outline of her mother stepped onto the sand in a bright orange cover-up. Behind her, Evan, Samuel, and David followed, carrying beach chairs, umbrellas, and more coolers. Leave it to Flossy to have arranged and assigned the men. Paige followed with the kids.

"How's the water?" Flossy called.

Clem waited as they made their way down. "Beautiful," she said, realizing she hadn't stepped foot in it yet.

"Uncle Sam! Uncle Evan! Look what we got," George shouted, grabbing the blue pail with the urchin. He rocketed past his mother, Maddy in hot pursuit.

"He's mine," Maddy told them, a warning rather than an invitation. She glanced back sheepishly at her mother. "For five more minutes."

Coolers were opened and towels laid out. Sam cracked a beer open, and Evan set up the umbrella.

"Where'd you find it?" Sam asked. "I haven't seen one of these in years."

"Some guy," George said.

Flossy frowned. "Which guy?"

Clem pointed next door. She realized she hadn't even introduced herself or the kids. She had no idea who he was. "The guy next door. I think he's a summer renter."

Flossy considered this as she set up her beach chair. "At the Weitzmans'?"

Clem nodded.

"Oh, that's not a summer renter. That's their youngest son."

"Fritzy? The baby?"

Flossy sat down, a look of amusement crossing her face. "Well, I don't imagine anyone's called him that in a long time, but yes. He just graduated from Duke."

Clem reached over and plucked Sam's beer out of his hand.

"Hey," he protested.

"I need this more than you," she said. She'd been ogling baby Fritz.

Paige

Damn it. Her mother had given her a grocery list, which it seemed she'd left somewhere back at the house, where Flossy was supervising the painting of the entire place for a mere birthday party and bossing said birthday boy around the yard with a shovel. She was not going back for it.

Paige remembered limes (likely for Sam's evening gin and tonics), milk, cereal, bread, and fresh berries, which she'd stop and pick up at the farm stand. She listed these out loud to Clem as they stood outside McQuade's Marketplace in the hot sun. "What else did Mom want?"

But Clem was distracted by George's sudden departure toward a giant bin of beach balls near the entrance doors. "Do they sell wine here?" she asked.

Paige really did not want to call Flossy to ask what else was on the list. Her mother seemed frazzled enough already with the party planning. And needier. Paige found herself being pulled aside to not only answer inquires about Clem but also David. Was everything *okay?* David looked *tired.* In fact, so did she. Was *she* okay? It was exhausting.

Late last night Paige had tiptoed out of the kids' bunkroom after checking on everyone one last time and come face-to-face with her mother, hovering outside the bunkroom door. Flossy was brushing her teeth in the hallway. "How did it go?" she'd asked, her mouth full of toothpaste.

Paige blinked in the bright light of the hall. "Shhh. They're fine, Mom. They're asleep."

"No, I meant the interview," Flossy pressed. "Any good news?" The toothbrush dangled out of her mother's mouth at an irritating angle.

"Just as I told you at dinner, no news on the interview. But I'll come wake you up if we hear something during the night." She'd felt bad after, when she climbed into bed beside David. It was the kind of thing she used to share with him, the kind of thing they'd lie nose to nose and laugh about in the dark: her crazy family, her nosy mother. But not recently. Besides, when she'd climbed into bed and pressed herself against him, she'd realized with disappointment that David was already sound asleep.

Maybe he'd hear some news about the interview today. Maybe Emma, who'd been somewhat reticent since arriving at the summer house, would let her mother join her for one of her mysterious long walks. Now, frustrated and determined to get in and out of McQuade's as fast as possible, she grabbed a grocery cart. "C'mere, George—want to go for a ride?"

George spiked a swirly blue beach ball into her cart before hopping onto the front, and they sailed into the refreshing cool of the produce aisle.

Clem lurched toward the cart, as if Paige might suddenly lose control and swerve into a display of watermelons.

"Oh, I don't let him do that at home," Clem said.

"You're not at home," Paige said flatly, winking at her nephew.

Maddy skipped beside her mother holding her hand. "What's that yummy smell? I'm hungry."

Paige knew that smell. When they were children, her father used to pile them all into their woodie station wagon and take them to the market, where he made a beeline for the seafood counter and ordered four bags of clam fritters, covered in tartar sauce. They were served in small brown paper bags, stained with the grease and salt. Clem usually dropped hers, and Sam practically swallowed his whole. But Paige would savor them one at a time as they followed their father's wandering path up and down the grocery aisles as he plucked jars of caramel syrup and bags of chips from the shelves, forgetting all the staples Flossy had written down for him to buy. Her mouth watered at the memory.

"Want to order fritters?" Paige looked expectantly at Clem.

She didn't seem enthused. "I'm not hungry. But you can get some for the kids."

"Come on, we can share one." Paige had noticed Clem picking at her dinner the night before. Flossy had made a deconstructed lobster salad, arranging the split crustaceans with spears of lettuce over ice. It was as succulent as it was lovely to look at, and yet her sister had only managed to eat maybe a claw or two.

Paige stopped at the fish counter and ordered three packets of the fried clams. "Careful," she warned the kids, passing each their own bag. George frowned doubtfully into his, but Maddy took a game bite.

"Did you realize Mom invited more than sixty people to Dad's birthday?" Clem asked, inspecting the fritter Paige had handed her. Paige gave her another so each hand was full, a technique she'd used on her own kids when it came to eating vegetables. "Where is she putting all those people?"

"Under a tent in the backyard. We need cereal. What aisle is the cereal in?"

"What if it rains?"

The large celebration was a surprise. A picnic of six seated on a large blanket by the water with wine and cheese boards was more Flossy's style. Or at most, a smattering of neighbors and Richard's Fairfield colleagues mingling in the backyard over a lantern-lit table of seasonal greens, grilled seafood, and oysters. Through all the years of anniversaries, birthdays, and promotions, there had been no grandiose celebrations Paige could recall. Certainly nothing requiring the Irish crystal and heirloom linens her mother had asked her to search for in the attic. Aside from the fact that her father was turning seventy-five, Paige wondered why this year.

"It's a lot of work," Clem went on. "And have you noticed her knees seem to be bothering her? When she took the kids out to cut hydrangeas in the garden I noticed she had trouble getting up."

"It wasn't our garden she was cutting the hydrangeas in," Paige said. She'd been horrified to find Flossy standing at the fence that morning in the backyard, whispering into the dense shrubs separating their property from the Cookes' property next door. The Cookes had not been around, as far as she could tell, but it didn't excuse Flossy's hacking into their hydrangea bushes. She'd sent the children in, at least.

Paige had noticed the knees, though, and even though her family teased her about being an animal doctor, ACLs were ACLs, and she'd suggested her mom see an orthopedist. "And Dad's back is bugging him, though he'd never admit it in front of us. They're just getting older."

"But they're getting *older* older," Clem said, pressing a finger to her brow.

Paige inspected her sister's furrowed forehead

out of the corner of her eye. Frankly, she was surprised it wasn't more creased, given the year she'd endured. Then again, Clem didn't have teenagers. "How much longer do you think they'll be able to keep the summer house going? None of us are close enough to help them open it and close it up each season. It's a lot of work."

They were in the dairy section, and Paige put two cartons of milk in the cart. She eyed George and Maddy, who were now devouring their fritters, and grabbed another carton. "It's not like they can't afford to hire someone to do that stuff. Mom's just too stubborn."

Clem looked at her. "I have a confession. I really didn't think I could do this this summer. But I think it's good we're all here."

Paige smiled with relief. It was the first time her little sister had actually shared something of substance. "Me, too." She reached for Clem's hand to give it a small squeeze.

But Clem moved away, not noticing. She'd already turned her attention and the grocery cart sharply toward the cashier.

"Now, can we *please* go to the liquor store?"

Twenty minutes and two stops later (Sam had requested "tonic syrup," not tonic water, necessitating a trip down Main Street to the more expensive liquor store), they were back in the driveway, unpacking groceries from the hot car. "Go get one of the uncles to help," Clem told the kids as they careened toward the front door.

Only there was no sign of David or any of the others. Flossy had left them a note: *Down by the water.* Clem grabbed it off the fridge and pressed it to her chest after reading it aloud. "Remember these?"

"What?" Paige asked, wishing Clem would help put away groceries before the milk got warm.

"*Down by the water.* It's like the title of our childhood summers!"

Paige raised an eyebrow, something that drove her sister crazy, both for its intent and the fact that she'd never been able to do it herself. "You're suddenly in a good mood."

Clem ignored this. "Remember how Mom used to leave these same notes for us when we came home from playing with friends or being in town?"

Paige snorted. "Yeah, probably hoping the three of us would leave her there in peace."

"Not so." Clem showed the note to her kids, who didn't seem to get it, but seemed happy to see how happy it made their mother. She trotted outside to the back porch and plucked their swimsuits from the railing where they'd been left to dry. "Let's catch up with Grammy on the beach. It's a gorgeous day."

Paige crammed the last of the perishables into

the refrigerator and shut the door. It hummed loudly. "This thing is on its last legs. I know Dad takes comfort in the fact that it was here when Grandma Mae was alive, but seriously. They need new appliances."

Clem frowned. "I love that fridge. It's part of this house's history."

"Precisely."

Clem ducked into the small laundry room and emerged with an armload of fresh beach towels. "Come on, kids, I'm going to teach you how to make dribble castles, just like Mommy did when she was little. Remember those, Paige?"

Paige folded the grocery bags and tucked them neatly into the cupboard beneath the sink. "What I remember is you crying when the waves washed them away. And how I had to carry you all the way up the beach path one day after a crab pinched your toe."

"Really? I don't remember that at all."

"You don't remember how it got infected, and the local doctor told Dad to carry you into the waves so you could soak it in salt water every day?"

Clem clapped her hands. "That's right! I almost forgot about the fiddler crabs. Kids, we should have crab races!"

Paige laughed. "There you go again."

"Don't listen to your auntie," Clem told Maddy and George, who were following their banter curiously. "She forgets what it's like to have fun."

Paige knew Clem was teasing, but it sounded like something her own kids had begun saying to her lately. "I didn't forget. I just don't have a need to sugarcoat everything."

Clem looked up from the rug, where she was tugging Maddy's purple swimsuit up her bean-shaped body. "It's not a need, Paige. It's how I remember things."

"Lucky you," Paige muttered. She opened the cupboard in search of a water glass. Her mother's mismatched Depression-era tumblers were stored precariously close together. She began to rearrange them.

It wasn't fair. Paige knew how to enjoy life as much as the rest of them. But as the oldest of the three, it had been she who toted the cumbersome lunch cooler across the hot sand while the others ran heedlessly down the dune path with their pails. Just as she had been the one to drag Clem out of rough water and remind her to reapply sunscreen before her freckled shoulders burned. Which had actually happened to Paige's one day, because she'd been so focused on protecting Clem's that she'd forgotten her own. Interesting that Clem never seemed to remember *those* things.

"Okay, we're off." Clem heaved her beach bag over her shoulder and ferried the kids out onto the back porch. Maddy streaked across the dry lawn straight for the beach path, her bright-purple figure disappearing into the dune grass. "We'll meet you *down by the water,*" Clem said, peering back through the screen door.

"Down *where?*" Paige called.

George paused on the back porch beside his mother. "Doesn't Aunt Paige remember where the beach is?"

Clem ushered him down the porch steps, and turned to stick her tongue out at her sister. "She remembers, honey. What she forgets is where she left her sense of humor."

Flossy

The birthday party had been a ruse to get the kids back to the summer house. And it had worked. Sure, it was also about Richard's seventy-fifth birthday, which she cared deeply about, even if he did not. Family needed to be celebrated, and seventy-five years on this earth was noteworthy. Seventy-five good years was just plain remarkable.

She was aware that she and Richard had lived a life not only comfortable and successful by anyone's gauge but unscathed as well. There had been none of the major upheavals some of their peers in Connecticut had experienced—no jobless years stemming from corporate layoffs, no scandals or affairs. The kids had each been raised to be not only productive citizens of a certain means and education but also good people—people Flossy and Richard were genuinely proud of and whose company they enjoyed. Unlike her friend Rhoda, whose eldest daughter had been class valedictorian and coasted easily into Dartmouth on an academic scholarship only to become pregnant her sophomore year and drop out to move home. Or Eddie and

Elaine, whose marriage had been ruptured by a redheaded paralegal in his firm with coltish legs and an extramarital invitation Eddie had not been able to turn down. Yes, there had been hard years. Years when the children were young and Richard was teaching classes that ran from morning until evening, returning home with his tie loose around his neck as he collapsed into his wing chair and shut the study door, in spite of the three sets of little hands that pounded on it and needed to be busied, then washed and tucked beneath blankets by eight o'clock. Flossy had felt a chasm open and widen between them during that time, one that she'd initially been too tired to consider, and later regarded with no small amount of resentment.

But there had been milestones and vacations, and they'd somehow muddled onward, then upward, as the kids had grown. Richard's mother, Mae's, illness, in later years, had been difficult. They'd moved her closer to them in Connecticut, after his father had passed, to an assisted-living facility with tennis courts and Spartan apartments that Flossy had eyed warily, silently beseeching her own children to keep her from this when she grew older. When Mae began to convalesce, they'd made all the arrangements for her care, visiting her weekly, then daily; sitting for hours at her bedside to hold her hand or read a book. Oddly enough, it had softened their bond rather than straining it, moving it from a place of committed practicality to one of demonstrations of gratitude. After Mae had passed, Richard surprised Flossy with a trip to Bordeaux, where they wandered cobblestone streets and sought out tiny outdoor cafes where they ate—and drank too much wine. Flossy felt lucky: their partnership had been strong and staid, if not remarkable. But as the kids began to graduate from college and enter the workforce, she took pause; all the collective labor to get the children to this point was largely done, and yet her worry did not recede with the tide of work when they left home. It rose. Like a wall of panic, as the grandkids came, Flossy realized the obstacles were greater and indiscernible: she felt out of touch, too tired, too old to protect her children and now her grandchildren from them. In the seventies it had seemed so much simpler. Yes, there were the Halloweens when the kids' candy bags were delivered to the local hospital to be X-rayed for razor blades. The years of Cold War fear, but even that seemed so remote in both probability and proximity. On the daily scale of things, her advice had been simple: If a van pulls up, don't climb into it. If your sister falls out of a tree, run to get me.

Back then, the dangers had been obvious and blunt. Nowadays they were invisible and more cutting: there was the Internet, and with it predators, cyberbullies, and identity theft; drivers who texted on devices she wasn't familiar with; drugs she couldn't name. It brought with it a tide of anxiety so acute there were moments she couldn't breathe. And yet also a measure of freedom that she had learned to embrace. If those horrors were unseen, then perhaps it was best she attend to what was in front of her: her grandchildren, minus all those perturbing "what ifs." As for her grown children, this year had nearly felled them. The struggles and the suffering had kept them down, individually and as a whole. Flossy could not protect her offspring from the world, just as she could never shed her role as mother. No matter how many tiny shoes had been tied or graduate degrees earned, the past year had imparted, in no gentle way, that she could not protect her offspring from the world at large. But the summer house had always been their way to try to escape it.

Ci Ci Le Blanc was a member of the summer Sea Spray Supper Club. The club had begun in the mid-eighties with a small group of summer residents. There had always been backyard barbecues and beach tailgate parties among the families and couples who lived along the same narrow strip of beach. The engagements were rustic and simple, where everyone brought a side dish and a bottle of wine. Within that loose amalgam of visitors and summer residents, a smaller group of women formed. The rules were simple: twelve members only, for the twelve weeks between Memorial Day and Labor Day. The supper club would meet each Friday. And each member hosted one time during the summer.

Over the years, the members rotated somewhat, but the premise never had. Outside of Ci Ci, Flossy and Judy were the two longest-standing members, which meant that they held some effect of rank. Though none of the women would ever dare to claim authority over any other, it was silently acknowledged when menus were discussed and opinions were sought. Flossy knew she was the member the others aspired to emulate in terms of presentation and detail. She knew which triple-cream cheese paired best with which region of grape. Her gardens were lush and robust, the hydrangeas deeper blue and denser than those of any other yard, a fact she suspected was due entirely to the sandy soil at the summer house, though when asked, she had perhaps on occasion made mention of salinity treatments. Judy, on the other hand, was known for the herb and fruit gardens that she tended and the menu she sourced from the suffocating interior of the greenhouse her husband, Ronald, had built for her. Unique, perhaps, but unnecessarily ostentatious, in Flossy's opinion. Judy seemed to take great pleasure in complicating things, blithely tossing out culinary institutions that thus far had prevailed over every New England picnic blanket or dinner table. What had tartar sauce ever done to her?

Judy's homemade concoctions stemmed from untraceable lists of foreign herbs, an international assault on the tongue. Her grilled lobster sauce was like a forced marriage: why smother an unassuming crustacean with Kaffir lime rind when a perfectly good lemon from the grocery would suffice?

Ci Ci Le Blanc, who held her Supper Clubs in the vaulted and chintz-upholstered sunroom of her cottage on the tip of Sea Spray, was the other longstanding Club member. The lone European in the group, she brought a Viennese flair to the menu. Or, at least, her cook did. Ci Ci's most notable, and often-requested, contribution had been her stuffed oyster recipe. It was unlike anything Flossy had ever tasted; a fusion of creamed spinach and buttery mollusk that nearly melted on the tongue. The Le Blancs' was the sole supper club meeting that Richard, who loathed being dragged to the weekly gatherings, had ever asked Flossy to attend, in the hope they'd be served the delectable dish. Sadly, Ci Ci had decided to move back to Austria with her husband, Hans-Peter, last May. As soon as Flossy had heard the news, she'd popped by to wish them well and to ask the question all the members had been wondering for years: would Ci Ci share the stuffed oyster recipe? She'd laughed, almost giddily, and for a moment Flossy had feared she would not. But Ci Ci assured her she'd write it out and leave the recipe card in Flossy's mailbox before they closed the cottage for the season.

In the interim, Flossy had checked her mailbox daily. On the last day of the season, she'd walked up the street and knocked on Ci Ci's door. The movers were there, and Ci Ci looked positively flustered when she finally answered.

"I left it in your mailbox," Ci Ci assured her. "The red one with the gold whale on the side."

Flossy blanched. No one on the street had such a garishly colored box, let alone with something as tacky as a brass whale affixed to it, except Judy Broadbent. "That wasn't my box," Flossy stammered.

Ci Ci was suddenly distracted by men coming down the stairs with an antique headboard. "Please do be careful!" She turned back to Flossy. "I'm so sorry, but I have to attend to things. Why don't you just ask Judy? I'm sure she'll be happy to give it to you."

But Flossy knew the answer to that. For twelve summers Judy had inquired about that recipe, just as Flossy had. Judy was proprietary about such things; when asked whether her salad dressing had a hint of rosemary or tarragon, she'd lift one shoulder noncommittally and smile.

Judy guarded ingredients and measurements like a hawk guarded its nest of eggs. Judy would not relinquish the stuffed oysters easily. When Flossy finally did ask, her suspicions were confirmed. Judy claimed she could not find it. Lo and behold, at the last supper club of the season, what did Judy serve? Ci Ci Le Blanc's stuffed oysters. Everyone had oohed and aahed. Flossy would have rather choked than eaten one. When she'd caught Richard standing by the greenhouse with one in each hand, she'd pinched him.

This summer, with Richard's seventy-fifth birthday on the horizon, Flossy was determined to get her hands on that recipe for his party. If only she could reach Ci Ci Le Blanc. Her communications with Ci Ci, while friendly, had been purely seasonal and held to matters of the gastronomic. Although the supper club had an email list of members for correspondences, when Flossy had tried, her message was returned as "undeliverable." Apparently, Ci Ci had severed ties with the Internet in the same season she had with her chintz sunroom. Flossy made inquiries with some of the other members, but not one could procure a way to contact her.

Briefly Flossy had wondered about social media, such as they called it. She, herself, was not on The Facebook or that Twitter. Though Judy likely was. Judy probably posted pictures of all her kids and grandkids propped up against the dunes in matching white linen shirts and khaki bottoms, an assemblage of towheads and teeth. Didn't people realize khaki blended in with the sand? Nevertheless, Flossy had made a call to Sam; he could help her explore The Facebook. But that only ended in a maddening slew of unreturned calls that were finally answered by Evan, who, bless him, had not only offered to help her create her own page (Lord, no!) but had then spent a two-hour phone call searching for Ci Ci Le Blanc. Alas, the search proved futile. The woman had vanished along with her stuffed oyster recipe. There was no other way around it: Flossy would have to call Judy Broadbent.

Sam

The sounds next door awoke him. If he'd ever truly been asleep, that is. In recent weeks, all Sam had managed through the night were long stretches of dozing, interrupted more and more by periods of wakefulness. Like the one he was experiencing now. He could hardly blame the loud music next door.

Their second chance was what was weighing most heavily on him. They'd gotten the word from the adoption agency six weeks ago about an expectant nineteen-year-old named Mara. Did they want to meet her? It had come more quickly than Sam had expected, and had only moved faster since. Evan was buoyed. Sam wanted to share in his enthusiasm, for both of them, but he still couldn't seem to shake Austin.

Things seemed to be going well; Mara was still in the process of deciding between prospective parents. They should hear something soon. But it wasn't just the waiting that was keeping Sam awake that night. He tried to push the thought away.

He rolled over and reached for Evan, who was sleeping facing the other way. Evan's broad back was warm, the sheets pulled snug around his waist despite the balmy summer night. Sam rested his hand at the base of his husband's spine, feeling his deep, slow breaths. How he envied Evan's restfulness.

Outside, animated voices rose and fell, coming in muffled bursts from the beach below. Probably a group of teenagers like he had once been a part of. Sam closed his eyes, picturing the bonfire crackling against the sand. The illuminated faces twisted in laughter and enveloped in smoke, the flash of crumpled beer cans littering the stony base of the hastily made fire pit. In spite of his pressing worries, he smiled against his fatigue at the memory. The summer house had a way of doing that to him; it brought everything back.

When they were teenagers, Richard had turned a mostly blind eye to the antics they had pulled during the summers at the house. Well, mostly Sam. Clem, being the youngest, had given them a run for their money by the time she'd reached that age. Paige, as eldest, had given them little to wonder about. For such a smart girl, her lack of imagination was sorely disappointing. It was Sam who had had to not only pick up the baton but carry it, and that he did, starting around his thirteenth summer, when he'd begun working in town on Bay Street. He'd met some older teenage boys, summer kids like himself, who were more interested in having fun wherever they could find it, and if that was on the shores of a private and mostly protected beach, all the better. Small and wild with dune grass, it afforded the teens a nightly gathering space that was not likely to be seen by residents like the larger Charlestown beach or tourist-trafficked Misquamicut. Sam liked to think they took him up on his invitation to come to the beach because they liked him; Sam was easygoing at work, sarcastic, and quick to draw laughter from even the older teens. He doubted they knew he was gay, but he was still wary. He had been since Brad Aaron. Brad was Sam's age, but where Sam was lean and leggy in body, Brad was burly in the way of his father, who worked at the mill in town, just as his father had before him. The boys had become playmates simply by way of geography; on their quiet road, he was one of only a handful of kids Sam's age.

Brad's house was the most modest, an unchanged fishing cottage set across the street from the waterside, unlike the other houses, which had been tastefully enlarged and renovated over the years. But these were not things young kids noticed. What Sam did notice was that Brad's parents were largely unseen; they did not mingle with the other, mostly summer residents on Sea Spray, never joining the back-deck barbecues or gatherings some of the other families hosted during the summer. Brad was what Sam's parents referred to, in no prejudiced way, as a "year rounder," a fact Sam had thought made Brad lucky. He knew that Brad stayed home alone while his parents worked during the day—his father at the mill, and his mother at a boutique in town. Richard had made a point to tell the kids not to comment on his rusted bike, though the thought had never occurred to Sam. His father had gone so far as to suggest Sam invite him to use the boogie boards they'd brought one summer and stored in the backyard up against the deck railings. Sam noted the way Richard inquired more about Brad than he did the other kids they played with, and the placating tone he used whenever his name came up. Flossy had once stated that being a "year rounder" didn't qualify as an affliction, but Richard afforded Brad exceptions that he did not dole out to other kids in the neighborhood. When one of the boogie boards was found broken and dumped in their side yard alongside the trash cans, it was discarded and replaced without discussion. Sam felt it had to be Brad; but Richard insisted it could've been any of the kids.

The few times Sam saw Mr. Aaron, he was in the driveway working under the hood of his Chevy or mowing the lawn. His expression was stern, his words clipped as he advised the boys to stay off the grass and out of Mrs. Aaron's hair. But Sam never had the opportunity to get into

Mrs. Aaron's hair, as he'd not once been invited into the house. Brad was not his first choice of friend, but they used to ride bikes together in a small pack, frequenting the other summer kids' backyards without invite or preplanning. It was the essence of summer on the shore.

Unlike the others, however, Brad was a bit of a humorless child. He was the kid who plucked the minnows that Sam had caught from the rocky pools around the jetty from his pail and flicked them in the head, stunning them, before twisting off their fins. Whatever interactions they had over the years seemed to darken as they grew older. Brad picked on the smaller kids. He had a primal talent for sensing an insecurity in any given playmate and calling them out for it publicly. One time, he made Clem cry with a song about thumb-sucking babies, something she only ever did in the safe confines of her quilted bed at night. At first he exerted this power haphazardly—any kid on Sea Spray was fair game. But by middle school his focus had narrowed. Brad seemed to see in Sam a dissimilarity that others did not, and would not for years to come, and it instilled in Sam a primal wariness that he'd never felt among other boys until then. At that age, Sam's burgeoning sense of self and sexuality was materializing, but it was still an uncertainty, even to him. However, if the subject of girls or summer crushes came up, Sam would sometimes catch Brad staring at him in a way that made him feel shucked wide open. Was he just being paranoid? At first, he hoped so. But Brad was the same kid who, years later during a game of keep-away, pinned Sam down in the dunes, shoved his face into the cool sand, and whispered into his ear, *"You like it like that?"*

Sam was stunned. Had he somehow given himself away? Or was Brad just reaching indiscriminately for any kind of threat, and the one he pulled from his toolbox just happened to be sexual? Bullies weren't particular.

Sam had never told his sisters or anyone else about it, even when Paige found him wiping sand from his reddened eyes and grabbed his hand.

"What'd he do?" she'd demanded.

But Sam had yanked his arm away. He was angry with himself for letting a kid as dull-witted as Brad Aaron get the better of him. Brad was larger and huskier, twice the breadth of Sam's narrow frame. Richard had taught them the power of the word, of the mind; Sam hadn't anticipated how meaningless those things would be beneath the bulk of a sweaty-smelling twelve-year-old boy, and in that moment, he'd hated his father as much as himself. Over the years, there were worse things said to him, graphic things, dangerous things, but none had ever burned as long as that incident behind the dunes.

Luckily, Sam had found he could lure others

in, in the same way he and Richard lured in stripers when they surf-cast off Napatree Point at night. It came as naturally as his lanky gait and his deep laugh. It was just a part of who he was. Sam hadn't realized the social prowess he possessed until he was a teen. Teachers would let him off the hook for missing homework, and their elderly neighbor, Thea Cribbs, gave him the keys to her house so he could water the plants when she went away on vacation, even though he helped himself to the snacks in her pantry and left the door unlocked on more than one occasion. If the adults gave any indication of their disappointment in him, it was at most with a resigned sigh. Sam took pride in the occasions when it was accompanied with a wry smile.

Even his peers fell under his spell. This proved most beneficial in high school, when he was no longer just wondering or worrying but indeed quite certain of his sexual preferences. Being different in any high school—sexually, physically, emotionally—was warrant for concern. Unlike the larger suburban schools where kids could fly beneath the radar, or at least establish security in numbers by finding those of their kind, there was no place to hide at Sam's regional high school. Hugh McMahon was the only openly gay person in his class. While Sam didn't know him particularly well, he was keenly aware of the razzing his classmates directed at him. Sam studied this from afar. Hugh was effeminate, and insisted on wearing brightly colored women's scarves or ponchos to school. "It's like he's asking for it," Pierce Warner once said. Though Sam doubted anyone ever asked for it, he had to admit he'd wondered why Hugh was so insistent on drawing attention, knowing it drew ire. On some days he found himself muttering, "Dude, just drop the jewelry." But somewhere deep down, Sam envied Hugh's grit. Thus far Sam had kept his sexuality to himself; he sometimes allowed himself to imagine how liberating it would feel to let his guard down.

But he wasn't ready. Instead, Sam worked feverishly to disguise any whiff of difference between him and the majority. He wasn't stupid; he knew kids smelled fear. His efforts paid off, however. Peers fell into step with him in the halls, laughing at his outrageous stories or asking him whose house party they should check out for the weekend. Sam didn't understand his ease in social groups any more than he understood the way he could solve long division quickly in his head; it just was. His awareness of it came with age. Mostly, Sam tried not to exercise his charm in a manipulative way. But there was no denying it; it helped.

Paige had envied him this deeply. He grew to understand that as he watched her circle the same groups he did, both in school and at the summer house each year. She was affable enough, but there was something too earnest, too hungry about her that made others slide past her in the hall. Small groups of friends she could reach, if not quite grasp. It was a glaring difference between the siblings.

"You have charisma," Paige had once told him. It was a rare moment, as much for its generosity as for its intimacy, the two of them huddled over the kitchen island sharing the last of the Christmas libations, long after the others had climbed the stairs and retired for the night. Sam had momentarily sobered, thinking it a compliment. But this was Paige, and she had delivered it in pragmatic Paige-like fashion. She was noting a fact, in the same way she might note the bump in the center of his nose from a skiing accident. "Strong," Evan had called it. A real compliment.

"Be careful of charisma," Paige had warned, her eyelids heavy as she swirled her glass of Malbec. "It brings people to your door. But it doesn't mean you should let them in."

He thought about that now, about Mara and their second chance at adoption, and he wondered if his charm was why she'd called them back. And if he was truly honest with himself, noting just the facts as Paige had, he'd have to admit that he'd wielded his so-called charisma as one does a sword. Had Mara been swayed by his colorful childhood anecdotes? Was she swept away by the delicate inquiries he made about her health? He was careful to never get too personal, but read enough of the *What to Expect* book he'd seen in her bag that first time the agency introduced them so they could make small talk and commiserate, as though he, too, were six months along and lamenting the swell of his ankles. He'd intended these things genuinely at first, just as Evan had with his soft questions about the kinds of parents she hoped to place her baby with, or what was important to her as to how her baby would be raised. But Sam had to admit he'd binged on the book's early chapters on the drive in for their second meeting. In the same way, he'd forgotten how far along she was. Evan had corrected him in the car. These things were important to Sam in what his mother had often referred to as mailbox moments. Sam allowed family news to pile up. It was something he tended to ignore, keeping it safely tucked away in metaphorical envelopes until he was forced to clear the stack to access his desk. Only then did he pay attention to things that mattered so much to others. Just as only on the way to their meetings did he cram like a hungover student walking into a midterm exam. Yes, Paige had that on him. Like him, she knew his weaknesses better than his strengths. And he used the latter to distract from the former every chance he got.

After Texas, when Tania had decided to keep the baby and they suffered the first blow to their dream of becoming parents, Sam's bent became one of business. At work, Sam's time was at a premium; he could barely bring himself to spend it, and certainly not to waste it. So he'd approached the adoption process with the same mind-set he approached an acquisition in the boardroom: close the deal. When the agency called again to ask if they were interested in meeting another prospective mother named Mara, he'd hedged. Evan was insistent—jubilant. But Sam weighed the situation before deciding. Mara was a nineteen-year-old girl in community college who did not plan to keep her baby. He and Sam wanted to start a family. The only thing standing between them was convincing her that *they* were that family.

The first meeting went very well, as had the previous ones with Tania. Evan remained stalwart. Sam remained cautious. When they were called back for a second interview, Sam felt the early pull of desperation. He liked Mara. She was smart and plucky, she laughed at his offbeat jokes. She shared with the two of them that she wanted to go to nursing school: it was a dream of hers, and she wanted to pursue it but was struggling to make ends meet, working double shifts at Gap. Suddenly Sam saw a need not just to find a home for her baby but for something beyond that. Mara had what they wanted. Maybe he could help her get what she wanted, too.

Was it wrong of him, what he did in the end? Maybe it was a mistake not telling Evan what he'd said to Mara. But Sam reassured himself that if his sister, Clem, had been privy to the details, she would probably have understood his reasoning. Flossy likely would have, too. But when he tried to imagine telling Richard, an overwhelming sense of dread rose like a plume in his chest, and he pushed the thought from his mind—just as he'd pushed away the thought of telling Evan. No, *wrong* was too subjective a term. Besides, was anyone ever truly wrong if they acted for the right reason?

On edge and unable to fall back to sleep, Sam rose and went to look out the window for the source of the noise that had roused him. A movement caught his eye across the yard. A lone figure was bobbing up the dune trail. A girl. Or was it a woman? Slight and quick-footed, she emerged from the path and trotted across the moon-splashed grass. She paused once in the middle of the silvery yard and looked back toward the beach. Sam swore he could hear her laugh. Then she darted toward the deck below. He pressed his forehead against the window, trying to get another look. She'd already disappeared from his view, but he was sure of it. It was Emma.

Clem

W e need to go over the checklist," Flossy announced as she set down the last of the dinner platters. They were all seated at the large farmhouse table off the kitchen, which overlooked the backyard. Outside, the sky seemed low and overcast, large gray clouds tumbling in off the water.

Richard pushed his glasses up his nose and squinted down the table at his offspring. "We need to do no such thing," he told them all. "All I want is a simple dinner with my family." He looked around, making satisfied note of the sun-kissed cheeks and freckled noses.

"Well, good!" Sam said, raising his glass. "So this counts?"

Everyone laughed, except Flossy and Evan, who managed a halfhearted smile, which made Clem's own smile fade. Evan's joviality ran deep, and the absence of it this summer was a reminder of her own loss—something still so three-dimensional that she never knew whether to navigate around it or give up and simply pull out a chair for it at the table. On the harder days, it could easily have filled a seat. Being in the summer house was good for her—the company, the impossibly bright July sun that spilled into every room, the sound of the surf always in the background. It reminded her that she was alive, her heart pounding in her chest just as surely as the waves pounded the beach. But sitting beside Evan reminded her that others bore their own grief.

"Fine if no one sees reason to celebrate you or your seventy-five years on this earth, then I'll cancel." Flossy lifted one shoulder as though it didn't matter to her either way, but they all knew their vacation week at the summer house depended on it. There would be no living with Flossy if it didn't happen.

Paige interjected. "Of course we're going to have the party, Mom. Dad, you want the party, right?" She looked so earnest; Paige never liked it when plans fell through. That didn't happen in her orderly world.

Richard sighed deeply. "Darling, you know I appreciate all this hard work, but that's just what it is—hard work. I don't see why we can't just invite the Weitzmans and the Russells for a simple gathering. I don't want you wearing yourself out over a silly birthday." His voice was soft and filled concern for the trouble he knew this celebration was causing his wife, but there was also an air of bewilderment.

"It's not just another birthday," Flossy reminded

him, her eyes traveling around the table and landing for a guilt-inducing beat on each person sitting there, grandchildren excepted. "This is a milestone for your father, and we should honor him accordingly."

Sam smirked. "Whether the birthday boy likes it or not."

"Sam," Paige warned.

Richard raised a hand. "I do like it," he replied, as if settling the matter. "And I'm sure it will be a wonderful evening. But I want you all to remember why you're here first. It's our family vacation here at the shore, something that has brought your mother and me great joy over the years, and something we're grateful to be able to still share with you. So all I ask is that you don't let the party planning take away from that."

"Daddy, you say that as though it's our last," Clem said. From the expressions around the table, she wasn't the only one who had heard it. Flossy narrowed her eyes at him. What was going on?

"No need to be dramatic," Richard added quickly. "I just want you all to make the most of the house. It's been in the Merrill family for many decades, and we've been fortunate." He turned his attention abruptly to his salad, leaving them all wondering.

"Can I go down to the beach tonight?" Ned asked, switching the subject.

"No!" Paige and David answered in unison. Clem averted her gaze and pretended to help Maddy cut up her chicken.

"Oh, come on. You heard what Grampa said. He wants us to have fun."

"You've had plenty of fun lately," Paige said firmly. "Let's play a family game tonight."

"That's boring!" Ned protested. "Only the little kids like it."

"Ned!" Paige snapped. She turned to Clem apologetically, but Maddy and George were too engrossed in their chicken nuggets to have heard.

"I'm with Ned," Sam said. "It's not like we didn't go to parties on the beach."

Paige threw him a look that could have melted tar. "Thanks, Sam. Even though you were the life of the party, I think you'll likely change your opinion on that topic if you ever have kids." As quickly as the words came out of her mouth, silence fell. She put a hand to her mouth. "Oh, Evan. I didn't mean . . . "

Evan met her gaze without ire. "It's okay. I know you didn't."

But Sam didn't. "What the hell does that mean?" he snapped.

"All right," Richard said, clearing his throat. "That's not what she meant."

"It's not, I'm sorry." But she was talking more to Evan. To Sam she said, "Maybe if you didn't stick your nose in where it doesn't belong all

142

the time. You have no idea what kinds of issues teens face these days, issues none of us had to contend with. And besides, if I remember correctly, you got off by the skin of your teeth with some of the stunts you pulled."

He jumped up so quickly the table shook. The little kids startled, eyes wide.

"Both of you, please," Richard admonished.

Sam tossed his napkin on his plate. "It's okay, Dad. I'm not hungry anymore."

Later, Clem and Evan stood side by side at the sink. Tradition was that two family members took turns each night doing dishes, and they'd decided she would dry and he would wash. "Rough night," she said quietly.

"Yeah, that's a fair statement."

Clem watched Evan scrub Flossy's copper-bottomed frying pan until it shone. "You know Paige didn't mean it like that."

Evan handed her the pan with a resigned look. "I know. Sam's been under a lot of pressure at work, and he likes to point to that. I think it's the adoption that's really weighing on him."

"What about you?"

Evan submerged a plate in soapy water and paused. "I have a good feeling about it. I don't know; after what happened last time, I wondered if we should take a break, you know?" He looked at Clem. "But this mother, Mara, is different.

She's a little older. She's got plans, things she wants to do. Which makes me think she's maybe a little more sure of herself."

Clem leaned forward to wipe a spot of soap off Evan's cheek, and then kissed it. "I want this for both of you," she said. There was a thunder of kids running down stairs. Maddy streaked into the kitchen, wearing nothing but a pair of Ned's swim trunks. She snatched a freshly cleaned serving spoon from the counter and the pot Clem had just dried. "Hey, now," Clem said, reaching for them. "Uncle Evan just washed those!"

But Maddy held both over her head and clanged them together before scooting out of her reach. George rounded the corner, his eyes wild with pursuit. He snatched a colander off the counter before Clem could stop him and took off after his sister with it on his head. "Bedtime!" Clem shouted.

Evan laughed.

"Oh, you think that's funny?" Clem asked. "Laugh now, brother. Laugh hard. Soon it will be your turn!"

He rolled up the dish towel she'd tossed on the counter and snapped it at her retreating behind.

Clem scooped Maddy up and motioned for George to follow. At the top of the creaking staircase she paused to both catch her breath and inhale the intoxicating scent that was her child: a sweet, gamey combination of hard play and seashore, tinged with baby shampoo. It gripped Clem with a visceral sense of calm, stilling her frenetic thoughts in a way she had not felt since the kids were babies and she used to linger in the rocker beside their cribs well into the night.

"You sleepy, baby?" she whispered. Maddy's legs dangled, and she'd grown suddenly heavy and still against her chest.

"Mmhmm," came the muffled voice. It was just like Maddy to go from full-tilt to near-collapse.

Clem herded George into the bathroom to wash faces and brush teeth and carried Maddy to bed. There would be no protest about bedtime tonight. This summer had been tougher with the gap in ages; in past years Clem's children were toddlers to Paige's elementary-aged kids, so everyone was usually tucked in by the same hour of eight. Now, however, the teens stayed up closer to ten, an ungodly bedtime for her little ones, but one they were determined to mimic. Luckily the long beach days worked their magic, and by dessert they were sun-weary, water-logged, and wrung out by the sea air.

Clem tucked Maddy in with a quick prayer to the tooth fairy gods for not possessing the strength to rouse her child to brush her teeth. George hoisted himself into his bunk above, and she climbed onto the bottom rung and kissed his head. "'Night, sweet boy." But he didn't answer. As soon as he had turned over, he was already drifting off and away from her. She stared at his boyish features: his broad forehead, his freckled nose. George was all Ben, a fact that left her forever heartsick and terribly grateful at once.

Below, she could hear the rattle of dessert dishes being washed in the kitchen sink and the creak of the screen door as people came in and out from the deck, probably getting another bottle of wine. She'd planned to go back down and have a bite of the peach cobbler Flossy had set out, but she was suddenly seized by a fatigue she could not deny, so instead she padded down the hall and washed up in the bathroom. Even the Ambien didn't allow her a sense of tiredness this complete, and the thought of getting to bed without taking one of the small yellow pills was too good to skip. If only she could keep the feeling. She'd just slid beneath the crisp sheets and switched off her bedside lamp when she heard it: the faint strum of guitar music and muffled laughter outside her window. It was so dark.

She got up and went to the window. The sash squeaked in protest from years of salt air and humid summers, but she finally managed to tug it open high enough that she could lean out into the night. The breeze was brisk and the sound of the shore stronger up here, echoing up over the bluff. Below, in the distance, she could see the orange flicker of a bonfire down on the sand, and her heart gave. Someone was having a party on their beach.

When they were teenagers, their annual summer departures to Westerly never failed to begin with vocal adolescent objection. Sam wanted to hang out with his school friends; Paige and Clem didn't want to miss a whole summer at home in Connecticut. But once they arrived at the shore, they always picked up right where they'd left off the summer before, with the bonus of having grown up a year. Like the summer Sam got his driver's license—before he crashed their father's vintage VW Bug along Shore Road after a beach party at Weekapaug. Or the year Paige took a job scooping ice cream behind the counter at St. Clair Annex—the same summer Clem could finally fill out her bikini in a way that made the college-age lifeguards at East Beach turn around in their chairs. The Merrill kids wasted no time rounding up summer comrades: Sam was trailed home regularly by swathes of freckle-skinned Irish students who worked as Ocean House hotel maids and busboys. Paige made friends with the teenagers at St. Clair's, and Clem spent her days linked arm in arm next door with Suzy Weitzman and the other local summer families who shared their narrow strip of beach. Each season became a reunion. As the years went on, their bonfire parties on the beach became legendary among the summer crowd, and though Flossy sat sentinel in the checkered wingback by the fireplaces running her fingers edgily over the threadbare arm covers until everyone stumbled safely back up the dune path and into the house, their parents did not forbid them those weekend forays. It was the one part of their childhood that was silently acknowledged and never commented upon, as long as the flames were smothered by sand and the beer cans were picked up before high tide washed away the last set of departing footprints.

Now, Clem kneeled at the open bedroom window and breathed in the salt air, remembering. Somewhere in the distance she could make out the faint lyrics to "American Pie." Her mind drifted to Fritz. Was he was sitting at home next doors reminded of the parties they'd shared as kids? She wondered if he recalled them with the same breezy longing that she did.

There was something about nighttime at the summer house. A sudden burst of laughter wafted up over the dunes, and she turned her face toward it, relishing the comforting rush it brought. Unable to resist, she tiptoed downstairs in her nightgown.

Outside, the backyard was so still, contradictory to the backdrop of roaring surf and voices coming from the beach below. A salty wind rose over the bluff. She paused on the edge of the porch and wrapped her thin bathrobe more tightly around her.

The grass was coarse and damp beneath her bare feet as she trotted across the yard. It had been how many years—ten or more—since she'd crept out of the house during the night like this, and the realization gave her spontaneous exit an air of deviousness. She paused at the opening of the sandy trail and glanced back at the house. There was a lone glow from Sam and Evan's window, but all the others were dark with what she imagined to be slumber. Still, as she stepped onto the beach path, it occurred to her that the kids might wake up and go looking for her, and she froze. It was the exact kind of fear that kept her close to home on weekdays or waiting in the car at after-school practices, always wary of leaving the children, even for a quick run to the grocery. Because no one knew better than she that anything could happen in the most ordinary of moments.

But Paige's room was right next door to the kids', and her parents were at the end of the hall near the stairs. Surely Maddy or George would know to go to them if they found her bed empty. Besides, after the long day on the beach, she doubted seriously that either would awake. And so she headed down the path, her heartbeat quick in her chest.

Ahead there was a faint glow by the water. The smell of wood smoke drifted up, and she pictured the large driftwood logs they used to pile up to burn. The voices grew louder as she approached; this definitely wasn't a group of grown-ups gathering with wine and picnic baskets. Too boisterous. The trail snaked back and forth through the dune grass and eventually opened up at the head of the beach. She halted as the bonfire came into view. A group of teens, maybe ten or fifteen of them, mingled around a roaring fire in small groups. There was the tinny flash of beer cans being lifted in the firelight and the pelt of laughter. Clem grinned; it felt like yesterday that she had been one of those very teenage girls racing down to the firelight to join them, welcomed by a chorus of shouts.

Not wanting to intrude, she stayed in the shadows. There was a sheltered spot at the base of the trail; it was an alcove between the dense thicket of dune cover and the grassless stretch of open sand, out of sight from both the house and the shoreline. The same cozy spot she'd taken shelter in as a child to watch the sunset or the moonrise. A spot she'd stolen away to for private moments over the years, whether for a good cry or a sun-drenched escape from her siblings. And later, a hideaway that teens would steal away to, to make out unseen by others. Now, she sank down into the cool sand and wrapped her arms around her knees. By the looks of the group down by the water, there was little to distinguish them from the group from her own teenage summers:

the denim shorts, the baseball hats on most of the boys' heads, the bare limbs that took on an apricot glow in the fire's light. Most of them were seated around the fire, faces alight with both youth and sunburn. A few kids stood off to the side, huddled together in conversation. Clem had no intention of walking down there, but something about the group made her want to stay a minute and take it all in. It was then she heard the clink of a bottle somewhere off to her right. Her gaze jerked in its direction, eyes narrowing at the tangled shadows of dune and sky.

"Didn't mean to startle you," a man's voice said. Clem sucked in her breath as his outline took shape against the blue-black summer night.

"Hello?" She stood up, taking a step back toward the dunes. He was seated in the sand, about five yards away, at the base of the Weitzmans' beach path.

"It's me," he said, raising one hand in greeting. "Fritz."

Fritz. She exhaled with relief, followed just as quickly by a rush of embarrassment. How long had he been sitting there? Clem crossed her arms, suddenly aware of her gauzy nightgown. The dune grass stirred in the breeze.

"It's Clem," she said shyly. "From next door?" she added, unsure if he remembered her.

"I know," he said. His tone was friendly, playful. Then, "Want a beer?"

Clem glanced at the group of teens down by the water, then back up over the bluff. She hesitated. The kids were tucked safely in their beds. It was late. At that moment, there were no jobs that demanded her attention, no hands to be held. She became aware of her crossed arms and let them fall to her side. She took a step toward him. "I'd like that."

Fritz opened a beer and stood, handing it to her. She could see him better now, in the distant light cast from the bonfire. Their fingers brushed. "Beautiful night," he said, holding his bottle out. They clinked the necks of their beers together, and each took a swig, their eyes meeting. Even in the chill of the shore air, Clem could feel herself blush. She averted her gaze.

"It is," she agreed, sitting down in the sand. "I see we had the same idea."

Fritz sat beside her. "Well, I don't know what your idea was, but I was just taking in the music. You seemed about to go and join them if I hadn't intervened."

She turned to him, unable to hide her smile. "Excuse me? I was coming down for a walk."

He kept his eyes on the bonfire. "In your nightgown?"

She pulled the hem of her robe over her knees. "So? Like you said, it's a beautiful night. And it's dark out."

He turned to look at her. "Not that dark."

Clem stared at the teens and took an indignant sip of her beer. Was he really going to be that obvious?

"Sorry," he added. "I wasn't looking."

Clem smiled in spite of herself.

"But it is a nice nightgown."

"I thought you said you weren't looking," she reminded him.

Fritz tipped his head back and laughed. "Touché."

There was something so easy about his playful tone, or maybe it was the flutter of beer in her stomach that egged her on. "You might do well to keep your eye on the group ahead. I think they're more your age."

"Hey, now. I just finished law school."

She nodded. "Yeah, yeah. Duke Law."

He watched her with amusement. "Something like that. My point is, I'm not as young as they are."

Clem shrugged. "You'll always be baby Fritzy to me," she said, and as soon as it came out of her mouth she began to laugh. Did he remember them calling him that? Had it bothered him? Instead of stopping to wonder, she covered her mouth with a hand to stifle the giggles that followed.

"Oh, you think that's funny, huh?" He was still smiling, but she wondered if she'd leveled the playing field too much. If maybe this reminder of being one of the older kids now was a disadvantage. Because, let's face it, that's exactly what she was: older. A widowed, *older* mother of two.

She turned to face him. "Not as funny as it used to be," she said quietly.

He studied her, wondering at the change in the tone of their banter.

"You've got two great kids," he said, as if reading her mind.

"Thanks. I think so."

"The last time I saw you was when you were in college. So, did you ever become a nurse?"

She wrinkled her nose. "Is that what I used to want to be?"

He shrugged. "Or was it a vet?"

Clem groaned. "That was Paige. Now *she's* older." She glanced at him sideways. "I'm not that old."

He watched her for a beat. "I know. You and Suzy are the same age. Thirty . . . "

Clem held up her hand. "Thirtysomething!" she said before he could finish.

"I don't get it," Fritz said, shaking his head. "So you're thirty . . . "—he waited for the look that he knew she'd throw him—"something," he finished. "You're young. And beautiful."

Clem lifted her beer quickly to her mouth and finished it. "I'd better get back."

Fritz stood with her. "Can I interest you in another? Night's young."

She nodded toward the group of teens. It had grown smaller, and those remaining had begun kicking sand onto the fire. "Looks like the party's over," she said softly. She felt a little deflated.

"Next time," he said, his eyes fixed on her. "Hey, I'm sorry if I made you feel uncomfortable."

"You didn't." But he had, even if it was unintentional. Clem hadn't sat with another man since Ben. She hadn't even looked twice at one. Sitting here with Fritz commenting on her children and complimenting her looks was suddenly very personal. And yet there was something also personal about it being with Fritz, in a good way. Fritz had never met Ben, as far as she knew. But he'd known her, the younger version of her, her whole life. He'd leapt off dunes and swam in the waves and run with her through the months of July and August as far back as she could remember. And there was something both familiar and comforting about that fact that kept her there on the sand. Something she needed.

The breeze picked up, and Clem shivered. She didn't really want to go, but she couldn't stay.

"Here," Fritz said. Before she could object, he unzipped his hooded sweatshirt and placed it around her shoulders. She put it on, but it was he who zipped it up for her, just as she did for Maddy. His face was so close she could smell the beer on his breath.

"Better?"

She nodded gratefully.

"Thanks for the beer, Fritz. And the company. Both were really nice."

It was dark on the beach, but the faint lights coming from the houses above silhouetted the two of them. She could just make out Fritz's expression. "It was my pleasure."

She started to unzip his jacket, but he held up his hand. "Please, keep it. It's chilly."

"Okay." Clem realized she was still holding her empty beer. "Well, good night."

Fritz reached out and took the empty bottle from her, but then he dropped it in the sand. Before she understood what was happening, he reached for her with both hands. Clem drew in a ragged breath.

She would not kiss this boy. She had not been kissed by anyone else, not since Ben. She didn't even think she knew how to anymore. It was too soon.

But as Fritz brought his hands gently to her face, she found herself closing her eyes, involuntarily, and raising her chin. She waited, shivering. But he did not kiss her. Instead, he pulled the hood of the sweatshirt up over her hair. She opened her eyes and blinked, stunned and ripe with embarrassment.

"Good night, Clementine," he said. And before she could answer, he stepped back, raised his hand, and turned up his beach path. She exhaled, awash with relief. And something else.

Heart in her throat, Clem turned toward her own path and climbed it hurriedly, her legs pumping in the cold sand. What had she been thinking? Fritz was a family friend. A mere boy from childhood. They knew nothing of each other, after all these years. But images flashed through her muddled thoughts: his smile, his broad hands. She was halfway to the top of the bluff before she realized what else it was that she'd felt down there on the beach when he pulled away: disappointment.

Paige

H er last orthopedic canine patient had been successfully discharged. She'd received a text from the vet tech before she'd even awakened saying that his owners had come to pick him up. The drains remained in place, and they'd taught them how to keep them clean. Paige breathed a sigh of relief.

Downstairs, she found Emma bent over her phone in the kitchen. She plucked a bowl and a box of cereal from the cupboard and glanced at her daughter. Her legs were getting brown already, something from David's side. She peered at her own: still fish-belly white, protruding from her pink running shorts. "What happened to Huck Finn?"

Emma laughed out loud, and Paige glanced her way. She was laughing at something she was reading from her phone.

"Did you finish Huck Finn?" Paige asked again. She didn't seem to hear. "Em?"

"What?" Emma snapped.

Paige set her cereal bowl on the table and looked into her daughter's upturned face. At least she was making eye contact with her mother, something that was like pulling teeth from Ned. But she looked annoyed. And tired. "Hey. I asked about your book. Why the tone?"

Emma lifted one shoulder and tucked her phone in her back shorts pocket.

First Sam and her mother. Not Emma, too. Paige was growing weary of everyone's energy; this was supposed to be vacation.

"Nothing. Sorry." Emma blinked, looking uncomfortable.

"Are you having a good week?" She felt like she'd barely seen her.

"Yeah. I guess."

All through middle school, Emma had given her almost no trouble. She knew she should be grateful that this sudden distance was all she'd shown of her thirteen years thus far.

"Good. Daddy and I were talking about taking a day off from the beach and doing something else. Any interest?"

Emma piped up. "Can we go shopping?"

"Oh. I was thinking we could go up to Napatree and do some hiking. Get some exercise."

It wasn't the answer Emma wanted to hear. She slumped back into the chair. "I thought we were on vacation."

"Yes, at the shore," Paige reminded her. "Come on, honey. Remember the ocean views from the point? We can't get that at home. Let's—"

Emma stood up abruptly. "Take advantage of

it!" she said curtly. She pushed her chair back and walked out to the deck.

Paige turned to see David watching from the kitchen sink. "I didn't hear you come down."

He nodded silently as he poured himself some coffee. "If she wants to shop, I can take her into town," he said.

Paige stared into her cereal. Here it was again: she was the pushy one, the ringleader, the . . . what had Sam called her? The dictator!

"If no one wants to hike, we don't have to hike. I would just like us to do something together today." She gestured toward the window. "It's gorgeous out."

David didn't come to the table to join her, but followed Emma's path to the deck. "We know," he said. There was no ire in his tone, but she heard it. As though they were on two different teams, his being the one with their kids. Outside, David settled into a deck chair beside Emma. She looked up and smiled at her dad, her expression bright and welcoming. Paige couldn't hear the words, but they fell into conversation the moment he pulled his chair in. She knew it was irrational, but it felt like a betrayal of sorts—by both of them. It seemed like yesterday that Emma had looked at her that way; when she managed to get out of the clinic early and pick her up from kindergarten. When she sat down next to her on the living room rug with a favorite book. Their bond as mother-daughter had always come so easily. Now, it was something she had to coax, to tease out, like a wary animal from its dark warren.

When had it happened? She stirred the remnants of granola in the bottom of her bowl before dumping the rest in the trash. Fine; they'd go into town and shop on Bay Street. She'd always liked to look through the stores, despite the crowds. Granted, most were resort-type boutiques chock full of coastal-themed home goods like tiny cheese knives with seashell handles and pillows stitched with whales. She supposed she could use a new Watch Hill T-shirt.

As predicted, the sidewalks of Bay Street were clogged with tourists moving at a snail's pace. They'd piled into Clem's Suburban—Paige, Emma, the uncles, and Richard. Ned had stayed behind with the little kids to help Clem at the beach. With four days left until the party, Flossy had remained sentinel in the house watching Joe—who was probably the least likely among them to require any form of monitoring—paint. On their way out the door, Sam had joked, "If she stares at it long enough, maybe she'll scare the paint a decidedly whiter shade."

They parked midway up the drag, in front of the Olympia Tea Room. Patrons lingered at the small wrought iron tables on the sidewalk, sipping iced tea and spooning chowder. Paige inhaled contentedly. Coming to town wasn't such a bad idea, after all. She glanced at Emma, whose mood had improved as she surveyed the storefronts. Across the street from the line of shops, the Watch Hill harbor sparkled in the full July sun, the boat masts gleaming white batons against the cloudless blue sky. Paige smiled. "Let's walk along the harbor wall and check out the boat names," she suggested.

"Let's!" Richard said. "And maybe some ice cream." It was something Richard had loved to do when Paige was little. She glanced at Emma.

"I want to look in there," she said, pointing to a storefront down the sidewalk. Racks of bathing suits and swim cover-ups framed its pink doorway. Before anyone could answer, she was heading that way. Paige fell into step behind Evan and Sam, who also seemed at ease out of the house.

"Remember that set of ivory dishes we liked last summer?" Evan asked.

Paige didn't correct him. It was two summers ago, but she did remember. "The ones with the fish motif?" she said.

Evan smiled. "Yes! Do you remember which store that was?"

Paige glanced up and down the sidewalk. "Wasn't it across the way, at that home goods store?"

Sam shook his head. "Let's see what Emma's found, and we can head over."

But Evan wasn't listening. He'd stopped abruptly in the middle of the sidewalk, in front of a store window, causing others to have to shift around him.

Sam patted his arm. "Ev?"

It was then Paige realized why. She followed Evan's gaze. It was a children's clothing store, the bump-out bay window filled with red, white, and blue coastal kids' wear. Seersucker shifts. Sailor suits. The cutest pink lobster onesie hanging in the center of the window over a gossamer-lined bassinet.

Immediately her eyes went to Evan's, whose were locked on the display. But it was Sam's who tore her gaze away. He was watching Evan with such tenderness, allowing him this moment without interruption. Finally, he put his hand on Evan's arm. Evan blinked, then stepped away. "Emma's up there," he said.

"Evan," Sam said softly, his hand still resting on his partner. "We can still go in and look."

But Evan shook his head, moving out of Sam's reach and down the sidewalk. "Emma's up ahead. Let's catch up before we lose her."

Unsure of what to say, Paige remained frozen by the baby store window. She should've had the sense to walk ahead, but now she couldn't leave him.

Sam stared at the onesie a moment longer, then jammed his hands into his shorts pockets. "Let's go," he said, bitterly. "Before *we lose her.*"

The hip clothing store where Emma had gone was narrow and deep, as were most of the storefronts on Bay Street. And like the others, a tanned young teen worked the register—her impossibly white teeth flashing hello at each customer who entered. Not now, thought Paige, as she followed Sam into the store. He'd not said a word on the walk over.

She found Emma and Evan at the rear, standing by the dressing rooms. Emma was looking in the mirror.

"What'd you find, honey?" Paige asked.

Emma stood in front of a mirror wearing a small black bikini, triangular top. Evan stood to the side, eyebrows raised.

"Oh, Em. I don't know," Paige began.

"Isn't it cute?" Emma turned around to show her, but her face fell the moment she made eye contact with her mother. "You don't like it."

"That's not what she said," Evan offered softly.

"I do like it," Paige said, trying not to narrow her eyes. The triangles were so small, and the black lace looked like something out of a lingerie catalogue. Emma had always favored tanks— solid-colored, modest tanks like the swimmers wore. "It's just a bit much, don't you think?"

"You hate it." Emma strode into the dressing

164

room and tugged the blue curtain behind her. Paige stared helplessly at the rainbow-colored fish, her brain swimming with them.

"I'll give you girls a minute," Evan said. He squeezed Paige's upper arm on the way past.

"Emma," Paige said, standing outside the curtain. "You look beautiful in it. But it doesn't seem practical. How can you swim or boogie board in a suit like that?"

From the other side of the curtain was the angry sound of hangers clanking.

Emma swept it aside. "When was the last time you saw me boogie board?" she asked.

True, Paige couldn't say she had noticed her boarding yet this vacation. But, by the same token, she hadn't noticed her *not* boarding. It was something the whole family did. Something they'd always done!

"You love to board," she said. She was not about to let a silly swimsuit take over their beach activities.

"Not anymore," Emma muttered, walking past her.

Paige noticed with relief the swimsuit had been left hanging in the dressing room. She pointed to a wall of suits. "Let's look for another one," she suggested.

"No, thanks," Emma said. She paused by Sam, who was on his phone.

"Find anything?"

Emma shook her head. "Nope."

"Not yet," Paige said, reaching for a sherbet-colored tankini. "What about this?"

Emma rolled her eyes and wandered off to where Evan was looking at board shorts.

"What's that all about?" Sam asked.

A group of teenage girls crowded in, bumping into them. "She found this horrendous bikini and she's mad at me because I won't get it," Paige said.

"Horrendous how?"

The music was too loud and the racks too close. Paige was getting irritated.

"Never mind, Sam. I need to go talk to her." She pushed around the racks in search of Emma.

Sam shrugged. "I'll get it for her."

"Emma doesn't need a tiny black bikini. It's too old for her." She found Evan and Emma at the storefront. Emma had her arms crossed.

Evan held up a pair of board shorts. "Thoughts?"

"Cute," Paige said, barely glancing at them. "Emma, if you want a new suit, we can look at some more."

Emma kept her expression neutral, but stared right past her mother to the sidewalk outside. "No, thank you, Mother." There it was again—the stone-faced politeness that reeked of fury.

"I think I'm going to buy these," Evan said, excusing himself.

166

"Emma, please," Paige said.

"Mom. Stop. I said I'm fine."

Paige gave up. Clearly Emma didn't want to talk or shop. She glanced at her watch: 12:30. She needed to eat something. They'd all feel better if they ate something. "Let's wait for the uncles outside and go find Grampa." Emma didn't argue.

It was hot, and Bay Street was thickening with the midday crowd who had left the beach and come into town for ice cream and a little shopping. Older couples dressed in pressed white shorts and collared shirts passed. Paige swept the back of her hand across her sweaty forehead. How did they stay so crisp? A young couple pushing a stroller with red-faced twins went past. Both babies were holding melting ice cream cones and crying. The father looked like he was about to join them. Paige smiled at Emma; thank God that phase was over. "Things could be worse," she said, patting Emma's back. Emma took one step out of her reach. Paige tried not to sigh.

When they finally emerged, Sam and Evan each had a bag. "Did you get the red suit?" Paige asked, trying to sound enthused.

"Blue," Evan corrected her. "That and a golf shirt." He pulled a pink vineyard vines collared shirt out of the bag. Evan could totally pull off pink.

"Nice," Paige said. "What about you?"

Sam shook his head. "Oh, nothing for me."

She was about to ask him what was in the bag when he smiled broadly and handed it past her to Emma. "Something for you, my dear."

Emma's face lit up. She peered inside and lifted out the black triangle bikini. "You didn't!" she shrieked. She flung her arms around his neck. "Thank you, Uncle Sam!"

"Just a little something from the uncles," Sam said.

Evan's eyes traveled from Sam's to Paige's. "Uh, from *one* uncle, anyway," he rushed to add.

Paige could feel her blood rise into her ears. Emma caught herself and tucked the bathing suit back into the bag. She averted her gaze sheepishly.

"What?" Sam asked, holding up both hands.

He knew what. "I told Emma she couldn't get that suit." Paige's voice was clipped with the strain of keeping her tone even. "I didn't think it was appropriate for her."

Sam shrugged. "It's a swimsuit. She's a teenager. What's the big deal?"

Here it was again: someone in the family undermining her authority, someone questioning her judgment. But worst of all, someone else bringing the smile to her daughter's face that she could not.

Evan leaned in. "Sam, we should take it back."

168

Sam turned to Emma. "Don't you like that suit?"

"Sam!" Paige snapped. She was a child. *Her* child. How dare he thrust her in the middle of their rivalry, let alone position her like that against her own mother? She'd deal with him later. Now, she looked at Emma, eyes round and threatening to fill with tears. Not here on Bay Street, not in front of her daughter.

Emma stared at her flip-flops. "I do like the suit," she said in a small voice. Paige wanted to grab Sam by the neck and shake him. "But Mom said no," Emma added. And then she handed the bag over calmly. Not to Sam, but to her mother. Paige exhaled.

"Thank you."

Emma looked away. But before she did, her eyes grazed Paige's, and in them Paige saw a flash of it: that undulating ribbon that still connected them. The fabric of familiarity as visceral as the flesh they shared.

Sam pivoted on the sidewalk. "Fine," he said, holding up the bag like it contained something offensive. "I'll take it back." He was such an ass.

Paige ignored him, putting her arm around Emma's shoulders. She turned her up the street toward the sound of the carousel and the beach. It was a narrow victory, but the only one that counted. "Come on," she said, her voice false, too bright even for the midday light. "Who's hungry?"

Flossy

Gravlax
Quail eggs and cucumber
Roasted Fig Crostini
Stuffed Oysters
Grapefruit Gimlets

Flossy pored over the appetizer course for the party for the hundredth time, and sat back contentedly in her Adirondack chair. She took a deep sip of her mint-iced tea. It was all coming together, finally. The kids, the food, the party.

At the edge of the yard, dune grass stirred in the breeze. It was a sensational morning, but then all July mornings at the summer house were so. She'd been relieved when the kids had gone into town to do some shopping. Clem, Ned, and the little ones had stayed behind to play on the beach. Clem sure was intent on getting the most out of the beach this summer; she was the first one to suit up and head through the back door every morning, and the last one to straggle up the beach path, sun-soaked and sand-weary. Well, there was nothing as healing as the ocean, as Flossy had been telling them all for years. At least one of her offspring had figured out that their mother knew a thing or two.

She wandered inside, adjusting piles of notes and images she'd compiled on the kitchen counter. She ran her finger down the spines of her hardest-working cookbooks: Julia Child, *The Joy of Cooking*, and *Jean-Georges,* whose exquisite lobster tails with mace butter had gone to waste that first night everyone arrived. No matter; she'd put Jean-Georges back on the beat. There was still his Black Pepper Shrimp that she'd seize upon if she had to.

Joe was finishing up the trim work in the front hall, whistling quietly as he worked. Flossy sighed. She'd made peace with the paint. Now it was time to tuck one more conciliatory feather in her cap. She picked up the phone and dialed.

"Hello, Judy, it's Flossy. Such a gorgeous day. How are you?" She was at risk of babbling.

Judy Broadbent did not reply right away. "Hello, Flossy. It is indeed."

Wasn't Judy going to ask how *she* was?

"Well, things are going very well over here," Flossy went on. "The kids are in town doing a little last-minute party shopping. So excited for their father's big day! You know how Paige loves to shop." She faltered. She had no indications that any of her children gave a hill of beans about their poor father's birthday. And Paige hated to shop. That was Clem. She grimaced at the kitchen sink.

Judy cleared her throat. "That's all very

nice. But I should share that I'm expecting an important call this morning. Although I despise call waiting, since it's my doctor I'm waiting on, I'm afraid I'll have to take it should he call in. You understand, of course."

Was that a question? And what were the odds of Judy's doctor calling in at that precise moment? Flossy glanced at the wall clock. Eleven thirty. Everyone knew doctors didn't return patient calls until during lunch or after hours. Judy was rushing her. Well, fine. Flossy had no desire to extend this conversation, either. Judy could've saved them both this annoyance if she'd just handed the recipe over months ago.

"Of course, I understand. Anyway, I'm going over some final notes for the party menu, *which is coming together beautifully,* and which the caterer needs today. So, I'm hoping you've had a chance to locate Ci Ci Le Blanc's stuffed oyster—"

"Oh! Just a moment," Judy interjected.

Flossy let her breath out. Could it be that easy? Was Judy poised to pluck the recipe from her files and dictate it over the phone, right then and there? Flossy scrabbled furiously through her kitchen junk drawer in search of a pen.

Judy came back on the line, her voice bright. "Wouldn't you know, it's my doctor's office. I'll be just a moment." And before, Flossy reply, there was a sudden click, followed by silence. Judy had all the nerve.

Flossy retrieved her coffee mug from the kitchen sink and took a deep swig of the lukewarm liquid at the bottom. As soon as Judy came back on the line Flossy would cut right to the chase. Judy had held her appetizer list hostage long enough.

When Judy came back, Flossy would make up her own interruption to cut off any more possibilities for stonewalling. *Oh dear, Judy, wouldn't you know? That's my painter, Joe. Did I mention we're having the whole house repainted? I'm afraid he needs me, but I'll pop over in an hour to pick up that recipe. Thanks, again!* That's what she'd say.

Suddenly the phone clicked again. She cleared her throat to speak. And then the line went dead.

Flossy stared at the receiver and put it back to her ear. "Hello? Judy?" There was nothing but a dial tone. The call had ended.

Flossy huffed. Surely Judy Broadbent had not hung up on her. Even she wouldn't stoop that low. Had she forgotten Flossy was waiting on the other line? Would Judy call back? Flossy returned the phone abruptly to its receiver. She stared at it, waiting. Willing it to ring. It did not.

Flossy slammed her coffee mug back down in the porcelain sink, where it promptly cracked right down the middle. At that moment Joe poked his head in the kitchen doorway. "Heading out for lunch," he said.

Flossy crossed her arms. "That *wench*."

Sam

He checked his phone again. The only message he had was from Adya detailing a contact error she'd caught, which she'd found and sent to one of the younger managers on the project, Craig. Shit. He'd forgotten to include those papers in the file he'd left for him. Thank God for Adya, she was worth twice her weight in bullion. At the end of the message she asked, "Any news?" He stuffed his phone into his shorts pocket. Adya wasn't asking about the Shanghai office.

Sam knew she meant well; she was thinking about them and worrying about them in the same way his parents were. This wasn't their first rodeo as adoptive parents. The last one had nearly broken them, and Sam wasn't sure if he and Evan could go through a disappointment like that again this summer. In fact, he was pretty sure they could not.

It was late afternoon, and Evan was upstairs in their bedroom napping. Sam had intended to join him—how he wanted to, when he walked in the darkened room and saw the shades drawn and Evan's supple limbs sticking out from the cool white bedding—but he was still amped up from town. Paige had given him such shit about Emma's bathing suit. Christ, with all the running she did, she should be far less strung out. He'd meant it as a gift for Emma, but he couldn't help it—seeing how worked up it made his sister still gave him some perverse kind of sibling pleasure. But when it was all said and done, he regretted it, and now it was under his skin. That, and the pressing thoughts on the adoption application. He needed to walk it off on the beach.

The last thing they'd heard from the agency was that Mara would be getting in touch with the couple she'd chosen by the end of the month. Sam and Evan had not commented on this; nor had they dared to celebrate having made it this far. This new sense of caution was something they'd acquired from the last failed experience. They would still be competing with the most innate urge of all: the visceral pull of a mother to her newborn. Sam tried to envision the process as a series of hoops, just as he did with his job. There was the scouting period, where product was aligned with a consumer. The period of educating said consumer or buyer about the services that could be provided, the need to be met. This was followed by an investment period, where a deal was made or a buyer hooked. The remaining stretch was the longest. Sam tried to imagine them at that stage. It was the news they were still waiting on. And it made him edgy. He needed to run.

As he stretched, he glanced back at the house, half expecting Paige to trail him outside and down to the beach, as she had in high school. He was the one on the cross-country team, but suddenly Paige had decided she enjoyed running, too—and lo and behold—she was good at it! While she never formally went out for the team (which he suspected had more to due with Flossy's intervention—he later learned that she'd redirected Paige's aspirations toward field hockey, a measure probably taken to give Sam some sense of athletic autonomy in the household of competitive siblings), Sam had loathed the fact that she often shadowed him on his practice runs. She didn't brag or taunt, but it was the nature of her being there, and keeping up, that taunted him most. The screen door slapped shut; it was Richard.

"Heading to the beach?"

Sam shook his head. "Just for a run."

His father nodded, gazing at the bluffs behind him. "Perfect weather this week. Your mother couldn't have ordered a better one."

Sam smiled. He wouldn't have put it past her.

Richard came down the back porch steps, stopping to sit on the last one. "We should grab the fishing poles and cast some lines."

Sam looked up. It was an invitation. Just as he

had when faced with his sleeping husband's form stretched luxuriously across the bed, he declined. "Sorry, Dad, I'm just taking a short run to clear my had. I've got a work thing I have to sort out."

Sam could feel the disappointment settle in the air between them. "Another time, then."

He felt guilty. He'd barely spent a moment with his father, certainly not one alone. How was it that every time he visited his family, he arrived with grandiose notions of long walks and meaningful conversations, only to be stymied by the constant charge of children's interruptions or inclement weather, or if he was most honest, his own reservations. Richard was aging; the fact of gathering for his seventy-fifth birthday was proof plenty. But still Sam couldn't seem to get past the divide he sensed between them.

"How about after dinner?" he asked quickly. "I'll make it up to you."

Richard stood and smiled good-naturedly. "Nothing to make up for, it's just an invitation to fish." But Sam knew it was more than that.

Chiding himself, he turned for the beach path, his thoughts returning to Adya's question. He was pretty sure it was the same question his father was hoping to ask him. Whether they acknowledged it or not, the truth was they were all keeping their own vigil, silently awaiting word.

Sam strolled down the dune path and onto the

beach. He turned left onto a mile-long stretch of sand ahead of him that snaked down the beach and eventually curved right to the point. He kept along the water where the ground was wet and firm, the balls of his bare feet creating small divots where they struck sand. How he loved the feel of the sand between his toes. It took him back to the endless summer afternoons of his childhood when time was as slow and thick as the humid July weather. The thing was, Sam was relieved there was no word. Because the news everyone else was hoping for was quite different from the breaking news he feared. Since that afternoon he'd uttered them two weeks ago at their last meeting with the adoptive mother, he'd been replaying the words he'd said over and over in his head. Trying to determine if they were as definitive as he thought. Had he really crossed a line? Because the power of suggestion was something quite different than an actual suggestion, and what Sam most feared was that he hadn't just made a flippant comment to this nineteen-year-old woman—that, in fact, he'd offered an outright bribe.

What remained was whether or not Mara actually understood what he'd offered. He realized that if she had not, he was in the clear. Mara wouldn't feel pressured and there would be nothing unethical that she could report to the agency or to her attorney; there'd be no repercussions and they could just wait and see how things panned out naturally. It should've been a relief to him. But Sam was in a boatload more trouble than just that because he realized that a large part of him actually hoped she had understood. In fact, he was betting on her understanding exactly what it was he had laid on the table and hoping that she'd take him up on it. Was that cause for culpability? They'd already suffered through the change of heart with Tania. Evan had gone into a depression so deep he'd taken a short leave of absence from work. For days he'd stayed home, sleeping through whole afternoons and pacing the loft at night. When Sam had tried to talk to him about it—proposed they return to the agency for the "support" sessions that Malayka had strongly suggested they do—Evan had balked.

One night, when Sam returned from work, the nursery was no longer. The small office desk was back from the storage unit, tucked in the corner of the room. The green chenille rug had been rolled up and the vintage baby toys stripped from the shelf, replaced with their old architecture and travel books. Evan would not speak of the baby. It went on like this for over a week, and Sam was ready to call the agency, or Flossy, or anyone, until one morning, Evan had risen early, showered, dressed, and gone to work. Everything had seemed to return to normal, except for the hulking dark space that had settled between them. No, Sam wouldn't let them suffer through all that again.

He quickened his pace. Sam was smarter than that. Regardless of what words had tumbled from his lips that day, it wasn't the delivery or the timing or the words themselves that held the power—it was how Mara perceived them. Inferences. Implications. Offers. He thought of the Nietzsche quote he'd fallen in love with during his freshmen year philosophy class. So much so, he'd had it printed and framed for his office wall as a reminder that in his line of work he was not dealing so much with the concrete transactions of funds and properties, but in the managing of mindsets. "All things are subject to interpretation. Whichever interpretation prevails at a given time is a function of power and not truth."

Evan would have hated this rationale. He would have railed against it being used in this context, accusing Sam of turning this into something as calculating as a business transaction. But he would've been wrong. Sam had acted out of the most desperate of influences: love.

He reached the end of the point and stopped short just before the rock jetty. Ahead the waves lapped against the rocks and he listened to the ebb and flow, willing his mind to follow suit. Normally the ocean made him feel small, secure in the knowledge that whatever was ailing him was also small and would pass. How many times had he sat on this very jetty as a kid? When he was fighting with his siblings or struggling with his emerging sexuality. But this was bigger.

Perhaps, he tried to reason, Mara would be organically inclined to choose the two of them as parents. Perhaps this was just an added incentive, he tried to tell himself. But even he wasn't that good of a salesman. He stood up, hands on his hips and surveyed the stretch of beach. A lone walker and his yellow Labrador edged their way along the water in his direction. In the distance, a small group of kids struggled to get a kite off the ground and into the air. If they lost another baby, Sam figured they could probably survive it. What they might not survive was if Evan found out what Sam had done, the secrecy of it being just as ugly as the offer. The first would require Evan to endure; the latter would require him to also forgive. It would be too much to ask of any human being, even one as exceptional as Evan.

He would have to take whatever was thrown at him, he decided as he walked toward home. What had been said had been said, and like the proverbial cat his offer was hanging out there somewhere in the universe, out of the bag. Either Mara would report him and the agency and attorneys would have to step in. Or not. He wasn't afraid of getting in trouble. It didn't matter how Mara perceived his offer or whether it was wrong; all that mattered to Sam was that he had done everything he could to tip the scales in their favor. That he might get the chance to watch Evan take their baby into his arms, and carry him into their home where they'd raise him together. He'd do it all over again, even if he had been wrong. In the end, Sam had decided he could live with that. What he couldn't live with was the alternative.

Paige

Paige tossed the shopping bags on the bed and flopped down among them. She'd spent too much money in town, but it seemed like the only way to guarantee some time with Emma. David set his book down and looked over at her, bemused.

"Was town that bad?" Upon hearing about the plans for their excursion, he had begged off and chosen to stay behind at the house. She'd hoped it was because he was expecting a call from the university, but she didn't want to ask. He had asked her to please stop asking.

When David didn't offer any update, she rolled over on her side to face him. "It was nice, actually. We grabbed lunch and did a little shopping. But Sam was his usual pain-in-the-ass self."

To her chagrin David nodded without comment. It was the glaring difference between them, and likely why he didn't understand her pressing need to request interview updates from him: she was forthcoming with information and he was not. Whether it was about the kids, work, household matters—Paige talked. She liked to talk and she

183

liked to compare notes. Take now, for example. David would not ask her what Sam had done to offend her because he did not have to. He knew she would tell him. *She* talked.

"Once again, Sam overstepped. Emma found this hideous bikini in one of the surf shops, and I told her she couldn't buy it. But then Sam went ahead, anyway, and got it for her." She studied David's face for reaction. He never liked it when adults tried to parent other people's kids. Surely this time he'd have two cents to put in.

"Well," he said, "what was wrong with the bikini?"

"Wait. You're not concerned with what Sam did, but rather you're questioning me about the bikini. Did I not say 'hideous'?"

David took off his glasses and rubbed his eyes. It was a sign that he was ready to talk, but not the kind of talk Paige felt like having. "Don't take it personally, Paige. I'm just trying to get all the facts."

"And I'm trying to tell you all the facts, if you care to hear them."

A flash of hurt crossed his eyes and Paige immediately regretted the jab. She hadn't meant it. Why was every conversation between them so strained? She hadn't even told him yet about the bottle in Ned's closet. "Never mind," she said, sitting up. "It's not a big deal. I took care of it."

David sighed. "Honey."

"No, really. I've already forgotten about it." She sat up and collected the shopping bags from the bottom of the bed, determined to steer them back on course. "Want to see what I bought?" She held up a peach T-shirt with a fish imprint.

"That's nice." But David wasn't looking at the fish.

She set the shirt down and reached for another bag. "Here, look at what I found for my mother in the shell shop."

"Paige, we should talk."

She unwrapped the tissue paper and held up the set of lobster napkin rings. Tasteful silver rings adorned with one tiny red lobster in the center. "Don't you think Flossy will love these? Especially after her lobster dinner was sort of a bust—we can try for another this week."

David brightened a little. "Yeah, she probably will. Listen, there's something . . ."

"Speaking of dinner, what if you and I get out of here tonight and go grab a dinner together. I was thinking the Ocean House. Just us!"

Flossy had already made reservations to dine at the Ocean House the night before the party, but she probably wouldn't mind if Paige and David went first for a little romantic dinner. She'd been watching them curiously, Paige could tell. Her mother would probably find it a relief to see them going off just the two of them.

"I'm not even hungry," David said, holding up one hand. He looked mildly annoyed.

"Not now, silly. I meant I could make a reservation for later. In fact . . . "

"Paige!" David's face flushed with frustration.

She dropped the lobster rings on the quilt and sat back.

He softened his voice, but she could tell it was a strain. "Please stop! I'm trying to tell you something."

She flinched. "What?"

"I didn't get the job."

"Oh." Her heart fell to her stomach. This was not good. This was not the news she'd been hoping for. But it wasn't awful, either. They'd managed thus far on her salary alone, and they could eek it out a bit more. There was still plenty of savings in their account. "Honey, I'm sorry." She edged closer to him on the bed; she wanted to touch him, but instead, she laced her fingers uncertainly together in her lap.

"I don't think I can keep this up much longer." David swung his legs over the side of the bed, away from her. He sat slumped, his head in his hands.

Paige studied the back of his head, where the deep brown hair had given way to silver-grey seemingly overnight. It was the spot where she used to run her hands through and down to his neck before she kissed him. When was the last time she'd done that? Paige shook her head. "There will be other interviews. And the practice is doing really well."

David swiveled around. "It's not about the money or the job, Paige. Although I think about that, that's not what's wrong."

She looked at his eyes, at the dark circles beneath them. When was the last time either of them looked like they'd had a decent night's sleep? "What's wrong, then?" Her voice was almost a whisper.

"It's us."

Paige sat back on her haunches. And then—she couldn't help it—she laughed. It came out as a snort, right through her nose, and she was as surprised by it as David looked.

"You think this is funny?" He was mad.

"No!" she shook her head vehemently. "No, of course not. But of all the things going wrong, the only thing you can point to is *us?*"

"We're not good, Paige. We haven't been good together for a while now, if you cared to slow down and take notice."

This was ridiculous. The whole conversation was. As if they didn't have enough to worry about, he wanted to point the finger at the two of them? She knew things had changed; did he think he was the only one who felt the chill between them? But they were carrying on, as people did. They'd circle back to each other, she was sure of it. If they could just wrap their hands around what was really eroding their relationship, like his unemployment and the house. "David, do you have any idea the things that I deal with on a daily basis, the things that are *really* going wrong?"

Instead of responding, David just stared, his expression set. "Tell me, Paige. I'm sure you've got a list."

A plume of ire rose in her chest. "What did you just say?"

David shook his head, and faced the window. There was something about it, the dismissiveness in his gesture, the act of literally turning away from her that made her head swell with fury. For so long she'd been treading water. And for what? He apparently appreciated none of it. All he could see was what she wasn't doing, no matter how hollowed out the doing made her.

Her voice cracked. "I'll give you a list. Ned is drinking, David. Our star lacrosse player is hiding vodka in his closet! But I waited to tell you because I knew how stressed you were about the interview. And Emma. Emma is distant and moody, pulling away from me in ways she never has. But I've kept that from you, too, because I didn't want to worry you. And the practice— well, the practice is the one thing that's great! It's thriving. So much so, that I'm working almost twenty hours a week more than I should be. We need to expand. Or hire new staff or something. But my office manager is new, and as I'm trying to train her and catch her up on the running of things, things are running away on *us!*" She scooted over to his side of the bed, her face very near his. But he refused to look at her.

Why wasn't he asking her about the vodka bottle? About Ned or Emma? The silence irked her more than the months of carrying the family and ricocheting between the animal hospital and the house. "There is only one of me, David. And I'm doing it all. Alone!"

He spun around to face her. "Do you know how emasculating that sounds? Don't you think I want to contribute, too? This job search is killing me. I hate sitting home idle every day, while you and the kids go about your business. But it's not something I can control."

"Then don't sit idly. Carpool the kids to their games and activities. Finish some of those house projects you've been talking about. Make dinner now and then. Or how about this: ask me how I'm doing. Ask me what I need. Because I can't do it all." She searched his face for understanding. For something. But he only looked more entrenched in his points.

"No one expects you to do it all, Paige. But you insist on it! You push yourself as hard as you push the rest of us. I don't turn to you because

I know you can do it all and do it better without me."

It was like a blow to the gut. "That's not true."

"Isn't it, though? You push yourself hard but you also push the rest of us too hard. It's exhausting."

Paige jumped up off the bed. "Would you rather I stopped? Let the house go. Let the practice fail? I'm exhausted!" she yelled.

Now, David hopped up beside her. "You must be! Because you're exhausting to be around."

There it was: his truth, along with the contempt in his eyes. David didn't see her sacrifices, and Paige was at a loss to make him.

Her eyes filled with tears. Downstairs there was the rustling of dinner preparations in the kitchen. Out in the hall she heard footsteps. Everyone in the house had probably heard them. "Maybe you're right, David. All you seem to see is that I have a list. Well, thank God one of us is keeping one."

Paige swiped the shopping bags off the bed on her way to the door. She wanted to throw them, but all her fight suddenly deflated, and seeing the contents spill from the bags across the floorboards gave her no satisfaction; it depressed her. When she opened the door to leave, David cleared his throat, and she hesitated.

"Paige, we need to work on us."

"Fuck you." She closed the door behind her.

In the hallway she ran smack into Emma coming up the stairs. Her stomach dropped. Paige rearranged her expression, forcing a smile. "Hey, honey."

Emma's eyes were round with inquiry. She glanced over her mother's shoulder at the bedroom door. "What's going on?"

Had she come upstairs because she heard her parents arguing? She didn't want to outright lie, but she also didn't want to burden Emma. That was the problem with arguments; the words went well beyond the adults hurling them, and navigating the aftermath meant assessing the damage. "I'm just heading downstairs to see if Grammy needs help with dinner." She made a silent prayer Emma would be satisfied with this.

Emma studied her, and Paige could almost feel her skin and bones giving way to the truth.

"What're you up to?" Paige asked, desperate to take her daughter's eyes off her face. If she had to hold herself together another second, she was pretty sure she would shatter.

Emma slid her eyes away from her mother's. "Nothing." She brushed past and continued down the hall.

Paige counted Emma's footsteps until the bunkroom door closed behind her with a *click*. Then she sank back against the wall and tried to breathe.

Clem

"Where should I set up the vases, Mom?"

Flossy waved a gloved hand absently toward the screen door. She was polishing the silver candlesticks that would accompany the hydrangea centerpieces as table adornments. Clem wouldn't cut the hydrangeas until the night of the party, which was still a couple days away, but Flossy had insisted they get out the table toppers and lay them out early to make sure everything looked right. "I'm planning to put them on the new serving table I ordered. The UPS man is in the driveway now, and your father and the boys are going to carry it out to the yard."

Clem looked outside. Her father stood in the middle of the yard, hands on his hips, staring at a giant cardboard box lying in the grass. Evan and Sam were on their knees attempting to open the flaps at one end with what looked like a screwdriver.

"What table?"

"You know, the one I've been waiting for all week. It was supposed to be delivered days ago. Well, it finally came. And, thank God, in time." Flossy bustled over, her hands still covered in her

192

stained cloth gloves. "I can't wait to see it." She squinted out the window. "What is *that?*"

Before Clem could answer, Flossy was out the door and halfway across the yard. She trailed her mother wearily.

"Please tell me that hideous flat box is not my new table."

Richard calmly pushed his glasses up his nose, and turned to his wife. "You are correct. It is not yet the new table. It seems that it has to first be assembled."

"Assembled?" Flossy's voice reached the pitch of panic reserved for botched Thanksgiving turkey and grandchildren's injuries.

Sam and Evan looked up at her.

"It shouldn't take long," Richard assured her, bending to retrieve the packing slip from the front of the giant box. "I think the directions are somewhere in here."

"Directions? I ordered a piece of furniture. A beautiful, teak serving table that cost more than Joe painting the porch!"

Richard looked at her over his shoulder, eyebrows raised.

Flossy jutted out her lip. "Well, maybe not that much. But it's high-end furniture. Not some cheap playset that requires backyard assembly."

By then Richard had found the instructions and unfolded them, holding them close to his face.

"I'm afraid it does, dear. Only we don't seem to have the table legs."

Flossy's lips formed a thin line. "Where are the legs?"

"Not in here," Sam said, grunting. He'd lifted the box up on its side and peered in the opening. "They must've been sent in a separate package."

"I already checked the garage," Richard assured her, flipping through the packing sheet. "It's not there, and it's not listed on here, but I'll call and see if they can track it. It's probably on this afternoon's truck."

Clem glanced sympathetically at her mother, who was watching as Sam and Evan slid the tabletop out from its cardboard sleeve and laid it flat on the grass.

"Nice driftwood color," Evan said, standing back appraisingly. "It has that coastal feel."

"It has no legs." Flossy glared down at the table top at their feet. "This is not a Japanese dinner party."

Clem tried to hide her smile. "Come on, Mom. Let these guys work on it. I'll help you finish polishing the candlesticks." She was about to turn back toward the house when a figure coming up through the dunes caught her eye. She knew the Wayfarer sunglasses and mop of hair immediately. A long rectangular box was hoisted on his right shoulder. It looked heavy.

"Fritz!" Richard exclaimed. "Good man."

194

Clem could see the sheen of sweat on his forehead as he drew closer. Sam jogged over to meet him. "It's okay, I got it," Fritz said. He set the delivery box down with relief between them all. "The UPS man dropped this off on my porch. I believe it's yours."

Flossy clapped her gloved hands together. "Thank God! My legs."

Fritz set it down carefully. "Whatever it is, it's heavy." He looked around. "Need a hand?"

Clem felt her tummy flip flop. He hadn't even looked her way. "You need a glass of iced tea," Flossy insisted. "The boys will handle this. Clem, take Fritz inside and give him a drink."

Fritz looked her way and grinned. "That'd be great."

Wordlessly, Clem led him inside. Clem was suddenly aware of her old cutoff shorts and ratty T-shirt. "Come in," she said, holding the screen door open behind her.

Fritz took off his sunglasses and looked around. "Wow, the place hasn't changed at all. Feels like I'm ten years old again."

Clem poured them both glasses of iced tea from the pitcher on the island. She thought about adding a slice of the lemon that Flossy had left on the cutting board, but decided against it. Too fussy. "Don't let my mother hear you say that. She's turned the place upside down just for this party."

She handed Fritz a glass and flinched when their fingers brushed as he took it from her. Had she ever found a man's hands attractive before? What was wrong with her?

"No, no, everything looks great," he explained. "I meant that it looks familiar. It's nice when things you remember fondly don't change." He looked at her over the rim of his glass. Damn, he had nice eyes, too.

Clem took a big swallow of iced tea and looked away. "Yeah, well my mother would have to agree with you."

Overhead the kids were thumping around, and Fritz glanced at the ceiling. "Remember when we used to play hide-and-seek in the bunkroom?"

Clem didn't, at least not with Fritz. "I remember playing dolls up there with your sister."

"No, we used to play hide-and-seek. All of us. Sam always picked the best hiding places. Once he pulled down the attic stairs and climbed up there to hide, but somehow the pull-down stairs snapped back up and he got stuck."

Clem put her hand to her mouth as it all came back to her. "Oh my God! I'd forgotten all about that! Didn't we give up looking for him and go down to the beach?"

"That we did." Fritz shook his head, chuckling.

"It must've been a hundred degrees up there! My mother reamed us out when we came back hours later." She laughed at the memory, reaching for Fritz's arm. "It seemed so funny to me at the time. I couldn't understand why she was so upset." Fritz looked down at her hand resting on his forearm, and she quickly withdrew it. "It doesn't seem so funny now. Guess we should've looked a little harder."

Fritz set his glass down on the island top. "I would've kept looking if it had been you."

Clem ignored this and grabbed his glass. "Want another?" What was Fritz doing?

"No thanks, I should go," he said. But he didn't make a move to. "Remember how we used to play flashlight tag in the dunes?" he asked suddenly.

She smiled at the memory. They'd run up and down the narrow paths they made in the dune grass, trying not to scratch their legs on the rough green blades as they ducked in and around the deep sandy grooves beneath the highest point. "You guys always used to spy on us from the highest point, and then when we tried to hide in the basin you'd jump down and scare us."

Fritz laughed. "The best was when the moon was out. Actually, there's going to be a full moon this weekend."

"Really?"

"My father got a telescope for the house this summer. I was thinking of taking it up on the dunes." Fritz looked earnest. Was this an invitation?

Clem took their glasses over to the sink,

making a show of running the water. What was he expecting, standing here in her mother's kitchen? She was always happy to see him on the beach. If she was honest, she was thrilled to have run into him the other night in the dunes—a moment her mind had been wandering back to ever since. But now, in full daylight in Flossy's kitchen, with her family outside and her kids playing upstairs and his eyes on her back, their interaction felt strange. Illicit, even. Feeling his gaze, she turned around. "Look, Fritz . . . "

"I'd better get back," he said quickly. "I've got an interview to prepare for." He jammed his hands in his shorts pockets and took two hurried steps backward toward the door. "Thanks for the tea."

Clem faltered. There were words tumbling around in her head, but she couldn't seem to articulate them. She'd wanted him to go. But now she didn't.

"Wait," she said, finally. But the screen door was already swinging on its hinges and Fritz was through it.

She watched him stop to say something to her father. It seemed Evan and Sam had already gotten three of the table legs on. Fritz picked up the last table leg and said something that made them all laugh. Clem went to the window, trying to hear. She wanted to know what he'd said. She wanted him to turn around and come back in the kitchen. She shook the thought from her head in frustration, and went back to the sink. Fritz was ten years younger. His law school degree was so fresh she bet he hadn't even framed it yet. All she really knew of him was from the past, when he was the youngest Weitzman they'd all outrun. And if she were completely honest with herself, no amount of years, college degrees, or catching up to adulthood made up for the differences between them. Fritz had barely begun living. And as for her, she'd already embraced death.

The screen door creaked again, and she spun around expectantly.

It was just Flossy. She looked out of sorts: still wearing her silver polish gloves and her cheeks were bright pink. "Well, thank goodness for Fritz! The table is done."

Clem looked past her mother and out through the window. Indeed, the teak table was finally assembled. The men were positioning it beneath the arbor now. Fritz had one end of the table and Evan had the other.

"How generous of him to carry that heavy box all the way up through the dunes." Flossy peeled off her work gloves and reached for the iced tea pitcher. "I invited him to the birthday party."

Clem exhaled, her eyes following Fritz's retreat as he waved good-bye and headed for the beach path. He jogged lightly on the balls of his feet in the same way her nephew, Ned, did.

Reminding her how young and untroubled his life was, how different. A fact that suddenly filled her with dread. "Did you, now?"

"Well, his parents are already coming, of course. I haven't seen much of the Weitzman kids in years, but whoever is at the shore is always welcome." She paused. "Fritzy certainly isn't the baby anymore. So handsome, don't you think?"

Suddenly Clem felt an urge to get out of there. "I thought you said we should refer to him as Fritz." She grabbed Flossy's gloves from the countertop and headed into the dining room, away from mother.

"Poor Cora," Flossy went on, absently following her from the kitchen.

"Why do you say that?" Clem asked.

Flossy swirled her glass of iced tea in her hand. "No reason, just that it's not easy to watch your baby grow up. It wasn't easy with you, either, though that seems like a *long* time ago."

Clem scoffed. "Well, *Fritz* does have his law degree, Mom. He's not *that* young."

"Yes, of course. But I wasn't referring to that. Schools and jobs are one thing. I was referring to letting Fritzy go."

"Go?"

Flossy seemed lost in thought. "Yes, poor Cora. She's going to have an awful time letting him go when some girl comes along and snaps Fritzy up."

Clem jammed her gloved hand in the pot of sticky silver polish and grabbed a candlestick from the table. Wordlessly, she scrubbed at the silver, flecks of pink goo flying.

Flossy watched in consternation. "Clem, dear. You're making a mess."

Flossy

Judy Broadbent's house was less than a mile up Sea Spray, set on the other side of the street from Flossy and Richard's. Not beach front, as Flossy's was. But any chance she got, Judy loved to remind everyone that she had the best of both worlds in her Rhode Island summer home: she was on the "safer" side of the street, away from the pounding surf during storm season, but she still had full view of the ocean. "It's marvelous, really. I wake up to water views but I never have to worry my house will float away!"

As compared to Flossy, whose house was set back privately on a low bluff overlooking the water—poor thing! As if.

Flossy snatched her to-do list off the ancient green refrigerator and ticked through it. In three days sixty people would be seated in their backyard to toast Richard's seventy-fifth birthday, and there was still so much to be done. So far, all the RSVPs had been affirmative, with the exception of the Mandevilles who were in Nantucket, and Richard's former Fairfield University history department colleague Noah

202

Barnes, who often came to Rhode Island for a weekend visit, but was visiting his grandchildren in Maine. They had yet to hear from Richard's college roommate, Hank. Flossy had asked Richard to call him no fewer than four times.

Still, she was thrilled that almost everyone was coming. Though Richard knew about the party, she'd not let him in entirely on the guest list, at least not the out-of-towners. She couldn't wait to see his face when some of the university crowd showed up. Which reminded her, she had better call the Inn at Watch Hill and check on their reservations. It was nearly impossible in the summer season to get a room anywhere near the village, but she'd managed to book a few rooms and the Weitzmans had offered their guest rooms to any extras. Luckily, most of the guests were summer people, as well.

Their landscaper, Lucas, was scheduled to come in to mow so that the backyard would be a fresh carpet of neatly trimmed green. She'd wanted to ask him to remove the hedges and replace them with some spike grass and sea lavender, but Richard said that was going hog wild, that they'd spent enough already, and he would trim the hedges himself. Flossy had given Sam and Evan the dull clippers to bring into the hardware store in town to be sharpened that morning, as a little reminder.

Outside the kitchen window, the teak bar table

was assembled and tucked beneath the arbor. She was very pleased with how it came out after the missing legs incident. She and Clem had been pulling down table toppers from the attic and the deep recesses of the old china cabinet in the dining room that no one ever used. But it had proven a much-needed trip down the memory lane of their family summers. She'd had the chance to handle some of Richard's mother's vintage fiesta ware (too bright), and the Irish crystal (too mismatched and broken over the years), and had finally settled on the silver candlesticks and heirloom linen table runners that had been stored away since she couldn't remember when.

"Remember these?" she'd asked Clem, holding up a baby's cup-and-bowl set adorned with white bunnies. There was a chip on the cup handle, and the glaze on both had cracked, but her chest swelled just looking at them.

"Weren't they mine?" Clem asked. For a moment, guilt filled her, and Flossy wondered if she and Richard were doing the right thing by not telling the kids about the sale of the house.

Flossy smiled sadly. "You all used that set at one time or another when you were babies. Goodness, the high chair you ate from is still in the attic, too." Flossy wondered briefly if she should offer any of the baby items to Sam and Evan, then immediately dismissed the thought. No, those boys already have enough burden of expectation on their shoulders. She studied the faded orange carrot on the bowl and sighed.

Flossy had known it would be hard, but selling the summer house was much more than just letting go of the building and the beach. There were so many invisible things her fingers ached to grasp onto that she had not anticipated. As she cleaned out the house and readied it for the party, material reminders kept popping up, harbingers of fleeting images that lingered here: a baby's sun bonnet found tucked in the back of a closet brought to mind an image of Sam in diapers, standing at the shore. A mason jar of sand discovered in the attic took her back to that frightening afternoon when three-year-old Paige toddled off down the beach path when she and Richard weren't looking, setting off a flurry of panic and searching. They'd found her half an hour later sitting in the dunes, fists full of sand, laughing. Flossy swiped at her eyes and set the baby cup back in its wilted cardboard box. When Clem pulled it back out, Flossy watched as she ran her index finger over the chipped handle. It was as if she'd touched some unseen crack in Flossy's very being. She could not put words to the relief she felt when Clem asked if she could take the set back to Boston and keep it.

At least the house was starting to come together. Joe had finished painting the trim upstairs and downstairs the day before, but then, in a fit of panic, Flossy had taken a closer look at the front porch where guests would enter and decided that touch-ups were needed.

Sea air was rough on a house exterior, she knew, but she'd always thought a little bit of chipped paint simply added to the coastal character. Oh, how wrong she was. It looked downright shabby, she decided. The entire family had been summoned outside to line up and weigh in, but to her surprise none of them seemed very concerned.

"Look at the railings!" she directed. "Can't you see the strips of missing paint on the posts?"

At least Evan made a show of squinting at the balusters; her own kids shrugged and wandered back inside. Richard looked defeated when she told him her plan. "We'll just dab a little paint here and there on the bald spots. It won't take a minute!" she tried to reassure him.

"We've already done so much to get the house in order. Surely that's something the new owners can do," Richard replied. "They'll probably want to change the colors to suit their own tastes, anyway."

Flossy did not like the thought of the new owners, but she especially did not like the thought of the new owners changing her paint colors. The summer house was beautifully done. These colors were timeless! In that mindset, she decided that she would repaint the porch. The new people would be less inclined to change it if it was freshly painted.

"It'll be fine," she told Richard, again. "A little dab here, a little dollop there."

But when she'd summoned Joe outside, he did not get on board. Joe calmly informed her that paint could not be dolloped or dabbed on to chipped areas. First, the porch railings and balusters had to be scraped down and sanded. Then primed. That would take several days. And only then could it be painted: two coats. There was a right way and a wrong way. Flossy knew which category her way fell into.

They didn't have several days. Surely there was another way?

Joe had just looked at her, the brim of his painter's cap firm over his unmoving gaze. Joe did things the right way. But she had at least managed to convince him to paint the hand railings. Those were the first things people would see—would, in fact, touch—as they entered the house. She'd just have to jazz up the cast iron planters on either side of the front door to keep the guests' eyes from sliding left or right to the chipped balusters. That would be something the new owners would have to address. Oh, the new owners.

Flummoxed, she pulled out her list. *Flowers for planters!* she scrawled. Which left only one item that needed to be dealt with immediately:

the stuffed oyster recipe. Sandy, the caterer, had called one last time to suggest that they use her recipe. It was a good recipe, she said, requested many times after by those who'd enjoyed it. Flossy considered Sandy's offer. She was tired of dwelling on the stuffed oyster recipe. Apparently, so was everyone else.

"Mom," Sam had scolded. "There's too much else going on. Ditch the oysters for clams. No one will care."

To which Evan had replied, "I'm sure the caterer knows what she's talking about. Keep the oysters, but go with her recipe."

But they were all missing the point. Flossy didn't give a flying cat's tail if she served oysters or clams. Sure, Richard had loved that recipe from Ci Ci. But, more than that, it was the principle. Judy Broadbent did not own the right to that recipe. Ci Ci had intended to pass it down to Flossy, not to her!

Flossy picked up the phone and dialed Sandy. "I'll have the recipe for you today," she promised the caterer.

Twenty-five minutes and one swipe of Chanel Ever Red lipstick later, Flossy found herself taking inventory of the contents of the shed. Richard had taken their car into town. Paige and Clem were out with the kids in the Volvo. It was too hot to walk at that hour, and she'd be darned if she was going to attempt to drive Sam's sports car, what with its keyless ignition and all those lit-up buttons on the dashboard (though she would've loved to show up in style at Judy's). No. She'd have to bike it over there.

She pushed her sunglasses up on her head and selected a faded blue Schwinn with a wicker basket—the only one that had mostly filled tires, as far as she could tell. She eyed the row of cobweb-covered helmets hanging on wooden pegs on the wall. No, she would not risk tangling with an arachnid on this already hot and frustrating venture. Judy lived just up the street. She wasn't biking to Newport, for God's sake.

Flossy wheeled the bike out into the driveway, swung her leg shakily over the seat and pushed her sunglasses up the bridge of her nose. Heavens knew when the last time was that she'd done this. No matter, there was a reason for the phrase "just like riding a bike," and she was going with that. She placed foot to pedal and pushed off. A little wobbling and a swift jerk of the handlebars to the left, and she was sailing up the street toward Judy's. How glorious the wind felt in her hair! If she weren't afraid of tipping, she would've taken one hand off the handlebars to salute the neighbors.

It had been a day since she'd left Judy that message about stopping by to retrieve the recipe. She imagined Judy having stayed away from the house all day, just to spite Flossy. Or better yet, sitting behind drawn drapes and peeking out the window at the herbs she couldn't water lest Flossy catch her outside—a prisoner in her own summer home. Flossy smiled. By now Judy would surely be pent up and assume she'd dropped the matter. Flossy might even find her unaware in the garden, windows and doors thrown open. Flossy pedaled faster.

Judy's house was not unlike the others on Sea Spray. Stately gray-shingled cottages of varying sizes set along the narrow beach road that led up to the Weekapaug Inn. Flossy admired the pillars at the end of some of the driveways: they were cone-shaped amalgamations of round beach stones and had always reminded her of the dribble castles the kids used to make on the beach when they were little. Judy's was not the most impressive on the street, but it was well situated at the end, neatly among manicured hydrangea rows. Flossy slowed her bike and eased into the driveway, the slow crunch of seashell satisfying beneath her tires—best to surprise Judy.

She rested her bike against the gate and let herself onto the walkway. The windows were all open to the ocean breeze, but the house seemed quiet. With her heart in her throat, she pressed the doorbell. Suddenly this excursion seemed a bit rebellious, if not rude. It was unlike her to just show up at someone's house, uninvited. It was not unlike her to stand up for herself, however. As she stood on the porch, Flossy wondered briefly what Ann Landers would say about this protocol predicament. Years ago, her mother had routinely clipped and mailed her the Dear Abby column when Flossy was a newlywed and her mother thought she should care about these things. Admittedly, she'd enjoyed reading them. Now, she imagined Abby frowning over her reading glasses. Weren't concessions made at times of family need? Because Flossy needed this family gathering to go off without a hitch, and in that vein she *needed* that damned recipe. At the very least, she tried to reassure herself it was summer—a season of relaxing rules and hemlines. Flossy could argue she'd taken a little etiquette holiday.

A minute passed and Flossy realized the only sounds she heard were not the footsteps of someone in the house coming to answer the door, but only the curious songbirds in Judy's lush shrubbery. She peered in the side window at the empty hall. How like Judy not to be home when Flossy finally got up the courage to go there. She jabbed the ringer again with her index finger. Nothing. Flossy glanced at her watch. By then, a precious hour of her day lay wasted, if she included the time it took to change out of her gardening clothes and apply a little lipstick just to come over here. What had she been thinking? She could've gone down to the beach with Clem and the little ones instead. She jabbed the doorbell button again, and when there was still only silence, she depressed it one last time—this time holding it down for several satisfying beats of irritation. *Rrrrrrring* you, Judy!

She'd just turned on her heel and was halfway down the front steps when the door opened. Flossy startled.

"Flossy? Heavens, what's the matter?" Judy was standing in the doorway, a mixed expression of surprise and consternation on her face. She was in crisp tennis whites, her muscled legs jutting out of the girlish skirt.

Flossy froze on the walkway. This was not how she'd imagined things. "You *are* home," Flossy stammered.

Judy crossed her arms. "So I am."

"Brilliant! I was just passing by and decided to pop in. I rang . . . perhaps you were out back in the garden?" Flossy hoped this would lend some reasonable explanation as to her laying on the doorbell like a complete lunatic. Though, as soon as the words were out of her lips, Flossy realized this made no sense whatsoever. If she'd really thought Judy was out back in the garden, Flossy could've walked out back to the garden. She'd been there enough times for

212

her book club meetings. Alas. Somewhere Ann Landers was rolling over in her grave.

Judy did not expand upon her whereabouts. Nor did she invite Flossy inside. *Very well, then,* Flossy thought. "I came for the stuffed oyster recipe. Thought I'd save you the trouble," she added for polite measure.

Judy didn't even blink. It was like she was expecting this. "Didn't I mention I was bringing it to the party?"

Flossy did blink. "The party? But my caterer needs the recipe in advance, of course."

Judy smiled broadly, and it raised the hairs right up on Flossy's neck. "No, silly. Not the recipe."

Judy had never called Flossy *silly.* That was reserved for schoolgirls. Or girlfriends. "I'm making the recipe to bring to your party. You said Richard loves them, correct?"

Flossy could not speak. Judy was bringing *her* oysters to *her* catered party? This implied generosity was all an illusion! Not only was Judy *not* handing over the recipe she had come all the way over and humiliated herself in an attempt to get, but Judy was doing far worse. She was masking her refusal to share it with an offer to make it herself. Judy had a nerve of grandiose proportion.

"I couldn't possibly allow you," Flossy said coolly. "The caterer was planning for ten dozen oysters. Think of the work!" She didn't add, *think of the expense.* Sandy, the caterer, had explicitly told her to plan on buying an entire bushel of local Watch Hills to feed the large crowd. Surely, that fact would shut Judy right up.

Judy cocked her head and Flossy imagined her calculating the one hundred-plus shellfish. It was preposterous. "It would be my pleasure."

Flossy was speechless. No one offered to bring ten dozen anythings to someone's party. Not to mention, how would Judy get them there? Serve them? No one was bringing platters of food. It was not that kind of party. Even Flossy's good friend, Cora, would never have dreamed to offer up such a lavish dish. And if she had, Flossy wouldn't have dreamed of letting her.

Flossy languished on the walkway trying to rationalize all this. She had to get back control of her own party. "Look, Judy, this is beyond generous, but Richard and I couldn't possibly hear of it. Besides, it would embarrass Richard, and it is his birthday," she reminded her. She waited a beat as this settled in the air between them. Judy seemed to be considering this. Richard was a man everyone liked, after all. He was the birthday boy.

With a wave of her hand, Judy stepped back in the doorway. "Nonsense. I insist." Before Flossy could reply, she felt the assault of Judy's gaze as it roamed up and down over her. "I just love what you've done with your hair this summer.

So low maintenance and . . . simple." She tossed Flossy one last beatific smile and then the door shut.

Flossy put a hand to her windblown hair and gasped. She'd been drawn and quartered in Judy Broadbent's front yard. An entire bushel of Watch Hill oysters—shucked, stuffed and baked— would be delivered and presented to *her* party by Judy. She imagined the cost. She imagined the volume. But most of all, she imagined Judy circling the oyster-eaters like a shark, seizing credit with each empty half-shell returned to the platter. *Clink.*

Flossy stalked down the walkway and yanked her bike away from the picket fence. This time she threw her leg over the seat and pedaled off so quickly the tires spun out from beneath her in the crushed shells and she just saved herself before becoming one with the driveway. Flossy righted the bike and caught her breath. She'd failed. Ci Ci Le Blanc's recipe remained in Judy's cold, manicured grip.

Before pedaling away, she glared back over her shoulder at Judy's. There it was: house, gardens, and sky. But she was so rattled it brought her little solace when she realized that she *could not,* in fact, see the ocean from here, as Judy always claimed.

Sam

Clem seemed fidgety, but Sam couldn't judge. He had been unable to ease into the summer house as he'd always done in the past. The one place that brought him solace and in which he could escape the strains of work and life in DC was straining to work its usual magic. But the day's weather was making an earnest effort.

Flossy had raced off on some mysterious errand, her face fully made up, which he'd made the mistake of commenting on. When he found Clem in the kitchen clutching a mug of coffee and staring out the window, he figured she'd have something wry to say about it. "Did you see Mom? She looks like she's heading out to a parent-teacher conference."

But Clem seemed not to hear. "Time to get ready for the beach," she said, rising quickly from the table.

"Is that an invitation?"

She turned, as if surprised to see him. "What? Oh, sure. Everyone should come." She breezed by him and set her coffee cup in the sink, before heading into the pantry. Her mug was still full.

"Where's the fire?" he asked.

From inside the pantry, Clem tossed the cooler on the floor at his feet and he jumped back. "Sorry. Can you start sandwiches?" she asked.

If anyone had a right to distractedness, it was his little sister. But Sam couldn't help but notice that beyond her high-alert mode of operation around the kids, she also seemed to have developed an itch beneath her skin. It was new. And unnerving.

He began pulling deli meat and fruit out of the fridge. "Who wants what?" he asked her.

She had already moved outside to the porch and was collecting beach towels.

"George likes cheese, no condiments, crust cut off. Maddy likes cheese and salami, a dash of mustard, but only on one side of the bread or she won't eat it."

Sam shook his head. "Crust or no crust."

"Crusts are fine for her. Oh, add cucumber," she shouted through the screen door.

"To the sandwich?"

"No, just slice it. You can put them in one of those little glass snack containers I brought. Less waste, no chemicals."

Sam rifled through the cabinet and pulled one out. "They weigh six pounds."

Clem skirted the island, laden with towels. "They have no BPA or phthalates."

Sam found a cucumber. "Peeled or skin on?"

"What?" She dumped the towels by the island. "Never mind, I'll do it."

Sam scoffed. "It's fine, I can do it. Peels on or off?"

Christ. Since when did making sandwiches become a process of algorithms. "You realize we've only covered two kids' sandwiches. And they're both yours." He winked at her, but she didn't seem amused.

"Evan wouldn't give me so much shit," she said, scooping the towels up and sailing by him as Evan sauntered in. He set down his book and eyed them both suspiciously.

"What wouldn't I do?"

"Millennial nutrition," Sam sneered. "Peel the cucumbers. And don't let the mustard touch the other side of the bread! *Poison.*"

"Still giving me shit!" Clem called out in a singsong voice from the stairs. They listened as she called to the kids, a thunderous rumble erupting overhead.

Evan was still wearing his reading glasses, which made Sam think of the two unopened books he'd brought sitting upstairs in his duffel bag. "We're supposed to take the hedge trimmers in to the hardware store for your mom. I want to pick up the champagne for the party toast, too. I thought that could be our contribution?"

Sam had forgotten all about the clippers. "Sure, but Clem just said she wants to go to the beach. Want to?" They'd been in the summer house five days, and Sam knew he hadn't exactly kept his promise about unplugging. Evan had been the one helping with dinners and playing games with the kids. Sam had only a few days left to do better. He wanted to do better. "I'll make you a cucumber sandwich," he added playfully.

"Sounds good, actually. We can run into town later." Evan pulled up a stool and reached for the loaf of bread.

"No you don't," Sam said. He grabbed a fresh mug and poured Evan a cup of coffee, pushing it in front of his husband; a little caffeinated olive branch. "Just sit and keep me company. It's my turn."

Evan took a deep sip and appraised him over the rim of his mug. "Thanks, honey. What's the occasion?" His tone was light, but still—it was deserved.

Sam set the butter knife down and looked at his husband. There were creases around his eyes from sleep, but his face was tanned and relaxed. Neither could be said for Sam, and he was running out of time to achieve either. There was so much he wanted to say to Evan, and yet every time he started, he returned to the day that Tania decided to keep the baby. To the week that followed, where Evan became unrecognizable, and Sam had had to step into a role he found both unfamiliar and uncomfortable. Until then, he hadn't realized how much he depended on Evan. The loft had turned into a sort of ground zero, and everywhere Sam turned he was faced with evidence of Evan: the white French ramekins lining the kitchen cupboard that he spooned Evan's yogurt into; the cashmere throws folded and neatly tucked into the linen closet, which he pulled out to cover his spouse with when he made it out of bed and onto the couch, only to fall asleep again; the hand-woven African basket where Evan stored fuzzy slippers for guests who visited, like a cottony embrace at the doorway. Evidence of Evan's hands and heart were all over their loft, and Sam found himself turning to all of it during that week, awed and ashamed each time he found another. Where was he? In the art on the wall? No, that was Evan's doing, too; Sam had only paid for the piece. And while he knew that his financial support was what funded much of their lifestyle, it was only that in the end—a style. The life—that was Evan. Now, standing at the kitchen island with crust-trimmed sandwiches between them he looked at his husband. "You and me. That's the occasion."

Flossy returned abruptly from her outing with lips pursed and in a silent steam, but there was no time to indulge her. Clem had rounded up the kids, sorted out swimsuits, and together they'd all assembled the usual slew of baggage and totes by the back door. As each person walked by, they grabbed one indiscriminately. Even Paige joined them, skipping her usual morning run. "You okay?" Sam asked her.

"Why wouldn't I be?" she said irritably, throwing a towel over her shoulder. She paused to hold the door open while Sam wrestled with the lunch cooler. It was so stuffed the lid wouldn't go on. "You coming or what?" When he didn't answer right away, she let the screen door slap shut.

David, a boogie board under one arm and Maddy in the other, turned back and pushed it open with his foot. "Here you go, Sam!"

"Dude's a saint," Sam said under his breath to Evan.

The water was rough. "Must be the full moon," Flossy said. Which caused Clem to glance back in the direction of the Weitzman house, Sam noticed. The little kids were shrieking and dancing back and forth, following the waves as they pounded the sand and then retreated. Ned had already dived in with one of the boards. David looked ready to follow.

"He's pretty fit," Sam said to Paige. She was stretched out in the beach chair next to him, and he'd decided to forgive her foul mood and try to be nice.

She barely glanced up. "Yeah, well he has time on his hands."

Evan raised his eyebrows and shot him a look, and Sam's stomach did a flip flop in reply. It wasn't that he was enjoying giving his sister a hard time, but the fact that Evan had turned to him. It was an undercurrent, a secret language just between them that had always come so naturally before. Something he could not remember the last time they'd had. Sam reached across the hot sand and grabbed his hand. When Evan squeezed back, tears pricked.

After lunch was finished and a smattering of sandcastles stretched along the water's edge in various states of erosion, the kids wanted to go for a walk. Clem had barely touched her food, but Sam noticed that she'd also given the kids a break, hovering less than usual. Maybe the vacation was starting to sink in for her, too. Her edginess, however, hadn't left. One leg jigging in the sand, she kept throwing backward glances at the dunes. "What's with you?" he asked, reaching over and laying a hand on her knee. "Do you need a pill?"

She went rigid, her expression with it. "What is that supposed to mean?"

Sam held up both hands playfully, but he knew he'd crossed some kind of line. "Easy, boy. I was just kidding."

"Well, it's not funny." Before he could stop her

she hopped up and strode down to the water's edge.

Flossy was looking at him, book in her lap. "What?"

Her mouth was a straight line. Never a good sign. "What do you think? Get your head out of the sand, Samuel."

Evan smirked beside him. "Jesus, everyone's sense of humor has gone out with the tide."

"Why don't you give your sisters a break. Take the kids for a walk."

He could. He'd been leaning toward stretching out in the warm sand and closing his eyes for a while; there was no nap like a beach nap. But he felt bad, so he stood up.

Maddy and George were digging a moat around one of their castles. Ned appeared to be passed out on beach towel. Only Emma looked bored and ready to do something. "Come on, kids. Let's go for a walk. We'll see if we can find something to maim or cage."

George raised both hands over his head and leaped to his feet. "Sharks!"

Sam stopped beside Ned and nudged him with a sandy toe. "Come on, sleeping beauty." Ned groaned, but he got up.

Clem was at his side in an instant. "Where are you taking them?"

Sam could see Flossy still watching him over

223

her book. He sighed. "Just for a walk up the beach. Is that okay?"

She lifted one shoulder. "Okay. Just keep Maddy's sun hat on. I don't want her getting burned."

"Got it."

"And keep George out of the water. It's too rough today."

"Okay."

She glanced back at the dunes again, and he wondered what had held her attention all morning. Her hair was tucked under her straw hat and for an instant, profiled against the white sand and flash of dune, the edges blurred and she could have been sixteen again. "Hey, sorry about what I said earlier," he said. "How're you holding up?"

Clem softened. "It's fine. I'm just tired. Must be all this quality family time." She tugged the brim of her hat down low, so he couldn't quite make out her expression. But then, to his relief, she smiled.

Sam started after the kids. "Family vacation! It's an oxymoron."

The little ones bolted ahead and Ned lumbered after them. Sam was pleased when Evan fell into step beside him.

"What's going on with you today?" Evan asked. The roar of the waves and the shouting from the kids almost drowned out the question, and for a moment Sam wasn't sure he'd heard right.

"Going on?"

Evan bent to pick up a shell. He examined it, turning it over in his hand, and Sam saw a flash of purple and white as he tossed it back into a wave. "Yeah. You're in an awfully generous mood."

Sam couldn't argue it. He was feeling generous. "I don't know. I guess I realized that the week is halfway over, and I want to enjoy it." He turned to Evan. "Does it seem disingenuous?"

Evan considered this. "No, I wouldn't say that."

"What then?"

"I was just wondering what took you so long." He slipped his hand into Sam's and they continued down the beach after the kids. Sam tipped his head back to the sun. *This*, he thought. This was what he'd been chasing.

It had been a long year, a year of starts and stalls, and steps backward. Sam wasn't used to the stepping back part. At work, as in his personal life, he'd always had to push. When one angle didn't work, he'd approach from another. There was always a way to get there, if he persisted. But that hadn't been the case with adoption, or with Evan. He'd entered into a process that required surrender.

"It's been hard," Evan said, as if reading Sam's thoughts. "I've been worried about us."

"Don't be. We are going to make this work."

Evan stopped. "That's not the part I'm talking about. I'm talking about us." His brown eyes softened and Sam felt his own insides giving, too.

"We're fine," he insisted. Though he didn't believe the words any more than he felt Evan did. They had not been fine, not in a while, and there was the thing he still hadn't told Evan. That was certainly not fine. Up the beach, George and Maddy were bent over the sweeping deposits of seaweed at the high tide mark, looking for treasures. Ned was knee-deep in the waves looking out toward Block Island. Sam squinted in its direction, but the horizon wasn't clear enough to see it today.

"Evan, there's something I need to tell you."

Maddy shouted up the beach to them. "Look what we found!"

Evan started toward her, but Sam grabbed his arm. He didn't want to say it, but he had to. Here, on the beach today, he'd known he had to. It felt right.

"Can it wait?" Evan asked, gesturing ahead. Both kids were waving at them.

Sam blurted it out. "I said something to Mara."

Evan stopped. "What do you mean?"

He'd been over this a thousand times in his head: to tell Evan or not to tell. The principles for doing so, the reasons for keeping it to himself.

In all the sleepless hours and distracted days he'd never once thought how.

"When we were in New Jersey the last time, at the end of our meeting, she told us that she wanted to go back to school."

Evan nodded impatiently. "To get her nursing degree."

"I wanted to help."

"Help Mara?"

Sam dug his foot into the sand. "Sort of. No." He met Evan's gaze. "I wanted to help us."

Evan's face fell. "What did you say to her?"

"I don't remember exactly, but . . ."

"Tell me what you said, Sam."

Sam had to look him in the eye, but when he did the words fell away. "I thought maybe I could help her out somehow. It started out as a gesture, but I guess she could have taken it a different way."

"Sam." Evan's voice rose about the beach.

"She was worried about getting in, and she said that even if she did, she wasn't sure how she was going to pay for it. And I insinuated that I'd take care of it."

Evan threw up his hands. "Take care of it? As in, get her accepted into the program? Or did you mean put her through college?"

"I don't know how she took it! That's just it. She didn't say anything, and she's not contacted me since. Maybe she just thought I was being nice." He reached for Evan's hand, but he pulled it away.

"You bribed her, Sam. That's bribery!"

"I know. It was wrong."

"Wrong? It's illegal!" Evan spun away from him and started walking toward the kids. Then he turned and came back. "Do you have any idea what you've done? You may have just jeopardized our chances of getting our baby!"

"I'll talk to Mara, I promise. I'll clear this up!"

"Mara? This goes well beyond her. I'm talking about the agency, Sam. God knows what the protocol is when this kind of thing happens, but I'm sure there's some kind of list. We're going to be flagged! We could be reported, or worse!" Evan stood as close as he could without making contact. His voice low, he spoke through his teeth. "You may have blown it for us." He turned down the beach, the way they'd come. Sam started to follow.

Sam had known Evan would be angry—furious, even. Because what he'd done was awful. But now, hearing Evan say these things out loud brought it all out into the light. And it was a far more dangerous beast than he'd acknowledged.

"Evan, I'm sorry!" he called after him. Evan did not turn around. Sam swiveled back to the kids, the roar of the ocean in his head. Ned was watching them curiously from a distance. The little ones had moved on down the beach.

Sam tried to lighten his tone as he waved the kids in. "Come on, guys! Time to head back."

Maddy sat down on her haunches. "But you didn't see my collection yet!"

He glanced back longingly at Evan's distant figure. Even from here, he could see the anger in his clipped stride and the roll of his shoulders. Then, against his will, he went to where George and Maddy were seated, cross-legged, in the wet sand. "Yes, Maddy. Show Uncle Sam."

Sam wanted to turn back down the beach for Evan. He wanted to yell at the kids to get up, get moving. What he most did not want to do was stand here a second longer and force himself to sit still during a five-year-old's show-and-tell of a bunch of broken sea shells. But he went over anyway.

Maddy held out her closed fists, palms up, and then opened them with flair. "Ta-da!" With great care, she deposited her treasures one by one in his open hand: twists of dried jade-green seaweed, a razor shell, a pink stone. As she did Sam stared at her cherubic hands, at the baby dimples across her knuckles. With each brush of her sandy little fingers his chest ached. What he really wanted to do was cry.

Clem

Fritz was wrong. The full moon wouldn't officially occur until that Saturday night, the evening of her father's birthday party, as luck would have it. But it was almost full— an asymmetrical yellow orb hanging low in the skyline over the bluff. It gave off just enough light that she could make out the dune grass tips bending in the evening breeze. She glanced at the clock: eight thirty-five.

It was an unusual night of early retreats at the house. The kids were tucked in. David and Paige had retired separately. Her to her room, "to call to the animal hospital manager and check in," and he to the back deck with a beer. Evan and Sam had also split that evening. Sam had gone for a walk, and Evan had begged off to read in bed, having claimed a headache. Leaving Richard and Flossy alone in the living room with cups of tea and a deck of cards, which probably suited them both at this point in the week. As much as her mother demanded (no, commanded) everyone's presence and participation, even Flossy seemed worn out from the party planning and the ever rounding-up of family members. Meal after meal, wet swimsuit after wet towel, the endless setting up and breaking down of activities grew tiring. If Clem had to face one more sand-crusted bottle of sunscreen that needed to be applied to each of her offspring, she'd cry. Which was exactly what had driven her to tiptoe upstairs with a magazine and the promise of a quiet night alone.

She preferred these kinds of nights, honestly. While the group outings and Trivial Pursuit evenings were fun in a boisterous way, Clem had long understood that of all her family members she was the most introverted. She loved to socialize, of course, but it required an energy she could not sustain long-term. And a family vacation was a nonstop onslaught of the senses: clanking of pots and dishes in the kitchen, voices rising and falling in conversations, children crying one minute, shrieking in a fit of laughter the next. And always, the incessant slap of the screen door as people strayed in and out, in and out. They were the comforting sounds of the summer house, all of them. Sounds that harkened back to her own childhood when her parents were gatekeepers of adulthood, and Clem's only real concern was which swimsuit to wear to the beach, or which flavor of saltwater taffy to purchase at the candy store off of Bay Street. How things had changed. Now she was not just an adult and a parent, but she was *the* adult and parent. If someone awoke sick in the night, it fell to her to fly out of bed and face it, sometimes leaving her racing between vomit-soiled sheets and a child retching over the toilet bowl. If someone was hungry, thirsty, sad, happy, in need of a nap, a hug, a scolding—it was all on her. Which is why she did not feel an ounce of guilt, as she might have any other year before, when she stole upstairs with a copy of *Better Homes & Gardens* tucked under her arm and an icy glass of lemonade.

Stretched on her bed, she flipped to an article on coastal gardens, allowing her eyes to roam lazily over hollyhocks and zinnias, a wave of rest following. But it did not last. At her open window, the curtains stirred. She sat up and listened; no music tonight, not even the roar of the tide coming in below. But the humid air was heavy with the scent of salt and the weight of water. She tried to settle back against the pillows. But the breeze picked up, the curtain dancing against the window screen. She rose.

Below, across the yard, was just a stretch of darkness. But beyond it, the reflection of the low moon over the water bathed the incoming tide in golden rivulets. She reached for her sweater on the chair, and it was then she noticed Fritz's sweatshirt. She stared at the faded red color and pressed it to her nose: it smelled of sunscreen and sun. And something else—that filled her with loneliness.

The night air was heavy, but as she trotted down the trail through the dunes, the wind picked up, so much so that by the time Clem stepped onto the sand a gust blasted the hair away from her face. Down here on the beach, the roar of the tide was thunderous. She knew it must be the moon.

To the right, the spot where the Weitzmans' beach path ended was empty. She zipped her hoodie up and looked up and down the dark beach in both directions, but there was no sign of Fritz or any other visitor out there. Clem walked down to the water's edge.

The ocean had always seemed fluctuating to her; during the day it was the deep green rolling playground from her youth. By sunset, it was placid—the waters flat and glasslike, stretching out in pink and yellow ribbons beneath the last of the day's light. But now, at night, it was ominous. The tides encroached, lapping hungrily up the beach toward the houses. It reminded her of a storm every time. Watching the crashing surf and listening to the pounding it made upon the beach was alarming, almost as much as the imagined sea creatures she pictured farther out in the quiet depths of darkness. When they were kids, Sam and Paige would think nothing of peeling off their sweaters and diving in for a night swim, catching waves and bodysurfing right up onto the beach, whooping as they rode in on invisible waves. But not Clem; she'd stayed on the safety of the sand, nestled among the dunes, or perhaps seated on a log of driftwood. She envied their brazenness. She still did.

Now, she walked timidly to meet the incoming surf. It surged in, swallowing her feet, tugging underneath her heels. She hopped back, regaining her footing. In the distance she could see the lights of a couple of boats, large yachts and sailing vessels. But even they were part of the sea, leaving her alone and vulnerable on the wet sand. In that instant, she longed for Ben. She felt closer to him at night, always had since he'd left them. And so she forced herself to lock her feet into the sand, despite the churning water that moved in and around her, pulling and pushing. She stood strong and still, eyes bent on the horizon line where black sky met black sea, waiting. But no matter how hard she tried, she could not feel Ben tonight, and the thought left her bereft. Clem raised her eyes to the almost full moon. Where was he?

A blast of wind came in off the water and, combined with the surf, she stumbled backwards. It was enough. Clem turned back up the beach. Her pace quickened as she approached the dunes, the wind at her back. The gusts were so fierce now, she couldn't differentiate between water and wind, and suddenly she yearned to be back in her bed. The summer house lights flickered above on the bluff, faint but present, and she ran up the sandy incline to the dunes. She was at the base of the beach path when suddenly someone caught her sleeve, pulled her back. She yelped.

"Clem, it's me." It was Fritz. She could just make out his profile against the filtered light coming from the houses along the bluff.

"God, you scared me!" She put a hand to her chest. Then, seeing the look on his face, she started to laugh.

"Sorry! I thought you saw me coming." He watched her curiously, as she doubled over in laughter. "Do you always laugh when you've encountered perceived danger, or are you amused to see me?"

Clem straightened, stifling her giggles. "Do you always sneak up behind women on a dark beach and grab their arm?" she teased. Seeing the worry on his face, she back-pedaled. "I'm fine, really, just a nervous reaction."

Fritz smiled. "Good. I was just coming down to take a walk."

She paused, hoping he'd ask her to join him. It was then she saw he was holding two bottles. "With two beers?" She didn't want to read into it, but had he been hoping to see her? But no, he could've easily polished off two beers on his own.

Fritz held the beers up between them. He didn't answer her, but instead asked, "Would you like one?"

"Drink and walk?" she asked.

"Preferred to drink and drive."

Clem grinned. Fritz's voice still held a note of boyishness, so familiar to her from childhood. It was the kind of voice she would enjoy staying up late listening to on the phone. "I was just heading home, actually," she said. Which was exactly what she did not feel like doing anymore. What was she doing? Fritz was so young. And she was so . . . tired. But despite the long day and the late hour, suddenly Clem wanted nothing more than to stay down there on the beach.

Fritz peered over her shoulder, toward the bonfire area below. A few orange embers still glowed in the distance. "Looks like I did a lousy job putting the fire out. I heard some kids down here earlier."

"Yeah, but the tide will take care of that," Clem said. "Unless . . . " Here was her chance.

"Unless what?"

"You any good at making fires?"

Fritz followed her gaze to the smoldering pile of driftwood, a smile spreading across his face. "I'm the king of beach bonfires."

"The king?" Relief flooded her chest. To hell with age differences and a good night's sleep. "Okay, then your highness. I think I'll have that beer."

They got the fire going again with a few pieces of driftwood and some dried seaweed Clem collected from the high tide area. As she scoured the sand for more pieces of wood, she glanced over her shoulder at Fritz, who was bent over the flames. She admired the strong curve of his back, the quick speed with which he worked.

If he was trying to hide his pleasure in the fact that she was staying, Fritz did a lousy job of it. As the fire crackled and spit, he talked animatedly about his family, about his mother, Cora, Flossy's dear friend, who was in Europe at the moment with her sister. About his sister, Suzy, and her kids, whom he was clearly crazy about.

"What about a girlfriend?" Clem braved. It was none of her business, and yet it was a question she'd been pushing to the back of her tongue until the beer started to soften her resolve.

Fritz shrugged. "What about her would you like to know?"

"Ah, so there is one."

He shook his head. "There was, but we ended things before graduation. Claire's down in Atlanta now. I guess we made more sense in the bubble of our campus life than we did in the real world."

"Geography can be hard."

"Nah, it was more about who she was. Claire was sharp but she was so indecisive. Her father was really well connected, and she landed a ton of interviews all over the country. She finally settled on New York. When she got a great job offer in Manhattan, she turned it down to stay in Durham and take a year off working at a clothing boutique."

"A clothing boutique? After three years of law school?"

Fritz shook his head. "If that was what she wanted to do from the start, fine. But I want someone who knows herself. Who has a little more pluck." He glanced at her. "Like you."

Clem snorted. "You have no idea what you're talking about. My compass has been spun completely out of whack this year. As for pluck . . ."

"No, I'm not talking about this past year. I'm talking about who you always were. Remember the dunes by the Spinner house?"

Clem did. Halfway up the beach was the highest point of grassy dune. Beneath it, the sand had been eroded away so that when you stood on top of the dune and looked down it was a straight drop of about ten feet. The kids used to line up at the edge and peer over, daring one another to jump. It used to scare her to death.

Fritz elbowed her gently. "You were the youngest in your family, but whenever we climbed those dunes, you always jumped first. I liked that about you."

Clem couldn't help it; she blushed. "Tell me about law school," she said, switching the subject.

He told Clem about his decision to go to Duke and how disappointed his dad had been that he didn't go to Dartmouth, as he had. When she congratulated him on graduating, he also told her that it was his opinion that anyone, really, could go to law school. It was a matter of discipline, yes, and a passion for the law, too. But also the ability to memorize.

"So what you're saying is that you have a good memory?" she asked.

Fritz feigned confusion. "When did I say that?"

Clem laughed and blurted out, "Ben is a lawyer, too." Then she caught herself. "I mean, was."

Fritz studied her for a moment. "I know. And I was so sorry to hear of your loss." He paused. "How are you doing?"

It was the invitation Clem had been waiting for. She did not know exactly how to answer that, as her answer changed moment to moment, but she began to try. And once she began, she talked for what seemed like hours. Clem told Fritz how they'd met at a sports bar in college and how she hadn't cared much for Ben when her friends introduced them (too fixated on the televised football game), but how he'd won her over at the very end of the night by listing every personal detail he'd picked up on over the course of the evening, from the name of her roommate's cat (Simon), to a novel she couldn't put down (*Mansfield Park*), while she'd assumed he'd been absorbed in the game. And how he wanted to memorize each and every one of those details. They'd started dating that night.

Fritz laughed and tapped his head. "See? Lawyer memory."

They talked until the fire they had built up faded, and the illuminated circle of sand around them grew shadowy once more.

"Thanks for tonight," she said. "It's been a while since I've talked to anyone like that. It's not that I don't want to, but sometimes I get the sense from my friends in Boston that they think I should be moving on more by now. And as far as my family goes, they get this fearful look if I say Ben's name. Like I'm this glass statue that's been broken and glued back together in so many places, and if we talk about him too much, I might shatter. But sometimes it helps."

Fritz was watching her carefully. "I imagine it's because they love you. It must hurt them to see you hurting."

"I know. But it hurts to keep it to myself, too."

"Well, if you ever want to talk, I'm here. We can talk about you, or the kids."

"Or sea urchins." She grinned at him.

"Or sea urchins. Or anything else you want." He turned to her. "I like talking to you, Clementine Merrill. I always have."

Clem's insides stirred. She didn't know if it was the beer or the late hour, or all their shared summers and history, but suddenly she felt a pull toward Fritz that went beyond gratitude for his kind words and company. He wasn't the kid brother of her summer friend. His hand was resting on the log beside hers, his tanned fingers open.

"Fritz . . . " she began. She placed her hand slowly atop his.

He stood up then, suddenly. "We should get you home," he said. "I imagine you need a few hours of sleep before George and Maddy come looking for you in the morning."

Clem watched in dismay as he began to kick sand onto the remains of the fire.

"Oh, right."

The last pieces of glowing ember disappeared beneath the sand, and the beach grew dark.

"Want me to walk you back?"

Clem stood, and wobbled.

"Woah, you okay?" He held his hand out to her, but she didn't take it.

"Yeah, I'm fine. Just tired." She shook her head. It wasn't the beer. It was the hour, and the sentiments that had been stirred up around the fire. He was probably right: she should go home.

"You sure?" He put a hand on her arm.

"I'm sure."

What had she been thinking? They'd spent the evening talking about Ben and their families, about children, and careers. So many things—

heavy things. Suddenly she just wanted to craw
into bed. She started back up toward the beach
path and he followed.

When they reached the base of the bluff where
he'd grabbed her sleeve only hours earlier, she
stopped and turned.

There was so much she wanted to say. She
felt a pull to this young man like she did to her
past, to her old carefree self. Fritz knew her in
ways others never would. Even in some ways
Ben had not. And yet he knew so little about
the woman she'd become. It was akin to the
draw of the tide, a force that you knew could
pull you in and down if you waded into it
"Listen, Fritz . . ."

Fritz slipped his hand into hers and she froze.
Another blast of wind enveloped them, throwing
her hair across her face, the sand spraying up
against her face. She squeezed her eyes shut and
bent into him for cover. It passed, and as soon
as it did his lips were on hers, his nose pressed
against her own. A warm flood of longing rose
up in her; she gave in. Clem wrapped both arms
around Fritz's neck, her fingers reaching across
his back. His breath was hot, his lips wet as he
pressed them against her own, again and again.
She opened her mouth, their tongues finding
each other, until she thought the surf and sky
would swallow them both. Fritz lifted her up
off the sand, and Clem moaned, unsure if it was

her desire or the driving wind that pressed them harder against one another.

"Please, Clem," she thought she heard over the pounding surf, but she wasn't sure if it was Fritz's voice or her imagination. She kissed him hungrily, unable to be satiated.

And then, just as quickly as he'd seized her, Fritz let go. Clem staggered backwards in the sand. Instantly, the cold air filled the space between them. Clem pressed her hand to her swollen mouth, staring back at him. As the next roar of surf crashed on the sand behind them, she turned and ran. This time she was sure she heard him call after her.

Clem did not look back until she was home. Safe inside, she found the living room empty, all lights turned out except for the lantern by the stairs. The house was too still, too quiet. She crept upstairs and checked the children, a wave of guilt washing over her as she adjusted their blankets, touched their cheeks. Back in her own room she shut the door, and fell back against it. She didn't cry until she slid down hard onto the floor, and when she finally did the stream of tears stung her bottom lip and tasted like ocean.

Paige

Paige balanced on the back deck on one leg, stretching her left hamstring up behind her. Her pink running shorts were loose on her waist; she wondered if she'd stress-shed a few pounds this week.

"You look like a flamingo," Sam told her, walking past with a cup of coffee. He slumped into one of the Adirondack chairs and focused on the horizon.

Paige ignored him. "Hey, Ned," she called through the screen door. Flossy was flipping pancakes at the stove, and Ned was hovering at her elbow with a plate. "When you're finished, why don't you come for a run with me?"

"No thanks, Mom."

She let go of her right foot, and switched positions to the left, without so much as a wobble. "Come on, you've got to stay in shape for lacrosse."

He didn't answer, but he gave her a baleful look that said he would. She squinted through the door for Emma, who'd just been sitting at the counter texting. Where had she gotten off to?

"Another gorgeous day." Evan came through

the screen door carrying hedge clippers. He set them carefully on the deck against the weathered shingle siding.

"Has Mom got you on the hedges, now?" she asked.

Evan chuckled loudly and shook his head. "No way. That's between your mother and father. We just got them sharpened for her." He winked. "I mean, him."

Paige noticed that Evan was sitting apart from Sam, though Sam seemed to be watching him intently. She wondered briefly what was going on there. Evan was so easygoing; Sam must've done something. But who was she to compare? She and David had spent the last night back to back in their bed, locked in wordless fits of sleep. They were civil, but the strain was wearing on her. That coupled with the news that Aubrey had shared the night before when she'd called to check in on the animal hospital. According to Aubrey, the clinic was running smoothly in her absence. The OR procedures were on schedule, minus a cat who hadn't shown up on time to be neutered, and a dog who'd swallowed a child's hair elastic and needed emergency surgery.

"What about the Tuesday morning shelter spays and neuters?" Paige had asked.

"All fine," Aubrey had said. "We had five."

"The delivery of Apoquel?" It was an allergy medication they'd been on a waiting list for, the demand for the surprisingly effective drug exceeding its availability. Clients were becoming so frustrated having to wait that she'd considered changing suppliers.

"That, too. Came in yesterday."

"Did the receptionists call the waiting-list patients?"

"They did. Now, you go enjoy your vacation! There's nothing here that needs your attention."

The updates should have come as a relief to Paige, but instead she'd hung up the phone feeling as if she'd been slapped. Her own clinic did not need her, any more than her family appeared to want her. She'd risen early, made notes of things to call the head vet tech about, and had already eaten an egg-white omelet by the time her mother had wandered into the kitchen at seven in her seersucker bathrobe. No, she didn't want pancakes. What she needed was a run.

"Come on, Ned," she called now, into the kitchen. "I want to get on the beach before the sun gets too hot."

He pushed through the screen door in unlaced sneakers and followed her across the backyard. The day was already getting hot, the sun a blinding white over the water. "Why are we doing this again?" he asked.

"Because it's good for you."

"Huh." When they reached the sand, he broke into a trot and headed down by the water where he footing was firm. She let him go out in front. Ned's legs were longer than her own this year, and it was a joy to watch him. But it was also another reminder of just how fast her eldest was growing up and away from them.

It was hard to keep up with Ned, even though she was in her best shape. No small feat this year, having to juggle the practice, home life, and squeeze in workouts. But they kept her sane. She liked to tell her coworkers, "I don't run because I love it. I run so I don't strangle anyone at home." Which was partly true. But she did enjoy the running, too. She liked pushing herself until her lungs burned and her quads ached. She loved the shaky feeling she got after a hard sprint, knowing her body could still do what she wanted of it, even if the rest of her life would not. Ned kept his head part way up the beach, but he was a sprinter, and a typical teen, so he'd already started to slow before he'd considered the length of the shore. Soon she caught up and pulled up alongside him.

"So, what do you think about the week?" she asked. She'd barely touched base with Ned all vacation; he'd been so busy with the little kids and off boogie boarding and swimming during the day. But he seemed happy enough, so much so that she hadn't given it any thought beyond occasionally checking in on his whereabouts and whether he was eating (which she need not have worried about).

"Think about what, exactly?"

Paige sighed. There it was, the teenage boy again. She rephrased her question. "What I mean is, are you having fun?"

"Yeah. It's been good." He puffed alongside her, saying nothing more, and for a moment she thought he was done. "Though everyone seems pretty stressed out. I don't get it."

Paige considered this. "True, but planning Grampa's party is a lot of work."

"Not about the party. About *other* stuff."

Paige felt her insides flutter. "What kind of other stuff?"

"Well, take Uncle Sam and Evan. I figured they'd be bummed about the adoption and all, but I think it's more than that. Sam seems nervous."

Paige pictured Sam: on his phone, talking work, sipping another gin and tonic. "You know the term 'married to your work,' right?"

Ned grunted. "Like you?"

"Neddy, hang on."

He must've seen her face fall, because he shook his head and threw her one of his lopsided smiles. "I'm just teasing you, Mom. But really—Sam's acting weird."

Well, that was a relief. But still.

"And then there's Grandma. I know she's getting old, and so I keep offering to help her set up stuff and move stuff and all, but she seems . . . I don't know. Mad."

He was right about that, she supposed. There'd been the dinners, the complaints, the usual guilt they all signed up for during their vacations each summer. But Flossy was more than her usual overwhelmed and over-expectant self. She *did* seem kind of mad.

"And Auntie Clem—well, she's the only one with a real reason to be bummed out. I was worried she'd be crying and stuff." He paused. "And she was a little upset, when we first got here. But actually, she seems really happy."

Paige studied her son as she ran alongside him. His handsome profile whose soft edges were sharpening: the boyish plushness of his face giving way to more masculine outlines, the cheekbones announcing themselves. Suddenly she felt a beat of guilt for always assuming that because he was gallivanting around like a kid, that he still saw the world as one. Ned deserved more credit. His perceptions were spot on. "Neddy, I'm proud of you."

He shrugged. "Could you please not call me that anymore? We talked about that, remember?"

Paige grinned. They had, and she did.

"At least not in public," he said.

"I will try my best. Even though it's hard." She reached over and slapped his arm playfully. Ned was doing okay. Moreover, she was relieved that the one couple he'd overlooked, or chosen to leave out, was his parents. She wondered if this came out of politeness or if he truly didn see what was happening to them, as she knew Emma had.

"Hey, I want to ask you something," she said slowing down.

"Yeah?"

"About that bottle in your closet."

Ned groaned, and she feared he'd run ahead But he didn't. "Mom, you were in my closet?"

"Hey," she warned, "that closet is in my house And you are my son. Let's talk about what it wa doing there, not what I was doing in your closet."

She was relieved when he slowed beside he and bowed his head shamefully. "I'm sorry Mom. It wasn't mine. I swear."

She wanted to believe it; what parent wouldn't But she knew it wasn't that simple. "Did yo drink any of it?"

He shook his head. "No."

"Then why were you keeping it? Because th last I knew you hadn't turned twenty-one, and you know the rules in our house."

"I know, I'm sorry. Dad already said all that t me."

This was a surprise. "Oh? So, Dad talked t you about it already?"

"Yeah, everything's fine."

Paige wondered what exactly Ned meant by "fine." There was nothing fine about it: not th worry it caused, not the way that she and Davi had handled it. They were better than this. They used to be united on family matters, or at least there was an effort to appear so. But, in spite of all of that, a bubble of hope rose in her gut. David had reached out to Ned, after all. Maybe their fight the night before had spurred him to it.

"So what did Dad say?"

"Didn't he tell you?"

Paige flinched. Of course their son would assume David had told her. That's what parents did. Or should do. Buoyed momentarily by the fact that Ned had such faith in his failing parents, she quickened her pace. She wondered if she should indulge him that sense of certainty. But she felt a pang of honesty surfacing.

"No, actually," she admitted. "Daddy and I haven't spoken yet. About your discussion." She glanced at Ned sideways to see if he was reading into any of it.

"Oh."

"But, your talk together went well?"

Ned halted. He swiped at his brow, looking pained. "Come on, Mom. I told him it was left over from someone's party, and it got put in my backpack. I don't usually do that stuff."

"Honey, I want to believe that. But there was a bottle of Ketel One in your closet." She didn't ask where they'd gotten their hands on such an expensive bottle. When she was a teen, kids drank Smirnoff.

"Look, we don't care where you got it or where you stashed it, Ned. Because I realize some one will always have it. We'd rather you didn' drink at all. But if you ever do, we want you to be smart about the choices you make."

"Because they can be life-changing," he said imitating her voice.

"No, because they can be life-*ending*."

They'd already had this talk many time at home over the years: what a serving o alcohol did to the body physically, how i affected the choices he made socially and emotionally, and what the consequences could be.

Ned looked embarrassed and mildly annoyed but still not as ashamed as she'd hoped. A soon as he'd entered seventh grade and they' gotten wind of middle-schoolers sneaking bee at school dances, they'd made it a point to show him articles on the news and in the paper— expounding on every grisly local cautionary tale they could get their hands on.

"Ned, are you listening to me? Because I'm worried about you. Dad is worried about you."

Ned halted in the sand and swung back around toward the house. "Well maybe you guys should worry a little less about me and a little more about Emma."

Paige scoffed. "What does that mean?" Surely he was joking. There were plenty of jabs he could've taken, but that was one of the more ridiculous ones.

"I'm serious, Mom. She's not the goody-good bookworm you guys think she is. Wake up."

With that, he broke into a slow run heading down the beach and away from her. Paige stared after him, dumbfounded. Emma was just annoyed about the swimsuit incident in town, and that was Sam's fault. And as for her being distant, that was true of every female teen. According to Paige's other mommy friends, Emma was a dream, a piece of cake. They'd been lucky to get so much angst-free time with her up to this point, from all the horror stories they heard about their friends' daughters. And if Emma was a little off this week, Paige was pretty certain it had to do with the distance between her parents lately. Girls were much more attuned to such subtle disruptions. As far as Ned was usually concerned, unless plates were thrown or curses hurled, he probably wouldn't notice. She couldn't decide whether that was a good thing or not.

The only concern that Paige and David had shared when it came to Emma was how socially quiet her life sometimes seemed. Her friends were good kids—kids like her who went to the library after school or volunteered at the vet clinic, talking in hushed tones to the animals in their crates. Emma was the kind of kid who had to be constantly told to put her book down, to engage in conversation at the dinner table. Unlike other teens, she wasn't on her phone texting all the time or scrolling through peers' social media pages. Paige had never worried about Emma partying or going out with kids they didn't know at night. In fact, she would almost welcome that.

She kicked off her running shoes and walked down to the water's edge. The waves were gentle today, small frothy curls that rolled in over her feet. She stood, relishing the feel on her toes and stared out at the endless blue horizon, Ned's words prickly in her ears. *Wake up to what?* she thought.

Flossy

Flossy sat at the dining room table, drumming her fingers on its cool mahogany surface. She glanced at her nails—the pink manicure she'd done the day before the kids had arrived was already chipped midway down each nail. They looked like she'd spent the last six days climbing the walls. *Well,* she thought.

She sipped her tea, eyes roaming over the mixed-and-matched serving ware laid out before her. Richard's mother had acquired many lovely pieces, all of which had been handed down to the two of them, since he was an only child. But Flossy and Richard were not formal people, and she'd always found it curious that her mother-in-law had kept such nice sets in the summer house, as the season was known for a more relaxed mode of entertaining. But entertaining was something Richard's parents had loved to do during their long Rhode Island summers. Flossy had some tender memories of her own during their early courting days when she had been a guest at Richard's parents' dinner parties. She remembered having been introduced as "Richard's special friend" by Mae. Mae

255

was known to set up intimate gatherings in the backyard, the table dressed in white linens and the lead-crystal punch bowl that had belonged to Richard's grandmother set in the center always filled with a sparkling pink lemonade spritzer. Mae had handed down that very bowl and ladle, along with a copy of the drink recipe carefully written out in her elegant hand on a monogrammed card, tucked inside. Now, the bowl sat on the dining room table ready to be filled with the same recipe for the party.

Flossy surveyed the rest of the dishes she'd selected for the birthday. There were the two-dozen Steuben goblets, lined up on the buffet like crystal soldiers. And the set of repoussé serving platters on which she'd planned to serve the oysters. Lined up were a host of large silver-polished forks, spoons, and serving knives in mismatched silver patterns. The overall effect was classic yet unassuming, just like the personal feel of the summer house.

She checked her watch. Noon. Now, she could focus on the children. And on this week that was winding down too quickly! Paige was irritable having dragged Ned out for a morning run. Sam and Evan seemed to be in some kind of tiff, though at least they were able to sit beside each other. Unlike David and Paige, who may have been in joint attendance at the beach or the dinner table, but who seemed to look past one another nonetheless. This worried her. Surprisingly, and thank goodness—Clem seemed happier than the rest of them. Suddenly so, in fact. Flossy had spent the better part of the last year worrying about Clem and Maddy and George. And she'd worried further about what this visit to the summer house would mean to them, as it was the first time since Ben had died that the three of them would walk through the door, across its sandy floorboards, and out back to the beach, no longer a foursome.

Richard was outside doing something to the grill. "Honey, what are you doing?"

"Just cleaning the grill. It needs it."

"Well, that's very nice. But can it wait? We really need to wrap up a few details."

He nodded in agreement and waved at her, but kept scraping the grill grate. Behind him, the rangy, half-dead hedges rustled in the ocean air.

She went to the screen door. "Since you're out there, how about these hedges? I can go ahead and call Lucas to do it. The party is upon us." When he didn't answer right away, she added, "The boys had the clippers sharpened. Shall we attack this project now?"

Richard turned and looked at her over the rim of his glasses. "Thank you, but beyond your offer to retrieve the clippers, I don't think there is any 'we' in this endeavor." His tone was playful, but Flossy did not care for his message.

"Richard. The party is in two days."

He returned his attention to the grill. "Yes, dear. We are all very well aware of that fact." *Yes, dear.* Richard knew it drove her crazy. Almost as crazy as those damned hedges.

No matter, Flossy had more pressing issues. They'd planned an intimate family dinner at the Ocean House. It was tradition, and this year it was also the eve of the birthday party, a night when the house would be cleaned and set up for the festivities, and she would not want to mess things up with any cooking. Plus, it would get them all out of the house and yard. How Flossy loved the low-key week loitering with sand between one's toes and lazy afternoons lounging on the beach. These were the aimless, lazy days she looked forward to all through the New England winter. But now, they were worn out from one another and worn down by the heat. It would do them all good to get out into town and "blow the stink off them," as her grandmother used to like to say. She called the Ocean House and confirmed their reservation: seven o'clock Friday evening. There. The only thing left to do was confirm Sandy. Sandy was going to cancel her catering contract if Flossy didn't finalize the details. She'd hoped to leave a message or at least get an assistant, but Sandy herself answered.

"That's correct," she informed Sandy. "Final headcount is sixty-one."

She listened vaguely as Sandy reviewed the menu, the linen service, the bartender's fee, the takedown fee, and the servers' gratuities. She did not bother taking any more notes—her spiral notebook lay open in front of her like a relic of some kind of scullery war, its pages crumpled and tea-stained. She glanced at the last entry: *Get Ci Ci's recipe!* and slapped the notebook shut.

She and Judy had reached a Mexican standoff.

"No, Sandy," she said. "No, there won't be stuffed oysters, after all. We've decided to go with the clams casino. Yes, I'm quite sure. Thank you."

Flossy knew that in the great order of things, this whole dilemma was ridiculous. A self-propelled dilemma fueled by the school-grade behavior of two grown women. She was better than this. And she should be ashamed. Her family had *real* issues to concern themselves with, and the refusal to grant a recipe by one book club member (however tyrannical) was not something that Flossy could afford to waste anymore of her precious time and energy upon. She simply would not do it!

However, before Sandy hung up, she asked for a clams casino serving count. And Flossy paused. Judy had said she was bringing a bushel of stuffed oysters. They really did not need the casinos. Flossy was merely ordering them to cover all bases, in case Judy fell through, fell ill . . . or just plain fell onto her knees and surrendered. Flossy couldn't risk having no shellfish appetizers at all. After tiring of the nonsense, Paige had suggested she order a mere four dozen—enough for the guests to enjoy a little taste, whether Judy came through or not. But now Flossy pictured another scenario: Judy, arriving with her fleet of oysters only to stumble upon a table teeming with silver platters of clams. Lovely half-shell pillows laden with crisps of bacon and a smidgen of pepper. One hundred shells arranged in an elegant arc across her mother-in-law's sterling repoussé serving trays. A lesser shellfish than the oyster, perhaps . . . but, oh!

Flossy cleared her throat. "Enough for the entire guest list," she said. "Just as many as we'd planned for oysters."

There. It was settled.

Sam

He'd been so intent on making headway with Evan and spending time with the family, being *present*, as their therapist liked to say, that he'd neglected to check his phone. Sam never forgot to check his phone.

There were two voice messages. The first, from Adya, saying that the paperwork from Shanghai had come in, contracts were signed, and they were good to go. Sam exhaled in a half laugh, half burst of relief. It was done! He had to tell Evan.

The second was a message from a Maryland phone number. The adoption agency. Sam's chest compressed against his heart.

The only words he'd managed to coerce from Evan since yesterday's reveal at the beach had taken place politely in front of family. *Here's a beach towel. Dinner looks great. Pass the ketchup, please.* It was infuriating and yet Sam knew he deserved it. Last night when they'd gone to bed, Evan had rolled away from him.

"Ev," Sam had whispered to his back. "Please. We've got to talk about this."

"Call Mara tomorrow and make it better,"

Evan had replied. "Make her believe this was all a misunderstanding."

The thing was, it may have been a misunderstanding. Until Sam actually got a chance to speak to Mara, he had no way of knowing what she thought. Maybe she'd not heard the implied promise. Maybe all this worry was for naught.

But there were other maybes that kept Sam awake as he listened to Evan's deep, slumbering breaths. What if she'd gone to Malayka at the agency? What if she was counting on him following through with his offer. No, *bribe,* Sam chastised himself. If he was going to be honest it started with himself: he'd bribed her, and he fucking knew it.

As he'd lain beside Evan, falling in and out of fitful sleep, images and sentiments came to him. Old hurts—wounds he'd caused, wounds he'd denied. It had been years since any of these had found him, though nighttime was as direct a route as could be taken to arrive at the threshold of his conscience.

His sophomore year of high school had been the first time Sam had been openly called out as gay by classmates. It happened on the bus, one spring afternoon.

"Sammy likes the boys!" Jimmy Durant had jeered at him, from the back row of the school bus. There'd been stunned silence by some and whispers by others. His best friend, Cal, had sat stiff-lipped next to him and stared out the bus window, saying nothing. For a few days they didn't talk until one afternoon in the locker room after track. Practice was over and the boys were planning to walk off school campus and meet across the street at Joe's Diner, like they did every Friday. Cal waited until the locker room emptied.

"So, is it true?"

He didn't have to add, *what Jimmy said on the bus.* Sam knew what he meant. He was tired of keeping it in, tired of wondering how others would react and if those who mattered most would accept him.

"Yes," he said, waiting for him to get up and walk away.

But he didn't. Cal remained on the bench, unlacing his shoes, slowly.

"I wondered," he said finally. Then, "You could've told me."

Sam looked at him for the first time. "Is this going to be a problem for you?" He hadn't meant it to come out so edgy, not to Cal. Cal had been his friend since grade school. And he was here, still sitting on the bench. If anything, Sam knew it would be more of a problem for *him* if Cal couldn't handle it. Because Sam couldn't imagine not having his friendship.

"No," Cal said. "No, it's not." He'd grabbed his

bag and stood. "Come on. If we hurry up, we can catch the rest of the team at the diner."

People's reactions at school followed. Luckily, Sam was quick, as deft with verbal comebacks as he was darting past opponents in intramural basketball games. Still, he knew what others were saying, and he never escaped the feeling that he was only one fast break ahead on the court or one shove back in the hallway.

There had not been, however, any official coming out at home. Paige knew, from school. She'd acknowledged this quietly by surprising him in his doorway one night while he sat at his desk doing homework. "You handling all this okay?"

He'd hesitated. "Yeah, I think so."

"Good. You know, I think Mom gets it," she added. "You could probably talk to her if you wanted."

"You think?" He honestly didn't know what his parents thought, though he knew he'd have to face it at some point. They seemed open minded, Flossy especially, and Sam seemed to recall a gay male couple who'd attended a few of their holiday parties in years past. But still—he knew it was different when it was your own family.

"Or me," Paige had said softly. "You can always talk to me, if you want."

It was a small gesture of enormous proportion. "Thanks. That means a lot."

But spring ended and their annual trip to the shore approached, and he still had not come out officially to his family. He wondered briefly if he should do it at the summer house. But he hedged; maybe one more summer would give him the guts to do it when they returned to Connecticut.

The safety he felt to be himself, mostly anonymous as any other fun-loving summer kid in Rhodey, was something he both looked forward to and took for granted until that summer. Sam was bussing tables at Olympia Tea Room, while silently counting down the hours of his shift until he got off. Then it would be he and a couple of kids from work, or the neighbors, at the beach. Swimming. Heading up to Narragannset Point. Building bonfires that stretched into the wee hours of the next day's morning light, like the teenage drinking crowd that partied and danced around them. They understood he did not leer at the girls surrounding the bonfire, and he did not feel inclined to lie about a girlfriend back home. He simply shrugged off inquiries and they seemed to be let go. There were too many other distractions of summer to concern themselves with—as long as Sam hosted gatherings, rounded up kegs, and kept everyone laughing, he was accepted without further pressing. It was a sweet spot.

Which is why the night that Brad Aaron from across the street showed up at a beach fire, Sam had no warning of what was to follow. A smaller group than usual had gotten together. Paige was there, along with the older Weitzman kids, their visiting cousins, and a couple of kids Paige worked with that summer. Someone had procured a bottle of Jagermeister that they passed around the circle and took swigs from when the beer ran out. The music was loud; to this day he could not hear Billy Idol's "Cradle of Love" without his skin breaking out in a prickly sweat.

Sam had had too much to drink. What he did remember was the blur of flames and the heat; he'd been sitting too close, talking too loud. Brad had suddenly walked up to their group, appearing as if out of the darkness. He'd been a neighborhood fixture in their earlier years, but Sam couldn't say he'd even laid eyes on him in the last season or two. Brad Aaron was stocky, a kid who made up in breadth what he lacked for in humor or sensibility. He walked up and sat down on a log like he owned it. Sam vaguely recalled him grabbing the bottle of Jagermeister from a girl.

What happened in the time after he arrived was nothing consequential. Brad Aaron was also loud, in an off-putting way. Those that had introduced themselves to him initially began edging away. His jokes were rude, drawing a few smirks from some of the guys. But Sam largely ignored him until he zeroed in on Paige.

Paige was a junior that year. She'd finally

grown into the rangy Merrill legs. It was August; like the rest she was tanned, her hair sun-bleached. Unlike the others, she was quieter, hanging back from the group. Which is how he probably got her aside.

What Sam remembered was looking past the fire at one point, seeing Paige toss her hair back and laugh. But there was something about the fixed expression that told him it was a show. She kept glancing back at her friend, Anne, who was also watching.

Brad passed her the bottle and held it to her mouth. This also got Sam's attention. Paige didn't drink the hard stuff. When she pushed the bottle away and turned her head, the liquor spilled on both of them.

"Ah, fuck!" Brad shouted. But then he laughed and threw his arm around her. Paige jumped up. Sam remembers standing up. He remembers walking around the fire, surprised by how it swayed hard to the left then the right as he steadied himself before proceeding. And then the glow of orange on Brad's face blocked out as Sam stood in front of him like an eclipse, the heat against his back.

He didn't address Brad. "Paige, you okay?"

She glanced nervously away and took a step back toward her group of friends.

"Oh, come on!" Brad jeered. "We're just starting to have fun."

Sam turned his attention to Brad. He doesn't recall the words that were exchanged. He knows there was some cursing. Then a shove. It came from Brad.

The next thing he knew, they were in the sand. Sam remembers the stars flashing overhead briefly then darkness as he was pushed into the sand, face first. He remembers the burn of the granules beneath his elbows, his knees, as they wrestled on the beach. Paige was shouting something. Then the stars, the fire, the roar of the surf in his ears. At one point he broke free and stood, swaying. Paige later told him that he yelled at Brad to just go home. That's when Brad swung.

This time Sam fell back, and Brad was on top of him. He remembers being flipped, so hard that the wind was blown from his chest, his arm pinned behind his back. He felt the cut of sand against skin on his face, in his eyes. And then Brad's mouth pressed up against his ear, his hot breath coming in short puffs. Then the laugh. "Fucking faggot." There was a blow to his side from Brad's foot. Paige's scream. And a scuffle overhead as others stepped in.

The next day, Sam awoke in his bed ears ringing and hair full of sand. There was sand on his pillow. In his sheets. His mouth was as dry as the beach. When he looked in the mirror he saw the red scrapes along his right cheekbone, the cut above his eyebrow. His ribs throbbed. For days he'd wondered if they were broken. When Paige came to his door and knocked he told her to leave him alone. When Flossy called the third time for breakfast, he knew he'd have to go down or she'd come looking for him.

When he walked into the kitchen Paige watched him worriedly from the table. Clem was the first to speak. "Oh my god! Look at Sam's face!"

Flossy was upon him. "What happened to you? Are you all right? Richard, come look at this."

Paige was saying something about the party, about a fight—it was no big deal. He'd been trying to break up some kids messing around. It had just gotten out of hand is all.

Richard was sitting at the head of the table, wordless. He asked Flossy to calm down, told Paige to hush. He looked down the table at Sam. "What happened to you?"

"It looks worse than it is," Sam said, his dry lips cracking with the effort. He needed a drink of water. He needed to crawl back into bed for a week.

"Was this the result of an accident or a fight?" Richard pressed. His brow furrowed with concern, but his tone was firm.

Sam had shaken his head, pushed away the frozen bag of peas his mother was trying to press against his cheek. "Mom, please." He met his father's stare. "It wasn't an accident. We were just down on the beach with some kids."

"Were you drinking?"

Clem was listening wide-eyed to all of it. Sam glanced at his lap, and nodded his head.

It was the question Richard asked next that had hit harder than any blow Sam had endured in the fight.

"Was this over a girl?"

Flossy had stiffened beside him. Sam would always remember that she was holding onto a dishtowel. It was red. She twisted it in her hands.

They'd all known. For months now—Paige, Flossy, some of his teachers, most of his friends. All spring, Flossy hovering outside his locked door at night. He could feel her there, see the shadow of her feet beneath the crack at the base of the door and sense the weight of her longing to come in. Only Richard had seemed deaf to the revelation of truths about his son. Sam never knew if it stemmed from a lack of awareness, or rather a lack of acceptance; one being involuntary, the other . . . well, unthinkable.

Richard, by the very nature of his professorship in the humanities department, was a man attuned to subtleties: the veiled symbolism in a stanza of poetry, the dry Southern arc of plot in a Faulkner novel. He was a man who nightly spent hours in his den, one eye searching the lunar image at the other end of his telescope, sometimes hurrying upstairs to wake the children, against Flossy's wishes, to share with them the milky view of a distant moon made closer. As a child, Clem used to say, "Daddy brings us the moon."

And yet, for all of his thoughtful consideration of words penned by long dead writers or the hours spent contemplating dimpled surfaces floating in a far-off galaxy, Richard seemed unable to read the very palpable signs spelled out by his only son under the same shared roof. Sam was right there, and yet his father did not see. The realization rendered Sam nearly invisible.

That morning after the fight, his face swollen and his thoughts askew, Sam looked at his father seated at the opposite end of the table. At the reserved plea in his eyes behind his spectacles. *Was it over a girl?*

Sam flew up from his chair, sending it toppling behind him. Everyone jumped. "You know it wasn't!" Sam screamed, his voice cracking in his throat. "You *know!*"

He seized the end of the table and flung it upward, plates sliding, coffee cups careening off the edge. It crashed back down, and the house shuddered. The din that followed echoed through the house, and would echo in Sam's memory in the years that followed: the cries of his mother to come back, the childish sobs from Clem, and his father's booming voice as Sam streaked from the house and out into the blazing August heat, the door crashing back on its hinges behind him.

He'd returned that night, after the sun was

gone. Flossy was standing at the kitchen sink, scrubbing dishes. The girls weren't around. She gasped when he came in, stepping toward him with her soapy hands then stopping.

"Honey, *please.*"

Sam had put his hand up. "I just want to go to bed."

She'd consented, her eyes filling with sadness. And she'd pressed her wet hands to either side of his face and looked at him, hard. "You listen to me, Sam Merrill. We love you. All of us do." Sam had looked down, but she pulled his chin up. "Don't you forget."

She'd let him go, and later left a plate of dinner outside his door with a gentle knock. But there was no word from Richard.

The next morning he met his father in the upstairs hall, coming out of his bedroom. It was then Sam noticed his hand. Richard had tucked it quickly behind his back, but not before Sam saw the flash of white bandage and medical tape.

"Are you all right?" Richard asked, pausing before him.

Sam had nodded, barely able to look at him.

"Your mother made breakfast. Why don't we get some."

And that was it. Sam had not apologized, though one formed like a lump in his throat. He was sorry for so much—for the way he'd acted, for the fact that his father had not seen him, for all of them. They went downstairs and they ate, Clem sneaking curious glances between the two men. The white bandage across his father's knuckles flashed as he forked egg into his mouth. Sam watched him switch hands, resting the injured one out of sight on his lap. He stared at it with regret; had he caused his father to punch a wall? Had his revelation made Richard that angry?

And then Flossy started talking, humming about the summer storm that had raged during the night and today's resulting high surf. Richard suggested they head to the beach.

"Oh, but the waves," Flossy said.

Clem asked if she could invite Suzy from next door, over to play, and Paige relayed a story about some kids who'd found a sand shark washed up on the beach after the last storm. They talked loudly, sometimes over top of one another, right through the last piece of bacon and crumb of toast. Sam had stared at his plate. That was the thing about the Merrills: for all of the talking they did, so much went unsaid.

Now, standing beneath the heavy afternoon sun in the backyard, the memory still brought with it a chill. But, they had endured that day and the days after. Just as Clem had endured Ben. And he and Evan had endured the lost adoption. He would do as Evan asked. He would make the calls and find out where things stood. Whatever fallout may come.

Clem

She boycotted the family beach.

"Guys, what do you think about hitting East Beach in town this afternoon?"

As predicted, the kids cheered. They loved the bustle of the carousel and the ice cream shop.

Paige looked at her dully over her coffee. "Really? It's late in the day, and it gets so crowded on the weekend. You hate crowds."

True, but what Clem hated more was the thought of crossing paths with Fritz Weitzman. Or the thought of having to watch the V-shape of his tanned back as he plunged into the surf and conducted his daily swim out to the buoy and back. What had happened the other night with Fritz was the fault of their beach; their private sanctuary of beach was a numinous place at night. Shrouded in the spit of salt air and surf, the pull of the moon on the tide. What chance did a mortal body stand against such forces? Clem determined not to assign meaning to what she had experienced with Fritz. She also determined not to return to the place where it had happened, at least not today. But hard as she

274

tried, she could not stop herself from replaying it in her mind. She'd kissed another man.

Guilt had shadowed her all morning as they helped Flossy get ready for the party. It made her hover, and she found herself watching George and Maddy like a hawk. When they'd started to argue over a game, she wondered if it was a response to the sadness they felt over their father's absence. When George, whom she directed to the outdoor shower after realizing he had not bathed in the last two days, lingered out there until Flossy worried out loud about the water waste, Clem wondered if he was remembering Ben. Ben had been the one in charge of showers after the beach; he'd scoop up both kids still in their swimsuits and stand under the shower stream while singing the theme from *Gilligan's Island* in loud disjointed verses as he shampooed their hair. Ben was not there with them this summer, and yet he was everywhere, and while she was afraid to bring him up to the kids too often, she was more afraid of what would happen if she did not. Would saying his name aloud keep him present? If they went on with life, referring to him less and less, would that allow his memory to drift away with the tide?

All along, Clem had felt Ben. She felt him at their Boston home each night as she climbed into their empty bed. When the kids were fighting and dinner was burning and she was about to lose it on all of them, she felt him in her ear, talking her gently back from the ledge. And when they had first arrived at the summer house, she'd felt him in every room, on every beach and corner in town. But as the week went on, Ben seemed to begin to fade. The first time she noticed it was at St. Clair Annex. Ben used to order the peach ice cream and split it with her. Clem liked the peach well enough, but it was Ben who really loved it. Now, back in Rhode Island without him, in some kind of ritual or homage, she found herself sticking with a single scoop peach ice cream every time. Until the other day, when standing in the long line and not thinking, she allowed her eyes to roam over the board of flavors and land upon peppermint stick. She ordered it. It wasn't until the kick of candy cane coated her tongue that her heart filled with dread.

To her consternation, the kids seemed to be following suit. Maddy had stopped wearing Ben's chenille blue shirt to bed. Suddenly it was too hot, too big. And George! George had become so preoccupied with tagging after Ned that he stopped asking Clem to hold his hands and twirl him in the waves, "like Daddy did." No, she was right to worry, she told herself. There *were* times and places when Ben was no longer with them.

Ben was certainly not there when she kissed Fritz. Not when she pressed herself up against him, Fritz's arms encircling her waist, his hands drifting down her back and across the top of her buttocks. His taste lingering in her mouth when she pulled away and staying with her as she ran all the way home. Something had sparked inside her last night, something that had been dormant. And while she felt herself rise up to meet it, hungrily even, she was doomed to come back down hard. Afterward, she had lain nearly paralyzed in her bed at the thought of not feeling Ben's presence again at the summer house, like some kind of punitive haunting.

She'd tossed and turned all night before stumbling across the dark room to the dresser. Frantically, she'd popped open the orange bottle of pills and taken two. The sleep that followed was like a whiteout.

Now, having slumbered, and worried, and mostly satisfied the party-planning chores on Flossy's list that morning, she was free to escape the beach and the house with her kids. She needed to get out.

Clem eyed her siblings, who were sprawled around the downstairs. The day was humid, and everyone seemed listless in the summer heat.

"What do you think, guys? East Beach?"

David and Paige were slumped on the living room couch like bookends to their kids who lounged between them, staring down at their phones. Emma, particularly, brightened. "Wait for me. I'll run up and get changed."

"I can get started on sandwiches," David offered. It was the most he'd said all morning, and Clem watched him rise and amble into the kitchen.

Paige shrugged. "Okay." She didn't make a move to take over or to help, however. Instead, it was Flossy who appeared with her notebook in hand to weigh in on the overheard plans.

"You girls go ahead and take the kids, but I need the boys here," she said, before any of the men could answer. The tent company was coming to set up that morning.

"Mom, all you have to do is tell them where you want everything and the delivery guys will put it there," Sam tried to point out. Despite having shared that his work deal in Asia had panned out, he'd been back on the phone all morning, and he seemed more edgy than usual to Clem. She wondered with whom, but was afraid to ask.

Evan shook his head. "It's okay, we can stay and help."

Clem noticed that Sam didn't press the matter any further.

"Okay, then," Clem said brightly to Paige, eager to get away before anyone changed their mind. "It's just us!"

Paige was right about town. Bay Street and East Beach were clogged, once again. They found a spot in the harbor parking lot, and it was a challenge to navigate the sidewalk full of tourists with their beach bags and coolers, the kids racing ahead between shoppers. She followed behind Paige who for once seemed immune to all of it. The line at the carousel was already long, but the music so reminiscent of carnivals and summer fairs that Clem felt her spirits rise. "Let's take the kids!" she said.

"On the way home," Paige said, over her shoulder.

The kids were waiting for them at St. Clair's ice cream window, eager looks on their faces. Before they could peep, Paige said, again, "On the way home."

Two hours later, sun weary and salty, they trudged out through the entrance gate and onto the sidewalk. Beside them, the flying horses swung past. Clem set her heavy beach bag down with a thud. "Can we now?" she joked. "Pleeease?"

Paige sighed. "Might as well."

The little kids hopped in line with Emma. "I think you're too big for the flying horses, honey," Paige said to her.

Emma made a face. "Mom. I know that." Clem hid her smile as Emma helped George and Maddy find the end of the line. It didn't matter how hot or tired or cranky any of them felt at the end of a long day, the sound and sight of the carousel made everything feel like happily ever after.

Except for Paige. "I'm toast. Maybe I should go ahead and start loading all this stuff in the car."

"Wait and we'll help you," Clem said. "The ride doesn't take long."

Ned, who was watching the carousel indifferently, perked up. "I can get the car?" he offered. "Save you the walk carrying all this junk."

Paige didn't hesitate. "It's not junk, and you'll do no such thing."

Clem laughed. "Thanks, Neddy. Maybe next summer, when you have your license."

"But I drove Grampa's VW last summer."

The sisters exchanged a look. "Which is the other reason why you aren't getting the car now!" Paige said. "But you can take the keys, and take a bag."

Ned sighed, but didn't argue. They watched him shuffle down the sidewalk with a tote in each hand, and a beach chair slung over one shoulder. "Ah, this motherhood moment. Watching your elder child carry his own shit *and* yours."

Clem laughed, but then switched gears. "How're you doing? Things with you and David okay?"

By now most of them had heard that David had not gotten the associate professor position, though of course it had never been formally announced or acknowledged. Clem had heard it from Flossy yesterday afternoon, who had been told by Paige, in the hallway that morning. Flossy told her that she'd texted Sam the news, since she couldn't get his attention in *real-time*. Clem hadn't known her mother knew how to text, though she couldn't argue the mode of arms-length communication. It was the Merrill way.

"Can I ask you something?" Paige asked, then without giving Clem a chance to reply: "Do you think I'm intense?"

Clem blinked. The carousel had started up again, and Maddy sailed by on a white horse. "Intense?" It was like the sun asking if it was lukewarm.

"Yeah, because David seems to think that I am. He said that I'm too hard on them, that I push all of us too much."

The carousel operator lifted the ring dispenser and swung its arm out. In reply, the kids extended their right arms and leaned out over their horses' necks reaching for the ring. Clink, clink, clink. She smiled as George snagged a ring and stacked it on his horse's ear. Maddy reached and missed.

"You're committed, Paige. You always have been. To school as a kid, later to vet school. And now, work and family. It's not a bad thing."

Paige was watching the carousel now, too.

"I didn't think so. But David does."

"Well, maybe try to balance it a little. David is different, you know. It's kind of why he's a good match for you. He's laid back to your drive."

"She did it!" Paige clapped. Maddy had finally snagged a ring! Clem waved as she flew by holding it up for them to see. Clem loved this about her sister: she *was* intense, but she was in it to win. She'd been there for Clem and the kids all year, calling in. Texting a simple, *Thinking of you.* Sending silly little care packages of pretty fall leaves and back-to-school stickers for the kids. Clem often thought how exhausting it must be to be Paige; she could never do it. But as much as it drove them crazy sometimes, it was all directed at them. It was how Paige loved.

"You guys need to talk. Have you tried therapy?"

Paige shook her head. "Who has time for that?" Then, looking quickly at her sister, she retracted it. "Shit. I didn't mean it like that."

Clem put a hand on her arm. "I know. But it helps. It's helped me a lot this year. You don't have to do it all alone. Or one hundred percent all of the time."

The carousel slowed and the kids held up their stash of silver rings. "Any golds?" Clem shouted.

George shook his head good-naturedly, undid the belt, and swung his leg over his horse. Maddy scowled and waited for the ride operator to come release her. "Look at Maddy," Clem said, sighing.

Paige shrugged. "She's going for the gold. Why not?"

Back at the house dinner prep was in full swing. Flossy and Evan were in the kitchen, scrubbing a bucket of mussels between them in the sink. "What smells so good?"

Evan nodded toward the open cookbook on the island. "Mussels and brown butter leeks."

"Fantastic." Clem grabbed the open bottle of Sauvignon Blanc on the counter. "Starting early?"

"Pour yourself a glass, girl," Evan said.

She poured one for each of them, and brought his to the sink. "Mom?"

"What? No, thanks." Flossy had a look of grit on her face that went beyond the scrubbing of shellfish.

"What's wrong?"

Evan gave Clem a look of warning, then nodded quickly toward the back door.

Outside the white tent was set up, the tables arranged neatly beneath it. She gasped. "Mom! It looks amazing."

The kids trailed in with Paige. "It's like a fancy

circus," Maddy shrieked, running out the screen door to check out the white awning.

But Flossy was not happy. "It's too big. I takes up the whole area of the yard I wanted open. And don't get me started on the forecast."

"What?"

"Rain," Evan mouthed, silently.

"No!" Clem said it, then slapped her hand over her mouth as Flossy spun around.

"I'm right here," she told them both, irritably.

By the time everyone had rinsed the beach off of themselves in the outdoor shower and come in to change, the family had congregated downstairs. The kids were attempting a game of badminton in the backyard, under the tent to Flossy's chagrin. Richard was outside coaching from his Adirondack chair on the deck. The kitchen filled with the steam of simmering white wine and creamy broth. Huge hunks of crusty French bread were torn into pieces and set in baskets for dipping. A pot full of linguine simmered on the stove. Two more bottles of wine had been opened, and Clem noticed that just about everyone had a glass nearby or in hand. A good sign, she thought. People were finally letting themselves relax.

She could hear Sam out on the front porch. She refilled her wine glass and went to find him, pausing at the door.

"I'm sorry to leave another message," he was

saying, "but there's something I think we should discuss." He left his number. "It's important," he added. "Please call."

He almost ran into her as she stepped outside. "Sorry."

"Here," she said, passing him her wine. "You look like you need this?"

Sam looked away, then took the glass from her. "Yeah. I guess I do."

She watched him sip curiously. "What's going on? I thought the Shanghai thing was done."

"It is. It's something else."

Clem waited for him to elaborate, but he didn't. "Want to sit?"

Sam pointed toward the rear of the house. "Sure. But the view is back there."

"Yeah, but I can't bear to watch the kids take down Flossy's tent with a badminton racquet." She plopped on to the porch swing and patted the seat beside her.

Sam handed her back her glass and sat down.

"So, Paige and I were talking in town earlier. She and David seem . . . "

"Clemmy, I've fucked up big." Sam put his face in his hands. He looked about ready to cry, and it took her by surprise. No matter what was happening, Sam might become sarcastic or snippy. But he always remained cool.

"What happened?"

285

"You know how we have this second chance to adopt. The girl named Mara?"

Clem nodded, her stomach flip-flopping. Had Mara changed her mind, too?

"I may have said something. No, I did say something. I offered to help get her into nursing school. And to pay for it."

"Why would you do that?" As soon as the words were out of her mouth, Clem knew why Sam was a dealer. He always had been.

"And Evan found out. I told him the other day."

Clem let a long breath out. "So that's why you guys are so quiet?"

"He told me to fix it. I'm trying, Clem, but can't reach her. And even if I do, I don't know what to say. Do I start with, 'I think there may have been a misunderstanding'? Or do I run with, 'Remember that bribe I offered? Well, I'm afraid it's off the table'?"

Clem sat back in the swing and tried to wrap her mind around it. "So you made the offer, but she didn't take you up on it yet?"

"Something like that. I don't really know how she took it, to be honest. Which is why I don't know what angle to take."

Clem closed her eyes. This was so Sam. Going for what he wanted, no matter the consequences. Paige was intense, but Sam could be rabid. "I don't think you should look at it as an angle," she said finally.

He ran his hands through his hair and looked at her. "What do you mean?"

"It's not business, Sam. It's a baby. I think you need to start with the truth."

"What? Tell her I want this baby so badly that I crossed a line?"

Clem leaned forward. "Yeah. That's exactly where I'd start. I'm a mom, and while that kind of thing is ugly, and probably also illegal . . . "

"Jesus, Clem. Thanks."

"Let me finish. It's an indication of how serious you are. I think this time you need to be real."

"Isn't it also an indication of my morals?"

"Maybe. But Mara herself is in a bit of a moral predicament. She's what—nineteen? With a baby on the way, and a whole life ahead of her. And the hardest decision she may ever have to make." She looked at him. "That's about as real as it gets."

The door opened and Evan filled it.

Sam stiffened. "Hey, honey, dinner ready?"

Evan glanced between the two of them, his mouth set. Clem wondered how much he'd heard.

She jumped to her feet. "Let me help. I'll come in and set the table."

"It's already done," Evan said coolly. He stepped back inside, letting the screen slap shut before either of them could get to it.

Clem look back at Sam's miserable face. "You guys will figure this out."

From inside, Flossy's voice rang out. "Everyone to the table. Family dinner!"

Sam stood, his voice dry with sarcasm. "Oh good! Because *that* solves everything."

For once, everyone arrived en masse at the table. The din of eating ensued. Chairs scraped the floor, spoons rattled against chowder bowls, glasses clinked.

"Who wants iced tea?"

"Salad dressing, Richard?"

"Oops. Maddy needs another spoon."

"Where is that salad dressing?"

"More bread, Evan?"

"Richard, will you *please* pass that salad dressing?"

What followed, for perhaps the first time in the summer house kitchen, was near silence. Between tentative bites, Sam stole glances across the table at Evan. Maddy stared doubtfully into the shelled depths of her bowl and promptly pushed it away. Clem handed her a piece of bread. Paige dove into her meal, expertly ripping each pink mussel from its case with the tines of her fork, pitching the discarded shells into the nearest bucket with a methodical *plink*. From the head of the table came the soft slurp of Richard tipping the juice of a half-shell contentedly into his mouth, while Flossy, seated at his elbow, directed her focus around thetable, measuring each family member like some kind of barometer. No one spoke.

George, sensing the disquiet, elbowed Ned gently. "Can you get me some more?"

Ned had already emptied his bowl and was busy dragging a hunk of crusty bread through the broth. "Sure, buddy." He looked to Clem for direction. "That okay?"

"Thanks, Neddy. Maddy, what are we going to do with you?"

Maddy slumped beside her. "Nuggets."

Clem sighed and set her fork down. Her own meal was just barely touched.

"I'll get them. Let me preheat the oven first."

Sam grimaced. "Seriously? It's ninety-five degrees in here and we're preheating an oven for nuggets?" He looked to Maddy. "Come on, kiddo. When your mommy was your age, you know what Grandma used to say to us?"

George piped up. "You get what you get and you don't get upset."

Clem, however, was. "Sam, please." She got up and stalked into the kitchen, followed by her mother.

Paige shook her head. "Give everyone a break. Clem knows what she's doing."

"No one said she didn't, Paige. I'm just saying that Mom worked hard on this dinner and maybe it wouldn't kill them if the kids expanded their palates."

"It's not your jurisdiction." Paige's tone was sharp with frustration.

Sam held up both hands. "Oh, sorry Sergeant Major. That would be your detail. Right, David?"

David, who'd been looking uncomfortably between the two, shook his head. "Hey, now."

Paige's cheeks flushed. "What the hell does that mean? Don't ask David to weigh in on this." She turned to her husband and whispered, "Ignore him."

Sam returned his attention to picking through his bowl. "So, you speak for him, too, huh?"

Paige slammed the flat of her hand on the table. "Shut the hell up, Sam!"

"Enough!" Richard said.

But they were too deep into it.

Flossy came roaring back from the kitchen. "Let's everyone stop and enjoy our dinner."

"Why don't you focus on yourself some more, Sam? The week's mostly over and you've barely put your phone down from work." She turned to Evan. "Right, Evan?"

Sam scoffed.

"What?" Paige's eyes blazed. "Your spouse is off limits, but you can go after mine?"

"Maybe if you went after your own spouse, he wouldn't be *off limits to you.*"

"Sam, that's low," Evan said.

Flossy interjected. "Does anyone know how

hard I worked on this meal? Now, please! Stop arguing."

"Your mother worked hard on this meal!" Richard repeated.

Sam pointed to Clem, watching from the safe distance of the kitchen. "Then why are we cooking another?"

"Because I like nuggets!" Maddy said, giggling.

Sam turned to her, his face softening. "I know, kiddo."

"Then let it go!" Paige said. "Every time you come here it's all about you, all about your job, your downtown loft, your cushy trips that are SO hard. Meanwhile the rest of us are limping through each day with our own damn jobs, and kids, and husbands to take care of!"

Clem appeared at the head of the table, just as it went silent. Her hands were on her hips, but tears streamed from her eyes. "Not all of us, Paige. Not all of us get to do that anymore."

Evan leaped to his feet. "She's right! What's the matter with all of you. You have kids. We have spouses." His face was contorted with emotion. "And yet all you do is dig up old wounds and look for slights. You're like goddamned archeologists!" He looked at Clem. "I'm sorry, honey. We all wish we had what you and Ben had."

"But . . . " Paige began.

Evan stopped her. "And you! What Sam and

I would give for a Ned or an Emma. You've got *both*." His hands dropped to his sides, limp.

Emma was listening, her arms crossed in validation. She glared at her parents.

"Evan's right," Richard said, looking around the table at all of them. He reached for Clem and pulled her closer, against his chair. Flossy sniffed, her hand to her eyes.

There was a moment of stunned silence as everyone stared at his or her laps.

"What I meant to say . . . " Sam began.

"Just stop it," Paige snapped. "You don't need to be right all the time."

"And you don't need to always get in the last word!"

Richard banged the table with his fist. "That will do!"

Evan let out a sharp breath. "I've had enough." He stalked away from the table and out the back door. But no one was watching.

"See what you did?" Sam shouted at his sister, rising from his chair.

Paige stood up, too. "Why don't you go after him? Because you're too busy trying to win an argument!"

"Mommy, I'm hungry!" Maddy wailed.

The scent of smoke began to rise in the air, and Flossy scurried back to the kitchen. "Oh no! I left bread in the oven. It's burning!"

She opened the door and a black cloud billowed out, filling the kitchen.

Maddy shrieked and Emma scooped her up onto her lap. "My nuggets!"

George covered his ears.

Richard hurried into the kitchen after Flossy, and gallantly pulled her aside. He reached barehanded into the oven and grabbed the bread pan. There followed a gasp and a spew of curses, and the pan clattered to the floor.

"Your hands!" Flossy cried.

Paige and Sam were still shouting as Flossy grabbed both of Richard's wrists and tugged him over to the sink. She flipped on the faucet and thrust them beneath the cold rush of water.

But Richard pulled them back out and swung around, holding both red-tipped hands out as if to the gods. "That will goddamned do!" his voice boomed.

There was a collective intake of breath as all eyes swiveled to Richard, his fingers dripping water. The only sound was the strangled sob that escaped from Maddy's chest. "Grampa's mad."

And then the sound of slashing metal came from outside.

"What on earth?" Flossy hurried to screen door.

The others followed to see what was the noise.

Outside in the darkening yard, against the last

shards of yellow sunset, Evan stood over the unwieldy hedges, clippers in hand. His forearms popped through his rolled-up shirt sleeves with every slash and clip, the hedges falling left and right as he tore through them.

Clem pressed her hand to her mouth, but no sound came. She looked for Maddy and George, and herded them both away from the window.

"My hedges!" Flossy cried.

The branches gave way like dandelions to a twister, leaves and dead branches flying out and around Evan's arms as he worked.

David let out a low whistle. "Jesus."

In seconds the long-debated bushes were slashed down to dirt. A spray of twiggy detritus was flung across the grass. Evan looked up at the window, his brow soaked in sweat, his chest specked in dirt. Everyone stepped back. He flung the clippers to the ground and climbed the deck steps. They crowded like sheep as he barreled back into the house.

Evan stopped, chest heaving, in the middle of the kitchen. He stared at the aghast faces of his family, and cleared his throat. "Now, let's eat."

Paige

Her father's birthday party was tomorrow. Paige lay on her side, the gauzy light of early morning hours slipping through the bedroom curtains. Behind her, David snored lightly.

She tried to go back to sleep, but her mind drifted. Paige wondered what it was like to be seventy-five. Flossy and Richard had been married for forty-eight years. She wondered what that was like, too. A thought that made her turn over and study her husband across the pillow.

David in slumber always looked like the young man she'd met when she was still in veterinary school. He was handsome in an unassuming way, his features symmetrical and pleasing, free of distinct qualities that might thrill one but turn off another like a Roman nose or dimpled chin. His brown hair and blue eyes were agreeable and straightforward. Just like he had been and what had attracted her to him in the earlier years. These days, there was a heaviness to his eyes. His smile never quite reached them.

Dinner had taken everything out of her. They'd finished the meal in silence, and after the dishes were done and pots washed, she'd retired upstairs with a glass of water and two Advil.

Why did she let Sam get to her? They weren't teenagers anymore, and she had no issue with him, beyond his scrutiny and criticism. If he would just stay out of everyone's personal matters, they'd be fine. If she could just ignore him, they might also be fine. But no matter what the subject, his ire was always on the tip of his tongue when it came to her, and she could not seem to help herself from responding with fire. She wondered how Evan ever managed to put up with him. But, she realized, he did not treat Evan this way, or any other person as far as she knew. No, Sam had always saved his venom for her.

The thing was, the two were more alike than anyone else in the family. They were driven by some unseen urge to succeed. They were physically inclined; he'd been a basketball player and track star, and she a soccer and field hockey player. They were intensely private, and just as committed to whatever was important to them. And, too, she realized, turning over on her back: they had spouses who were suffering alongside them, and marriages that were strained. For two people who shared so much in common, she wondered at the hard fact that they could not, indeed, *share* any of it. She tried to imagine herself confiding in Sam, having a cup of tea and sitting down in a café to really talk. But maybe that was the problem: when they looked at one another it was like looking in the mirror. If you didn't like what you saw, you turned away.

She reached hesitantly under the covers and slid her hand over David's chest, pausing to press it gently over his heart. His eyes flickered.

"What? Was I snoring?"

Paige shook her head.

He turned to glance at the clock and turned back to her, squinting in the breaking darkness. "It's only five-thirty."

Paige moved her hand up his chest and along the side of his neck. She grasped his chin gently, and turned it toward her.

He blinked in confusion. "What's wrong?"

"I'm sorry."

David sighed deeply. "Paige, it's too early for this."

"No. If anything it's too late."

He rolled over onto his side and her hand slipped away.

"I'm sorry," she said, again. "Things have been so . . . I don't know, hard. I don't recognize us anymore. Whatever I've done, was because I only meant to keep everyone together."

"We're going to do this now?" David stared up at the ceiling. She waited. "I know you meant well," he said finally. "And I wish I had been more help to you. That's the thing, I guess. I feel so helpless."

"But you aren't."

"Paige. Let me finish." He turned to face her. "You are a strong woman. Hell, you're probably the strongest person I know. And I've always admired that about you."

"But?"

"But nothing. It's just that this year, I haven't been as strong. I wasn't happy at work, and then I got let go. And now, I'd give my left arm to have my old job back."

"You would?"

"Yes. Do you know I called the school and offered to be an AP last month?"

Paige propped herself up on her elbow. "What? Why didn't you tell me?"

"Because it was demeaning enough to have to call that witch back and beg. Can you imagine how much worse I felt when Marcy told me they'd hired a grad student?" David's face crumpled, and her heart went out to him.

"Honey, I wish I'd known."

"There's nothing you could've done."

"But I would've tried!"

He shook his head. "That's just it, Paige. Sometimes I need you to stop trying and just listen. To let me say that all of this really sucks, without putting one of your happy spins on it.

And maybe now and then agree with me about how much it sucks."

"I know it sucks, which is why I'm trying to help."

"But I don't need you to figure this out. Sometimes what I need is for you to stand by me while I try to. I want you to have faith in *me*."

The sun was streaking through the room now, bright fingers reaching across the blankets. A ray flashed across David's face, and the blue in his eyes flickered. Paige lay back against her pillow. "I do have faith in you." She did, but he hadn't seen it that way. In trying to encourage, she began to see that maybe she had micromanaged him. "Jesus, all this time I thought you wanted me to cheer you on. Here I've been clipping job positions and emailing you teaching announcements."

David laughed sadly. "I know. My inbox is teeming."

Paige managed a small laugh, too. "You must hate me."

"I don't hate you," David said. He rolled closer, and looked down into her eyes.

"Sometimes it feels like it."

"Then, I'm sorry." He put a hand to her cheek, and it was the most tender thing he'd done in so long that she felt she might shatter.

Paige reached for him tentatively. She slid her arm under his side and around his waist, allowing her hand to travel up his back. When he didn't pull away, her eyes filled.

"I feel invisible sometimes," she whispered. "And I'm tired. I'm so damn tired." Tears ran down her cheeks, spilling on to the pillowcase. She pulled her hand back and swiped at them.

But David grabbed it in his.

"What?"

"Let them fall," he said gently.

It only made her cry harder. "I'm a mess."

"No, you're human, Paige Merrill. I'm afraid to break it to you. And, so am I."

Paige reached for him, then, clasping his face between both hands. She couldn't recall the last time either of them had reached for the other, and it filled her with self-consciousness. But when she pressed her mouth to David's, he pressed back. He slid over and on top of her, and the pressure of his weight made her heart feel like it would burst with relief. She rose up to meet him. David slipped his hand beneath the sheets, slowly across her tummy and tugged her shorts down. Wriggling free, she wrapped her legs around him, and squeezed. When he ran his hand over her breasts, she groaned. He cupped them, one, then the other, kissing her tenderly, then hungrily.

"David, please."

Their lips never left each other's as they made

love, slowly and sadly, until the room was filled with light and her mind stilled.

Later, when she awoke, she slid from his arms and tiptoed out into the empty hall. The bunkroom door was ajar, and she peeked inside. Ned snored on his back in the far corner bunk, and below him George was tucked in like a burrito. On the girls' side, Maddy was asleep face first on her pillow, arms and legs akimbo; her sheet had been kicked onto the floor. Paige went over and pulled the sheet back up, planting a kiss on Maddy's warm head. When she stood and peered up into the top bunk, she realized it was empty. Emma's bedding was still tucked in neatly, her pillow uncreased by sleep. After the disaster that was dinner last night, Paige had gone upstairs, taken two Advil, and fallen into bed. She'd completely forgotten about the beach party.

She roused David, roughly. "Wake up," she said. "Emma's gone."

Flossy

She awoke before any of the rest of them, something she'd long done at the summer house and something she'd relished just as much. For years, when the kids were younger, she'd tried to awaken early to sneak in some alone time before the chaos of the day began. Here at the Rhode Island house, it hadn't seemed as desperate as it had at the Connecticut house, for she didn't have lunchboxes to pack or children to dress hurriedly for school. Here, it had always been summer. Days were long and luxuriously lazy, belonging solely to them. But still—there were always mouths to feed, bodies to sunscreen, beach towels to be collected and floorboards to be swept free of sand before they all fell into their beds in a dreamless sleep and awoke the next day to do it all over again. Always, there was the looming work of motherhood, and so this private time in the morning felt like a stolen glance between lovers or a long-kept secret: it was hers, and hers alone, to treasure.

The fact that the house was being sold this year lent an additional air of preciousness to it for Flossy. These mornings alone in the dark kitchen as the sunlight spilled outside were dwindling, and so she rose early determined to keep them close. She flipped on the coffee machine, ran her hand along the cool stainless steel island and padded over to stand at the backyard windows.

Tomorrow was the day! The white tent was still standing, and overhead the rising sun cast a yellow glow of early morning light that ran across its top like gold ribbon. Beyond it the ocean surface rolled gently, and Flossy opened the back door to let the sea air in for the day. She inhaled contentedly. Tonight they would go to the Ocean House for their annual family dinner, just as they did the last Saturday of their vacation every year. Richard would order a Manhattan on ice, and they'd clink glasses and eat lobster bisque, and everyone would be on their best behavior as they somehow always managed for that last dinner. It signaled the end of a week together, of their summer season, and was a bittersweet harbinger of the packing up of suitcases and impending goodbye, before everyone returned to their own lives in their own states until Christmas. It was a favorite night of Flossy's, second only to the first Friday everyone arrived. And tonight would be all the more bittersweet, because it would be the last such one.

All week she'd wondered if they should've told the kids about the sale sooner, if perhaps Richard was right. Maybe if they had, the kids wouldn't have argued so much and would have cherished the week (and each other!) more. But no, after considering that shiny-happy-people improbable outcome, Flossy stood by her decision. They each had arrived that summer with their own strains, and the news of the impending sale would just add another. She had wanted her children to all be themselves, and be themselves they certainly had. Behind her, the coffee maker chimed.

She took her mug outside to the deck. The air was crisper today, less humid, to her relief. She sat in Richard's Adirondack chair and settled back. The decimated hedges stood before her in stark ruin. Flossy shuddered at the sight up close. Never had she seen Evan lose his temper; she'd practically thought him incapable. Her own children, well, they were headstrong and bright and stubborn—and also had inherited her Irish temper, every single one of them. She'd long admired Evan's stamina against it. He was like Richard in that way, unruffled by childish looks and carelessly tossed words, unlike her own lot. Oh, perhaps she could've done more when they were young to help them bridle such emotional displays. It wasn't good for any of them. But after last night, after what Evan had suffered, it got her thinking. Perhaps it was better to blow off steam and pull a few punches along the journey, rather than hold it all in. Look at poor, sweet Evan. Look at her hedges!

She'd have to call Lucas, the landscaper, now and pay whatever it cost for him to come last minute. She'd tell him what happened. She wondered if he offered a family crisis discount.

As she sipped her coffee a flutter of movement under the tent caught her eye. She squinted, and reached for her glasses in her bathrobe pocket. Was there something left on one of the tables?

Flossy stood, setting down her coffee mug. She stepped off the porch for a closer look. Yes, there was something green resting on one of the far tables in the rear of the tent. Or rather, at the table. What on earth?

Flossy started toward it, her pace quickening as the green shape took dimension. It was a person. Sitting in a chair, their head resting on the table. She halted, alarmed at the realization. She should go wake Richard. Or one of the men. Just then, the figure moved. Flossy stepped back, tightening her bathrobe. Who was this in her backyard at this hour? The person lifted their head and looked up at her through a film of long red hair, just as a scream escaped Flossy's chest.

Flossy gasped. "Emma?"

She hurried through the tent, the dry grass prickling her bare feet. "Darling, what are you doing out here?"

Emma blinked in the bright light, as if she were waking in her own bed. "Grammy?"

Her hair hung in tangles about her face, her

freckled cheek creased where her head had rested on the table surface. She was wearing the same green sweatshirt she'd had on last night.

Flossy swept up beside her. "What on earth, child. Are you all right?"

Emma swiped a clump of hair from her face and sat back, looking around the tent. "Sorry, Grammy." Her voice was a hoarse whisper.

"What happened? Have you been out here all night?"

"Yes. I mean, no. I'm okay, really." Emma's face flushed and she stood up, but the second she did, the color left her cheeks and she began to sway. She grabbed the table with both hands and plopped back down into her chair again. "Grammy, I don't feel so good."

Flossy bent down. The acrid smell of beer and vomit coming from her beloved granddaughter made her roil back on her haunches. "Dear God! Oh my. We need to get you inside."

Emma put her head back down on the table and held a hand up. "No. No, please don't get Mom. You can't tell her."

Flossy held her breath and put a steadying arm around her. "I'm afraid your mother is the least of your worries. Can you stand up slowly, honey?"

"I don't want to. I just want to lie here. And die."

"Good grief. Don't say that." Flossy let go gently of Emma and looked around helplessly.

No one else was up, as far as she could tell. It was too far to try to haul Emma into the house alone—she could never do it. But she couldn't leave her granddaughter outside, either. She looked desperately back at the house. Then down at the beach, where the roar of the waves rose up. From here, she could see the beach path and the wild roses. And there, walking across the sand, was a man in red shorts. She recognized those shorts. Fritz Weitzman!

She bent by Emma's ear. "Honey, can you hang on a second more? I'll be right back."

Emma groaned in response.

Flossy wrapped her bathrobe tightly around her, attempted to fix her hair, and headed for the beach path. This was perhaps not the best idea; in fact she was pretty certain it was an awful one. Paige and David were the ones she should be getting right now. But Emma had begged her not to, and after last night's episode Flossy was pretty sure that this would unglue Paige. It might be better to get Emma inside and cleaned up a little first. Besides, Fritz was right there under her nose. Over the years, Fritz had just about seen it all with her family—this morning making it official—and Fritz was young and strong and present. Right now that more than qualified him for the job.

She scurried down the beach path waving her arms and calling his name over the waves. "Fritz!

Fritz, good morning!" He was standing at the water's edge, looking ready to go in.

She had to run halfway across the sand until he heard her, and when he turned and got sight of her standing in her seersucker robe in the middle of the beach the look on his face told her this was perhaps not the best idea, after all. He sprinted up to her. "Mrs. Merrill? What's wrong?"

"Fritz, I need your help."

Emma was exactly as she'd left her, slumped in her chair under the tent. Flossy's heart caught in her chest at this view of her beautiful young grandchild, and for a terrifying beat she wondered if the child had passed out. She should've called 911 instead!

Fritz didn't hesitate. "Emma," he said loudly, kneeling next to her.

She lifted her head.

"Emma, are you all right?"

She nodded very slowly, as if doing so hurt. "I'm fine."

Fritz glanced at Flossy. "I can see that. Emma, what did you take last night?"

This got her attention, and she straightened, defensively. "Nothing. I just had a beer."

"One beer?" he asked. Flossy was impressed by his calm.

She shrugged. "Maybe three."

"Oh, lord." Flossy began to panic. She should really get Paige.

"Okay, Emma. Did you throw up?" Fritz asked.

"Yes. Don't say that word," Emma groaned, putting her head back down.

Fritz took her wrist and turned it over, pressing his thumb against it. "Her pulse is strong, her color is good. I think we should get her inside."

Flossy nodded, wondering how Fritz knew all this. He'd been a lifeguard in college. She supposed they had to deal with teens and beach parties all the time.

Without waiting for a reply, Fritz tucked one arm under Emma's back and the other beneath her knees, and before she could protest he had scooped her up and was carrying her toward the house. Flossy scurried uselessly beside him. "I'll get the door!"

She tugged open the screen door and Fritz carried Emma over the threshold and into the house. They were met in the kitchen by Clem, Evan, and Ned.

"What the hell?" Ned asked.

Flossy shooed at him. "Get us some water!"

Clem stared, mouth agape. "What happened to Emma?"

Fritz carried Emma to the living room and lowered her gently onto the couch. She turned over on her side, hugging her stomach. "You may want to get her a trash can," he told them all.

Ned appeared with water. "Jeez, Em. Good going."

This time Clem swatted at him. "Did you find her outside?" Clem looked at her mother for answers.

"Evan, would you please get some wet towels I think Emma will feel better cleaned up," Flossy said. She grabbed Clem's arm and pulled her aside. "I didn't know what to do! I found her outside just now. She was sitting at one of the tables, sound asleep."

Clem let out a breath. "And Fritz?"

"Thank goodness, he was on the beach. I called for help, and he came."

"You'd better wake Paige and David," Clem told her. "This is bad."

Evan brought a glass of water and a damp towel. "It's warm," he said. Ned handed Fritz the wastebasket, and they all stood back, allowing him to take charge.

"Emma," Fritz said, still kneeling by her. "Do you still feel like you're going to be sick?" She sat up and took a small sip of water.

"You look like hell," Ned said.

She did, but she looked better, Flossy thought. "I'm okay, I think," she said in a small voice.

Fritz studied her. "You're lucky," he said. "You need to be careful, kiddo." With that he stood, and stepped back respectfully, allowing the family to move in.

Ned plopped on the chair beside the couch, keeping a safe distance. "Where'd you go last night, anyway?" Then, "Mom is going to kill you."

Evan sank onto the arm of the couch and gently pressed a towel to Emma's forehead. "Okay, Ned. Let's save it."

Flossy needed to go get Paige. But she noticed Fritz had moved to the door by then with Clem. He turned and lifted a hand in goodbye. "Oh, thank you," Flossy said, rushing over. "I'm so grateful."

"I'm happy I could help," he replied. "I hope she feels better."

"Yes, and we'll see you tomorrow night for the birthday?"

"Of course."

"And this is between us?" Flossy added. "I seem to recall a night your senior summer when we found you in the dunes . . . "

"Mom!" Clem said.

Fritz smiled politely. "Yes, of course. I believe that was my brother, Jerry, but you still have my word, Mrs. Merrill."

Clem threw her an imploring look.

"All right then. I'm going to get her parents." Emma seemed to be in better spirits, sitting upright on the couch.

"I think she needs to sleep this off," Evan said.

Flossy's chest fluttered with relief at the sight of Emma sitting up and the input of surrounding family, but this was none of their jurisdictions. Paige would be furious that she'd not been alerted thus far.

As she started up the stairs Flossy noticed Fritz lingering in the doorway. Clem was beside him, and their heads were bent together in conversation. There was something about the arc of Clem's neck in his direction, the closeness of their foreheads. Flossy halted on the bottom step and watched them. Clem laughed. And in that moment, by the way Fritz looked at her, Flossy knew.

Good lord, she thought, steeling herself. She glanced up the stairs at the steep climb. Then back across the living room, as the screen door closed and Clem stood silhouetted in the morning light watching Fritz go. Then at the couch, where everyone else sat. "I'm going to be sick!" Emma cried out.

Ned leaped back off the chair, and Clem rushed over.

Flossy cringed as her granddaughter retched audibly into the bucket. At the head of the stairs, came the creak of floorboards. Flossy looked up to see Paige.

"Where's Emma?" Paige asked. She looked frantic, as if she already sensed something was wrong.

David appeared behind her, in a T-shirt and plaid pajama pants. The two pounded down the stairs, squeezing past her.

Before they hit the bottom step, Flossy managed to get out, "I was going to make pancakes . . . and there's something else you should know."

Sam

It was probably best to get out of the house. Sam had come downstairs to find the living room empty, despite a commotion he was sure he'd heard earlier that morning. Paige and David were conferring on the front porch in low voices, bent together in some kind of unified fury.

Richard had suggested everyone "Get out and enjoy the day," and he'd taken Flossy down to the beach for a walk. Clem and the kids had gone to swim. Ned was slumped on the couch, looking dazed.

"What'd he do?" Sam had asked Evan as he scoured the kitchen for breakfast leftovers. It didn't appear there had been any breakfast, period.

"Not him," Evan had whispered. "Emma."

"Whoa." Sam actually felt bad for Paige. And even worse for Emma, who he had yet to lay eyes on. There had been a gentle moaning coming from the bunk room, and he'd steered clear.

He was glad, however, that Evan was talking to him. Flossy had given him a list of liquor to purchase and he plucked it from the front of the refrigerator. "Want to come for a ride?"

They took the old VW Bug into the center of Westerly, Sam behind the wheel. Evan seemed more relaxed, his head tipped back in the sun. But with his aviators shielding his eyes, Sam couldn't be sure of his mood. He'd checked his messages at least every five minutes all morning. Still, nothing.

They parked on Main Street and walked to the liquor store. Evan asked to see the list.

"Fifteen bottles of Moet?" he read aloud. "That sounds more like one of our parties than Flossy's."

Sam shrugged. "Whatever. I'm not about to question Flossy today."

They split up and wandered the aisles, Evan on champagne detail, and Sam went to locate a case of red and a case of white. Flossy also wanted a few bottles of Grey Goose. There were two on the shelf, so he had to ask the manager to get one more from the back. While waiting, he grabbed two bottles of Bombay Sapphire, for good measure.

He was still standing in the spirit aisle when his phone rang. The caller ID said Maryland. Sam froze. He didn't want to take the call in the liquor store, with Evan standing around the corner. But he couldn't risk losing it.

"Hello? Sam Merrill." He pushed the cart to the far corner of the store.

"Hi! It's Mara." Her bright cheerful voice

was at odds with the dark aisle of the liquor store.

Sam's heart began to pound. "Mara, thanks for getting back to me. I'm sorry to have bothered you."

"It's okay. You mentioned something important. What's up?"

Sam cleared his throat. The manager was approaching him with the bottle of Grey Goose. He wanted to wave him away.

"Do you remember that conversation we had at the end of our last meeting? When you mentioned applying to nursing school?"

"Yeah. You mean when you offered to help me out?"

Sam's stomach fell. "Yes, that's the one." He paused. "What did you think I meant by offering to help?"

There was an uncomfortable pause on the other line. "Well, I guess I thought you were offering to help me get in somehow. You made it sound like you had contacts there, or something."

Sam winced. It was what he'd said, and she interpreted it as such.

"Why? Is something wrong?"

"No, not really," Sam said. "It's just that I wanted to clarify what I meant exactly. So that there isn't any confusion moving forward. I wanted to make sure we were on the same page."

"Okay." Mara's voice sounded doubtful. Worried. Sam needed to get through this.

"I wasn't suggesting that I could guarantee your entrance, exactly. More importantly, I wasn' suggesting that Evan and I could somehow help you—financially—through school. Because tha would be . . . "

Mara didn't hesitate. "Like a bribe."

Sam exhaled. "Yeah. Something like that."

At that moment Evan pushed his cart around the corner and found him.

Sam pointed to the phone with his free hand "Mara" he mouthed. Evan's face went solemn. He started to turn the cart around, then stopped. Sam was sure he could hear his heart pounding through his polo shirt.

"Mara, I was serious when I said I wanted to help you. I've been through school twice, as an undergrad and then in business school. So I'd be happy to help you with your application or with a reference. Whatever you need."

"But not tuition?" The specificity of the word made him take a breath.

"No, I could not help you with tuition. You do understand that, right?"

There was silence, and Sam imagined her processing what he was saying. He imagined her changing her mind, leaning away from them as prospective parents to her unborn baby. He felt like a cheater and a liar, and he wouldn't blame her if she felt the same way about him. It was all true. He looked at Evan, and closed his eyes.

"Well, the way you talked about it, I kind of did think you meant to help with tuition. If we were to move ahead together with my baby."

The word *if* froze in Sam's mind. He closed his eyes.

Mara went on. "But I never assumed you meant it as a bribe, per se. I just thought you were being nice. Because I would never adopt my child out to some couple just because they offered me something. That would be awful. That would be . . ."

"Illegal," Sam said. "That would be illegal." He may as well get it all out on the table. Evan, upon hearing the word, left the cart in the aisle and walked away. Sam heard the jingle of the bell over the shop door as it opened and closed. The air conditioner roared on in reply.

"Mara," Sam continued in vain, "I'm really sorry for making that offer to you. I know this is confusing, and I'm not entirely sure what I meant by it. Evan and I like you, and I was sincere in wanting to help you. I think your aspirations are admirable, and we love the fact that you are bright and earnest—you've got your whole life ahead of you. You deserve to go to school and get that nursing degree if that's what you want. But I think I also jumped the gun. You see, Evan and I want to have a family so badly. And we've been trying for a while now. And when we met you, things just felt right to us and it felt like maybe your baby, and in some way you, could be tha family for us. And I got carried away. I'm sorry and I want to be honest with you. Whatever yo decide with your baby, and your future, yo deserve that."

There. He'd said it all, as best he could. San slumped against the cart, his hand over his face.

Mara was still there; he could feel her. "Okay then. Thank you, Sam. I appreciate that."

He could feel that their call had ended. Ther was nothing more to say. But he panicked—ther must be something more he could say. He didn' want to get off the phone without some kind o answer, some sort of sense as to where Mar was leaning. He needed to assess the damage He needed something to tell Evan. Something concrete for them to hold on to.

"Well, I'll be in touch," Mara said, finally. "O Malayka will be, okay?"

Sam's heart pounded harder. No, it was no okay. He hadn't gotten the answer he needed or any real answer, for that matter. There wa no way to know where things stood, and San did not like not knowing where things stood. H had lived life in such a way that that rarel happened to him. But he knew he had to let he go—he had to giver her time and space to make her decision. No matter how much this woul cause both him and Evan to twist in the wind while they awaited news of it.

"Enjoy the rest of your vacation," she said, brightly. Sam nodded, even though he knew she could not see him.

"Yes, we will do just that," he said, trying to mean it. "And Mara?"

"Yes?"

"Thank you for hearing me out."

"You're welcome," she said. And then the call ended.

Sam pushed both carts to the front of the store and paid for the liquor with his AmEx card. He glanced outside at the sidewalk, searching for Evan as the cashier boy slowly bagged and boxed the bottles. "Here, let me," Sam said, offering to help. He had to get out of there.

The cashier consolidated the purchase into one cart, and Sam pushed it outside into the bright day. He went to the VW. Evan wasn't in it, so he loaded the backseat and returned the cart to the storefront. He found Evan sitting on a bench, halfway down the street outside a toy store. He stared straight ahead at the window.

"What's the word?" Evan asked, when he sat down beside him. His voice was low and deep, the voice of a man. A real man, Sam thought. A man of principle.

"I tried," Sam said. "I told her what I meant, and what I could and couldn't do. I told her how much we wanted this baby, and how I got carried away. I told her everything I could think of."

Evan didn't look up. "Is there anything else?"

"I told her I was sorry."

Evan stood. "Then we wait."

Back at the house, Evan helped carry in the liquor and went upstairs to read. Richard was puttering in the kitchen, whistling to himself, making a sandwich. "Ah, good. Your mother will be pleased. What do I owe you?" he asked.

Sam held up his hand and sat down on a stool at the island. "It's fine, Dad."

His father watched him a moment, then offered to make him a sandwich. "I'm not hungry."

Richard went to the refrigerator, and pulled out ham and cheese. He grabbed a jar of pickles. "Dad, really it's okay. I'm not hungry."

Richard kept whistling. Sam watched him spread grainy mustard on the bread. He arranged three slices of ham, folded in half on one side. Then he doused the other piece of bread with mayonnaise. He took his time, and Sam found himself watching his father's gnarled hands gently handling the bread and fixings, mesmerized. "You know, when you were little, I used to make you cinnamon toast when you were upset."

Sam had not remembered that, but the second his father mentioned it, he could smell the cinnamon. "With sugar."

"Yes, and butter. Extra butter was how you liked it."

Sam smiled in spite of himself.

"It was such a pleasure to me to make that toast for you, and your sisters. Whether it was a sibling dispute or a skinned knee, or even some kid at school, the cinnamon toast seemed to work its magic every time."

He pushed the sandwich in front of Sam, and Sam picked up a half. He bit into it, the pickles crunching, and realized he was famished. "As you grew, so did the nature of the problems you kids suffered. And there came a point where cinnamon toast didn't work anymore." He paused, watching Sam tear through the sandwich. "It's a helpless thing to watch your children struggle, realizing that you don't have all the answers. And the day the kids realize that—well—that's perhaps one of the worst days of a parent's life. Up until then, you kept them safe."

Sam nodded, his mouth full. He never ate sandwiches. But this sandwich tasted so good. His father went on, "I couldn't fix your problems for you anymore, but do you remember what I used to tell you kids when things went sour?"

Sam shook his head, thinking. "Tell the truth?" He wanted to get this right. More than anything.

Richard smiled. "Speak your heart. It's the hardest thing to do, at times. And I can't guarantee it'll grant you the outcome you want. But you will never regret having done so."

Sam felt tears prick at the corners of his eyes.

He licked the mustard from his lip and met his father's gaze. "Dad, I've made a mistake. A terrible mistake."

"I tried to correct it, but it may be too late. And on top of that, maybe worst of all, I may have let down the person I love the most." Sam's tears spilled openly as he spoke.

Richard waited, watching him with concern. When he regained composure, he reached over and took the empty plate. "Did you speak from the heart?"

Sam nodded. His father came around the table and pulled him into a tight hug. Sam was taken aback by the strength of his arms, the force of his embrace. And totally unprepared for the safety he felt in that second. As quickly as he'd pulled him in, Richard stepped back. He looked Sam in the eye.

"Then, whatever happens, I'm proud of you."

Sam glanced outside. The sun was at its midpoint, just past afternoon. Soon, they would be sitting on the deck of the Ocean House for the annual summer dinner reservation. Tomorrow they would be toasting his father's birthday. And then they would all be leaving. Everything was suddenly happening too fast.

"Want to take a walk on the beach?" he asked his father.

Richard pointed to the couch. "I think I'm going to steal a nap before supper, before everyone gets back. You go ahead." Sam regarded him more carefully. Richard's gray hair was thinning over his ears, his eyes more hooded.

"Sleep well, then," Sam said. He grabbed his running shoes at the door. Suddenly he needed to be on the beach.

Sam didn't like to run at midday; the sun was too high in the sky, the day too hot. But he needed to run. He saw Clem and the kids spread out on beach blankets and chairs. Flossy tried to wave him over, but he waved and pointed down the shore.

He didn't warm up. This time he went to the water's edge and headed down the beach at a solid pace. It felt good. He moved faster.

Mara had been noncommittal, and surprisingly unemotional. Sam had expected a challenge— for her to ask that he honor his offer, as she had taken it. Or that she would get upset and turn to the agency or her attorney to dispel the facts. He was awash with relief that she had done neither; but he knew it didn't mean she still wouldn't.

Halfway up the beach he saw a woman running in front of him. She was muscled, strong, and he recognized the stride even from behind. It was Paige. Sam wasn't sure if she wanted company after that morning; certainly not his. But after trailing her at a distance for a quarter mile, he was itching to move ahead. He needed to burn off his stress.

"Hey," he puffed, pulling up alongside her.

Paige swiveled, surprised. "Oh. Hi." She didn't slow.

"Doing okay?" he asked.

She nodded, her eyes fixed on the jetty down the beach. "You?"

"Never better," he lied. It was easier. He was here to run, not commiserate.

Sam wasn't sure how long she'd been out there, but Paige had barely broken a sweat. He, on the other hand, was drenched already.

She pointed to the jetty. "Come on, like old times?" It was a challenge, the same one they'd done in high school. A few times she'd beat him, but he almost always won. He was pretty sure he still could, despite her fitness level.

"Count of three. Three."

"Two . . . " she replied.

"One!"

They broke into full sprint, side by side. Paige was shorter, and she was running faster than him already just to keep up. But keep up she did. They hit the midway point of the beach and surged ahead, hugging the water. A few times the waves came in and lapped at him, sucking the sand beneath his feet, but he was moving so quickly it didn't stand a chance. Sam laughed out loud. He felt alive.

Beside him he could sense Paige starting to struggle. She was looking at him out of the corner of her eye. He could see the sheen of perspiration on her upper arms, across her chest. She was winding, he could hear it. The jetty was closing in. He pulled ahead, and in that moment he had second thoughts. He could let her have it. Without giving it more thought, he checked his pace. Predictably Paige surged up beside him. There was a mad grin on her face, but her head was tipped back with effort. She couldn't possibly have much left in her. And then something familiar in him clicked. Sam wanted to win. He wanted to win badly.

Sam burst ahead. He expected Paige to fall behind, to disappear all together. But to his surprise she kept her ground beside him. He was running as fast as he could, legs trembling with the effort. The jetty was roaring up to meet them. His lungs burned. He pulled ahead, by just a head, and was about to declare victory when she threw herself forward and flung herself past him. They both had to slam to a halt to avoid running into the rocks.

Sam was livid.

"Yeah!" Paige shouted between breaths. She threw her arms overhead, pumped the air once. Then she fell forward in the sand, heaving. He feared she might throw up.

"What the hell's wrong with you?"

"What?"

"It's not all a competition, Paige. Jesus. All that just to beat me?"

She stood up, hands on her hips, her breath coming out in ragged puffs. "You're just mad I did."

"No Paige, I think it's pathetic that you can't ever take second place. Like it'd kill you."

She walked along the jetty, into the surf. "Grow up, Sam."

"It's not all a goddamned race, Paige. Don't you get it?" he shouted after her. "You're racing to nowhere. You're the golden child! You win."

He paced back and forth in front of the rocks, trying to catch his breath. He was mad he'd given her the lead, and more mad that he hadn't gotten it back. But more than anything, he was worried about both of them. What did it say that neither of them could ever handle being anything but on top?

Paige turned back, heading his way. "What are you talking about?"

"You, Paige. You need to win everything. Everyone sees it. And Dad—Jesus, he loves that stuff—he eats it up. I give up. You win."

Paige came up next to him, her brow furrowed. She didn't look upset, as he'd thought. She looked like she was about to laugh.

"Dad does not. All he does is talk about your work, every time I phone them. Sam is traveling again—Dubai, Los Angeles, Shanghai. Come on, you must know that."

Sam sat down in the sand. "So?"

"So, if anyone is the golden child, I'm pretty sure you wear the crown." She plopped down in the sand next to him.

"No," Sam said. "Dad loves all of us, but it's different with me. It always has been."

She looked at him. "You mean because you're gay? Or because you're a pain in the ass."

In spite of himself, he smiled. "Whatever. You don't know what it's like trying to live up to other people's expectations and being . . . different."

"Sam, you can say a lot of things about mom and dad. But you can't say they treated you differently. When you came out, I remember them being right there. They never wavered. They never held you at arms' length. I was there, remember?"

Sam put his head in his hands. He was winded and the sun was too hot, and this conversation too much. "But you didn't see the look in David's eye that I saw. Don't you remember that night Brad Aaron made a pass at you? He beat the shit out of me."

Paige reached over and touched his arm. Sam flinched. "I know. I told them all about it after."

"Well, thanks. But before you did—do you remember what dad asked me? He asked me if that fight was over a *girl*. I mean, come on. All of you must have fucking known by then, right?" Sam could barely get the words out, his heart beating faster than it had during their sprint. He felt like he might be sick.

"I do. But I don't think Dad meant to assign any hope or expectation on you with that comment, Sam. I really think he was clueless. He knew you were hurting, that you were struggling with something, like we all did. But he didn't get it. That's Dad. He's always wandering around lost in a book, lost in a fog of thought. That's just who *he* is. It had nothing do with who he wanted *you* to be."

Sam heard the words, and he tried to believe them. Oh, how hard he wanted to believe them. But there were other signs, too.

"He hurt his hand that day, Paige. He was so mad or disappointed, or whatever, that he punched something and busted up his hand. That sounds to me like disappointment."

Next to him Paige shifted abruptly in the sand. She squeezed his arm, hard. "Wait, you didn't know?"

He looked over at her. "Know what?"

"What dad did to his hand?"

Sam shook his head. "He was so mad he hit something."

"He hit something, all right. Sam, he went over to Brad Aaron's house to ask about that night. To tell his dad about me and you, and the fight at the beach party the night before."

Sam sat back, studying Paige's eyes. The green flecks flashed like they always did when she got excited. "No one ever told me that."

"Sam, Dad punched Brad Aaron's dad. Right in the face. Broke his hand doing it."

Sam exhaled in a short burst. "What?"

Paige was nodding, smiling. "Yeah, our dad the bookworm professor, who couldn't swing a hammer or trim the hedges, walked across the street to talk to Mr. Aaron about the incident with Brad. I don't think he had any intention of getting into it, physically. But things turned bad."

"How do you know?"

"I was sitting on the stairs, listening to Mom and Dad talk about it, after what happened at breakfast when you took off that morning. Mom was actually against him going over there, but he was determined."

"Did she go, too?"

Paige shook her head. "No, but I did."

Sam's eyes widened.

"I was scared. You'd run off like that, Mom and Dad were arguing in the kitchen. I wanted to know what was going to happen. So I rode my bike over after he left, and hung out in the neighbor's driveway where I could sort of hear."

"What happened?"

"I couldn't hear all of it, but it started calmly.

Dad said he wanted to talk to him. You know Mr. Aaron—not the nicest guy. He seemed to dismiss the whole thing, started blaming us kids."

"I still can't see Dad hitting anyone. It's not who he is."

Paige paused. "It's not. Dad seemed to give up and started walking back home. But then Mr. Aaron said something."

"Tell me, Paige."

She bit her lip. "He shouted after Dad. It was about you."

Sam knew immediately. He wasn't sure which name or slang word or hateful thing it was, but he knew the gist of it right then and there.

"Which word?"

Paige didn't want to say it, he could tell. But she did. "He told Dad that he should teach you how to be a man. Dad turned around and asked him what he meant. That's when Mr. Aaron said, 'You're raising a fag'."

Sam sat back on his haunches and stared at her in disbelief. "Jesus, Paige."

"I know, I'm sorry."

"No, that guy was always an asshole. It's the fact that all this time, no one ever thought to tell me?"

"I know, believe me. I raced back home. Mom shooed me upstairs when Dad came through the door with his hand covered in blood. I tried to listen in, but you know them—there was a lot of frantic whispering and Mom gasped a few times. I got the sense Mr. Aaron said something pretty awful. Later, Mom told me I couldn't say a word to you or Clem, and not to dare mention it to Dad. It was this big secret."

"But why? The things I thought over the years. I thought Dad was ashamed, or wished I'd been different." Sam stood up angrily, brushed the sand off his legs.

Paige was watching him, her expression full of concern. "If I'd known you felt that way, of course I would've told you. But you know this family. It's a vault. They never spoke of it, but neither did you."

Sam did know. He had been one, himself, for many years. He also knew what a burden it was to keep quiet over time.

"I'm sorry," she said, again.

He stood up. "You were a kid. And you did what Mom asked you to." And then Sam did something he hadn't done any time he could remember. He hugged Paige, hard.

She clapped him on the back, and he let go. Wordlessly, they both turned back for home.

Clem

S tand still, baby." Clem pinned the oversized grosgrain bow to Maddy's hair and stepped back. Maddy twirled in her sundress, the periwinkle skirt billowing out over her tiny legs like a burgeoning flower on its stem.

"Cars, everyone! Cars are leaving," Flossy called from downstairs. She clapped her hands for emphasis.

Clem did a quick inspection of herself in the mirror. Her hair was pulled back in a loose chignon, and her white tunic looked flowy and loose. Just as she felt. It had been a good week, and her chest plumed with sadness at the thought of this being the last two days.

Richard was looking rather dapper behind the wheel of the VW in a seersucker jacket.

Flossy wiggled her nose. "Really, Richard? Where on earth did you find that relic?"

"I thought you'd appreciate that it still fits." He beeped the horn for good measure.

"I want to go with Grampa!" George shouted. Clem had already explained to the kids that their boosters wouldn't fit into the rear bucket seats. They did not care.

"I don't want to sit in that baby seat anymore," George whined. "I like Grampy's car. And tonight is special!"

Clem groaned. She tugged the boosters from the back of her SUV and managed to wiggle them into the back of the Bug, mostly in position. "All right, everybody in. Ocean House, here we come."

Bay Street was teeming with tourists on a Friday night. "Isn't it quicker to just turn up Plympton Hill?" Sam asked.

"Yes, but that's not tradition," Clem told him as she cruised behind Richard and Flossy. The kids kept turning and waving at her.

"We always go down Bay Street and drive up along Bluff Avenue," Paige reminded them all. "Let's turn off the AC and roll the windows down."

Sam groaned from the passenger seat, but Evan already had his down in the back. "Good. I love looking at all the old mansions."

"It's so sad that our week is almost over," Clem said as she slowed to let a family cross.

"Ha. We have yet to survive the birthday," Sam said.

At the end of Bay, they curved left uphill along Larkin, and onto Bluff Avenue and Little Narragansett Bay sparkled under the cloudless blue sky. Immense historic Victorian mansions rose up on their right, nestled along the steep bluff. Behind them, impeccable emerald green lawns swept down to meet the beach. "My God, this is a view. It's nothing but blue sky and surf."

"And old money," Sam added. "Look, there's Taylor Swift's house."

"That would be new money," David said. They drove past a gated drive where two security guards stood at the base of the road.

"She must be in town," Evan mused. "Let's drop in for a lemonade."

Ahead, at the highest point of the bluff, the colossal Ocean House awaited. "Oh, you guys." Clem always got a little choked up when it came into view. The old hotel had been the place of many special occasions for her family over the years: graduation dinners, the announcement of her pregnancy with George. David and Paige had even honeymooned here.

They pulled into the pebbled circular drive and the valets came down the porch steps to meet them. "Every time I'm at this place I think of the Titanic," David said. "It's so grand."

The family walked up the porch steps together, and onto the sweeping deck that overlooked the Atlantic. "It's summer," Paige said. "The sunny yellow hotel. The impossibly blue skies and water. It just screams summer."

"Come on everyone," Richard called softly. They followed him to the end of the porch and looked out over the water. Hotel guests were making their way up the beach path below. The cabanas were being closed for the day, and the clink of silverware and scent of dinner wafted out from the grand dining room. They crowded at the railing and looked out, taking in the majestic views. Flossy was standing beside Clem, and she looked radiant, the sun against her profile. "It's been a good week, Mom," Clem said, leaning in to her.

Flossy smiled and raised her eyebrows. "It's been a week, that's for sure."

Dinner was long and leisurely. As was their custom, they ordered something from every course. As the drinks flowed, so did the camaraderie. Sam and Evan seemed lighter, and more chatty. Clem watched with relief as Sam rolled back the cuffs of his linen shirt and draped his arm across the back of his husband's chair. Emma, who hadn't quite recovered from the events of the night before, at least had regained her color and was able to eat something. Everyone ordered something New England: Nantucket Bay scallops, caviar, Watch Hill oysters, lobster bisque. By the end of the meal, palates and conversation were satiated. Dessert menus were passed around, and crème brulee was ordered.

Richard sat back in his seat and raised his glass. "As you all know, tomorrow evening your mother has seen fit to pay homage to the old man you call your father. Since that lovely event is taking place on the evening of our traditional goodbye dinner, we wanted to take you all out tonight, just family, to thank you for coming together this week."

He paused, looking over lovingly at Flossy. "Getting all of you together is a feat of sometimes grandiose measure these days, but you managed to all do it. And for that your mother and I are grateful. Because family is everything."

Clem glanced around the table at the faces listening in earnest.

"The town of Westerly has been a special place for our family for many years. Our summer house began as a fishing cottage for your great grandfather Richard, after whom I am named. And it was inherited by his son, my father, and later passed down to me." He glanced around the Ocean House dining room, at the oversized windows overlooking the beach in every direction. It was a clear day, and across the sound was the green outline of Block Island, and to the right, Montauk. The light was mesmerizing at that hour, washing the white tablecloths of the dining room with rosy-pink hues. "Your grandparents used to come here to dine and to dance in the Ocean House ballroom, once upon a time."

Clem smiled at Paige. They had always loved this bit of family history. "And your father and I held our wedding dinner in this very dining room," Flossy added, glancing over her shoulder at the surf outside the windows.

"The lovely view has not changed," Richard said, looking adoringly at her. "And I'm not referring to Narragansett Sound."

Flossy waved him away, with a roll of her eyes, but she was smiling.

They were spooning the last custardy remains of crème brulee from their dessert plates, when Clem spied a familiar gentleman approaching their table.

"Richard! Flossy! How nice to see you all." Richard turned in his seat to greet the man, but Clem noticed her father glance uncomfortably at her mother.

"You kids remember Mr. Wright, don't you?"

That's who he was. Maurice and his wife, Virginia, owned the house across the street from theirs and had a son who was Paige's age. Clem remembered them as being friendly; the ongoing joke being that they wished they could trade views and be on the ocean side of the street.

Maurice raised a hand in greeting to them all, smiling broadly. Her father seemed to have forgotten himself, so Paige went around the table reintroducing everyone while Richard stared blankly at his plate. Clem was about to inquire about Maurice's son, but was interrupted by Flossy who had begun to fidget with her purse. "Where's the check?" she whispered impatiently.

After an awkward beat, Richard stood. "Was nice to see you, Maurice. Please give Virginia our best."

"Of course." He said goodbye and was on his way.

Again, Richard threw Flossy a look. If Clem weren't mistaken, the two looked relieved.

"Oh, Richard, one more thing." Maurice was back.

Richard spun around to face him.

"My attorney is in Nantucket for the weekend, but we should have the offer to purchase signed and ready by Monday." He looked up at the rest of them, his eyes twinkling. "I hope we'll have as many happy memories in the house as you have all enjoyed."

Beside her Flossy's eyes widened with something akin to horror, but Clem forced herself to nod politely and return Mr. Wright's warm smile. When she glanced around the table, she saw that the rest of her family was attempting to do the same. Except for Richard, who had ducked his head as Mr. Wright walked away.

"Dad?" Clem asked, a rush of anxiety settling over her.

Paige echoed her thoughts. "What was Mr. Wright talking about?"

It was Sam who put a hand to his forehead and said the unthinkable. "You're selling him the summer house."

"You can't!" Paige cried.

"No! Why would you sell it?" Clem echoed. "You and mom love it here. We all do."

Flossy looked perturbed. "Hang on. Your father and I asked all of you if you had any interest in the house last summer. Not one of you wanted it or was in the position to take it."

"We didn't think you were serious!"

"We didn't think you'd sell it out from under us!"

"When exactly were you planning on telling us?"

Flossy threw up her hands before putting them chastely back in her lap.

"You say it every year," Clem agreed. "But you never mean it."

Flossy looked pained. "We didn't want to ruin our last week at the house."

"So you lied to us?" Paige was almost shouting.

Richard raised one gentle hand. "Everybody calm down, please. Let's discuss this rationally."

Clem looked to Sam for help; Sam always had something to say, but tonight he was quiet, a look of grim resolution on his face. She elbowed him. "What?"

"Say something!" she hissed.

Flossy beat him to it. "We knew this would be upsetting news, which is why we didn't plan to tell you until after vacation. Your father and I thought you'd enjoy your week more without this hanging over your heads, and that's what the summer house is about. Enjoying ourselves."

"So you lied to us," Paige said.

"It wasn't a lie," Flossy insisted.

Finally Sam spoke. "It was a lie by omission."

"That's not fair!" Flossy said. Her neck was flushing a deep shade of red, which was never a good sign.

Clem couldn't help it. This was all too much. Hot tears rolled out of her eyes and spilled onto her dessert plate. "But it isn't just yours to sell! It's all of ours."

Flossy turned to Clem. "It always will be, honey. Think of all the memories you have there. That won't change."

Clem pressed her napkin to her face. "What about the kids?"

George's eyes were traveling over the expressions of them all trying to ascertain how he should respond. Maddy arrived at a decision before George. She promptly burst into tears. "I don't want to move!" she cried.

"Now, now, hush . . . " Flossy leaped up and took Maddy's hand. "Come on, let's go look in the gift shop."

"I don't want a gift!" Maddy howled. "I'm moving."

Flossy tugged her hand gently. "Oh, no, sweetheart! You aren't moving."

David, who'd remained silent and looking like

he'd rather be under the table than at it, cleared his throat. "Have you accepted the offer? Has it gone to contract?"

Everyone fell silent for a beat. Richard nodded.

Sam sat back in his chair. "Well, then it's done." He motioned to the server for another cocktail.

"When?" Paige asked. Her cheeks looked hollow.

"Nothing has been signed, but we indicated we wanted one last summer."

"So this is it?" Clem asked. She was stricken with the realization.

"Which is why we are going to enjoy it!" Flossy said, returning to the table. "We are not going to fret or argue or worry. Tomorrow night we are celebrating your father's birthday and our summers here in Rhode Island. We are celebrating family! And I want every one of us to remember that." It was a command as much as a request, and although she didn't cry, Flossy's voice broke.

As everyone sat digesting the news, the table fell quiet again. Ned and Emma took the little kids out to the porch to watch the croquet players on the green below. Richard motioned for the server, and after a polite verbal scuffle with Sam over the bill, paid it. Plates were cleared. One by one, they all stood—Paige excusing herself for the restroom, Evan and David to join the others outside. Until it was just Clem and Richard. He took off his glasses.

"Daddy, there must be some other way. What if we all go in on it together?"

"Sweetheart, it's too much. Your mother and I can put this toward retirement, and to our grandkids. We want to help you with George and Maddy, for college and that sort of thing. It'd be too much of a stretch, otherwise." His voice ell away.

"But you don't have to," Clem said. "Ben took care of us, there's money left for the kids." Which was true, but so was some of what Richard had said: there was no way to tell just how long the life insurance and investments would last. She would have to go back to work, she knew. And college was something that concerned her. No, she was in no position to go in on a summer home.

Outside they waited in silence at the base of the Ocean House steps as the valets brought their cars around. "So, we'll see you at home," Richard said, solemnly.

Even though they were all returning to the same house, their soon-to-be-sold summer house, there was a heavy pause and then they each hugged and kissed their parents and thanked them for dinner.

Flossy guided the little kids into the back of the Bug. The rest of them stood in the driveway and watched the Volkswagon convertible drive away.

Emma leaned against her father. "So, this is our last summer in Westerly?"

David put an arm around each of his teens.

"Let's take a walk and give your mom a minute with her brother and sister. Evan, you're welcome to join us if you want."

Sam put a hand on Evan's arm. "Please, I want you to stay."

"Well isn't anyone else going to cry?" Clem asked. She felt like she was ten years old again, unable to contain her feelings or her words. Her siblings just stared back at her miserably.

Finally, the valet pulled around with her car. She handed the keys to Evan. "I'm too upset to drive home." The news was too fresh, too hard to hold.

David and the kids took the Volvo, and the others piled into Clem's just as they had as teenagers. As they pulled away from the Ocean House and Clem looked back at its glowing portico and the sea behind it, her heart swelled. No one spoke on the ride home.

It was late when they got back. She tucked the kids into bed, and was relieved that both were nearly asleep by the time their little heads hit their pillows. Richard and Flossy had retired to their room, wordlessly. In the kitchen, Sam, David, Paige and Evan crowded around the kitchen island.

Sam opened a bottle of Cabernet intended for the party and gave each of them a deep pour. "We knew this day would come. They're getting older. I don't blame them for wanting to let go."

Clem swung around to face him. "You're not the least bit upset?"

"Of course I am, but I also see the sense in it. It's part of their retirement. It's a smart business decision."

Paige, who'd been silent, spoke up. "We all knew it was coming, but we've had this place so long, it just seemed like we would forever."

"You can tell it hurt them," Evan said, softly. "I think Flossy's right about honoring tomorrow. Your dad's birthday, the house, all of it."

"I just don't see why they didn't tell us all sooner," David wondered aloud. "It must've been a burden for them to keep to themselves all week."

"There's got to be another way," Clem said. She wasn't willing to talk realtor-free transactions or emotional burdens. She wanted to take action. "I have some money left from Ben's estate—what if we all . . . ?"

"No!" Paige said. "You can't, Clemmy. That's an emotional knee-jerk reaction."

"But you cried at dinner," Clem reminded her. "Fine, then what about you guys?" She looked at all of them, waiting.

David winced. "Clem, I like the idea, but I'm looking for a job."

She felt awful as soon as he said it.

"And I've expanded the practice," Paige added. "Ned starts college in two years."

"So that's it, then? We just toast Dad tomorrow,

wake up the next day and pack our bags and don't look back?" Clem was furious with them all. Where was the emotion she was experiencing? Was she the only one to cherish the years here—didn't any one of them want to hang on to that, or at least try to?

"What are our options?" Sam asked.

"I don't know, but quitting out of the gate isn't like you, Sam. Where's your fight? Yours, too, Paige. You two duke it out over every dinner, but you can't summon some of that to at least consider what we can do to save this place?"

"Save it? Clemmy, it's not like someone's dying," Sam insisted.

She felt the air go out of the room. Clem closed her eyes, as the kitchen swayed in front of her. She had to get out of there.

Sam turned to her and grabbed both arms. "Wait. I didn't mean it like that."

She let Sam hold her and let him look right through her, at all the hurt she knew was behind the green eyes Ben used to sing about. Everyone was waiting to see what she'd do.

Clem laughed. She couldn't help it. A small, strangled laugh escaped her mouth. Sam squeezed her hands harder. "You know, that's the funny thing, you guys. Someone did die." She pulled her hands gently from Sam's, first one then the other. He let her.

"He already died. So you don't have to worry

about me. The worst thing that could happen already did."

"Clemmy, honey." It was Paige, in her right ear. Then Evan. The kitchen was still swaying, but it was slowing down. She thought of the orange bottle on her dresser. She could feel the dry pill under her tongue. But no. She didn't want that.

"I'll be right back," she said.

Evan looked alarmed. "Where are you going? Want me to come?"

Clem shook her head. "Just to the bathroom. I'm okay. Really."

She felt the weight of their eyes on her back as she walked to the front of the house. She opened the bathroom door, splashed water on her face and stood looking in the mirror.

When she came back out, she stopped by the front door. She could hear them talking. Probably about her. No way was she going back in there. Quietly, Clem slipped through the front door and out into the night.

The beach path was rough beneath her feet: cold sand, sharp grass. But she ran. When she reached the base, she did not head straight for the water. This time she turned right, and headed up to the Weitzmans'.

Clem was done worrying—about the kids, about getting through each day and sleeping through each night. She was tired of the empty space at the base of her spine where Ben used to rest his hand, guiding her into a room or up a sidewalk on any given day. She was tired of being alone and lonely, two things so different but that caused an ache that anchored her in place, unable to imagine allowing someone else to fill that void. Tonight something in her shifted. Whether it was the news of their beloved home, and with it all of its memories, being sold, or the realization that time went on, no matter how many things, good or bad, took place within its hours. Clem did not have hours to waste worrying anymore. All she had was right now. And right now she wanted to take some of those hours for herself, without wondering for a single beat if it was selfish or wise, and spend it. She quickened her pace across the sand.

Her way was well lit as the back porch of the Weitzmans' summer place was illuminated by the hurricane lamps on either side of the back door. She climbed the sandy stairs. Clem had not been here since she was a teenager, but nothing had changed. Through the sliding door screen she could hear music. Inside, someone stood at the kitchen sink in madras shorts. She went to the screen door.

"Fritz."

He spun around, but didn't seem surprised. "Clementine."

Fritz crossed the floor to meet her at the door,

and she watched him move toward her. He was so boyish in nature, and yet he had the build of a man. He was a man. When he opened the screen door aside, she had one question. "Are your parents back from their trip?"

He shook his head. "They drive up tomorrow." And before he could ask her what she was doing there or what she might need, Clem stepped inside, pressed her hands against his bare chest and tilted her head up to his. She kissed him firmly on the mouth, her eyes searching his face. The planes of his cheekbones, the dark lashes over his eyes. Again and again she pressed her mouth to his and he responded. Clem was not a mother, not a widower. Clem was not grieving her life, her childhood, the summers that defined her. Here, in Fritz's arms, she was flesh and bone. And longing. When he lifted her up and carried her into the living room, she curled into him like a child. Tenderly he set her upon the couch and stepped back a moment, taking her in. Under his gaze, she felt herself yield. Clem did not think about slipping her shirt up over her head. She moved fluid as water, fabric rolling over hips, hair spilling over her breasts. A skirt spilling on to the floor.

Fritz waited for her.

She reached for his hand and pulled him in, like the tide.

Paige

It was low tide, and she hiked along the exposed rocks on the bay side of Napatree Point. Sandpipers skittered along the watery outskirts. The sun was high, and she lifted her binoculars to her eyes and looked east. In the distance a shore heron stood on one leg in the shallows of a tidal pool. It arced its neck, danced forward, and speared the water. There was a splash, and it emerged with a spindly legged fiddler crab in its beak.

Paige had slept little after the last twenty-four hours. She'd thought that finding Emma hung over and sick from a night drinking at a beach party had been the worst of it. Then her parents had dropped the bomb of their house decision on all of them, in the most elegant of white tablecloth dining rooms in New England, no less. She let the binoculars hang from her neck and made her way farther up the point. Tonight was her father's birthday, and though she was sure the house would be humming with activity upon her return, she was determined to soak in the quietude of Napatree. It would get her through the day.

She didn't know what to do about Emma. Emma, her reader, her easy-going kitchen helper, who never got sucked in to the catty issues between teenage girls at school or on social media. The kid hadn't even wanted a phone, though her brother begged for one for years, and when she and David finally gave both one at Christmas, it was Emma who had asked if she could download the Audible app over Instagram. Friends had told Paige it was a matter of time, she was just a late bloomer. Maybe, she'd thought. But she hadn't believed it. When Flossy met her on the stairs yesterday morning Paige was sure it had been a mistake. Surely she meant Ned. Or maybe it was that Emma was sick—some kind of stomach bug or food poisoning—because the thought of Emma staying out all night, alone, and vomiting from having been drinking, was not something Paige could compute. It wasn't just that she was disappointed in her daughter. She was most disappointed in herself. She'd missed the signs. She hadn't seen Emma.

Paige had raced to the couch and sat beside her, running her hands through Emma's snarled hair, the stench of beer and throw-up profound in her mother's living room. "Are you all right?" she kept asking, because none of this made sense and Paige, herself, was most certainly not all right. Had it been Ned, she'd have addressed him first with concern for his physical well being, reserving the emotional display for after. She was a veterinarian, a woman of science and medicine, after all. Part of her job was the intake of urgent cases—dogs who had been struck by vehicles, femurs protruding from skin, animals in shock. There was protocol to follow, and she was experienced enough to no longer feel the press of emotion in her chest when injured animals were hauled in to her waiting room by equally distraught people. But with Emma, she'd found herself useless. She'd burst into tears and wanted to shake her.

David was the one who had handled it. After determining that she did not in fact need medical attention, he'd sent her straight upstairs to shower and go to bed. Red-faced and in sore shape, Emma had obliged. He brought her water and Tylenol, along with a plate of dry toast and the subsequently requisite trash can. David was the one who stayed upstairs working on applications from their bedroom so he could hear Emma in case she became sick again or needed them. Paige had been dispatched to the beach, by all of them.

Before they went to dinner at the Ocean House, Paige had knocked on the bunkroom door and found her alone. She'd sat on Maddy's lower bunk while Emma stood in front of the mirror brushing her hair. By then they'd covered the

351

who, what, where, when. All Paige wanted to know was, "Why?"

Emma had been forthright. "Because I wanted to know what it was like." An answer that Paige could appreciate for its bare honesty but found terrifying. Proof that no matter the number of verbal warnings or graphic news clippings a parent procured and shoved under their kid's nose, there were some kids who still needed to see for themselves. Paige had looked her in the eye and said, "That's an honest answer, honey. It's also fucking stupid."

Emma had recoiled, but Paige was all right with that. They were not done talking about it. And she realized that with two teens, they never would be. She'd left to get dressed and find a decent pair of shoes to wear.

Now, there was the matter of the summer house. It was a shock, no matter how they tried to reason with their parents' decision. Paige was attached to this house in the way she was attached to her childhood self—she thought of it fondly and she felt most like herself here. But she also didn't give it much thought. It had always been there, some childish voice in her head had reasoned, and therefore it always would be. Clem, however, was most upset. Which made sense, after all she had lost that year. But it was more than that. Paige agreed with her on some level that there should be some way to keep

352

it in the family. She did not like the thought of Emma and Ned not being able to return here to the place where she, Sam, and Clem had run barefoot through the summers of their teens and through college. To bring their own children here to toddle along the shore, giggling at the waves that lapped their toes. She'd always imagined it so. The thought it would not be brought grief.

At the end of the point, Paige stood at the water's edge. Richard had taken them here to hike when they were children, when he came up on the weekends. They'd come armed with nets and binoculars and a large metal pail. He'd point out the Piping Plovers, more plentiful in number back then, and the sandpipers. Richard taught them that the most stagnant and pungent pools were most rewarding. "The stinky spots are where you find the good stuff." He was right, and Paige would follow him right into the slime and murk of low tide with her net. Unlike her sister and brother, she never minded the effusive stench. Richard delighted in that fact. When Clemmy and Sam covered their nose and howled about the smell, Richard would lean in close and whisper to her, "tourists."

They'd identify crabs and shells, dumping them gently into the basin of the bucket to best inspect them. Afterward, he'd have them all release their treasures on the sandy stretch of sanctuary before returning home. "Leave the wild in the wild," he liked to say.

It was time to go home. Paige's sneakers were soaked with saltwater, and the briny smell of low tide reeked on the warm day. On her way back, she passed a well-dressed young couple with two boys, about George's age. The boys ran ahead, picking up bits of seaweed and clamshell. As they approached a rocky out-cropping by the water, one of the boys waved his hand in the air. "Peew! Let's get out of here."

The parents caught up to them. They were standing over a pool that she knew to be full of hermit crabs. "What is that smell?" the father asked, wrinkling his nose. He pulled the boys away from the water.

Paige continued down the beach, smiling to herself. "Tourists."

Back at the house, Flossy was beside herself. The caterers arrived at four o'clock and began setting up. Outside in the driveway cars circled in and out, unloading. White tablecloths, white lights, white candles. The florist arrived with bunches of Endless Summer blue hydrangeas, to complement the ones Clem had cut from the family garden, and she arranged them in the crystal vases Flossy had set aside earlier in the week. The scent was intoxicating.

Sandy arrived next, in her white apron, hair

pulled back in a sharp dark bun. She was efficient and calm, unlike Paige's mother who hovered and fluttered at the edge of the preparations, asking questions and worrying out loud, before alighting to another perceived near-disaster. "Are you sure those won't tip?" she asked the florist. Before turning her attention to the bartender, "No, I don't want the ice kept in that ugly bin. That's what the copper trough is for." Then, "Good Lord, *where* is the copper trough?"

Paige had dressed and done her makeup early in an effort to assist her mother, not so much in setting up, as there were certainly plenty of competent people there doing just that, but to assuage her.

"Mom. Have you had anything to eat yet?"

"Eat?" Flossy's eyes were wild. "Have you any idea how much food there will be?"

Paige put an arm around her mother. "At six, Mom. It's been hours since lunch, and you barely ate then. Have some cheese and crackers, please."

Sandy addressed Flossy. "Mrs. Merrill, I'm going to set up in the kitchen now. If you would like to go get dressed, we will be fine. The menu is set, and we've started the grill."

"But there's no ice at the bar. And I want to check the table settings."

Sandy looked at her in the same way Joe, the painter, had all week. "All taken care of, Mrs. Merrill. Now, why don't you relax and get ready?" She handed Flossy a small plate of cheese, crackers, and thinly sliced cantaloupe and directed her to the stairs.

Flossy blinked in confusion, and submitted. It was the most polite demonstration of kicking one out of one's own kitchen Paige had ever witnessed, and suddenly she wanted to hug this woman. She would make sure Richard tipped Sandy well.

Evan came downstairs in creamy linen pants and a sky-blue button down. He looked as crisp and cool as a late winter's day standing among the heated flurry of deliveries and food preparation.

"Look at you!" Paige said. He took her hand and spun her around once.

"Looking lovely, yourself, Dr. Merrill." They went outside and helped themselves to a glass of champagne each at the bar.

"Is the bar open?" David joined them, planting a kiss on Paige's mouth before ordering a beer. Things between them felt better, if not exactly right, yet. Oddly enough the incident with Emma had helped bring them closer.

"Where are the kids?" Paige asked, looking around the yard. She spied Ned, in a pink polo shirt and shorts. "Shorts? What happened to the dress pants I ironed?"

David shrugged.

She was about to trek across the yard and tell

Ned to go inside and change, but she held herself in place. Let it go, she told herself.

Clem brought the children down. Maddy wore a gingham dress with two tiny sprigs of hydrangea in each pigtail, and the effect was fairy-like. George stood like a little man in his button-down shirt, his hands in the pockets of his khakis, and for a second Paige saw Ben. She snapped a picture of him and wiped a tear from her eye. This would be a good night.

Soon the backyard was transformed. The hulking white tent that had, until then, sat in the backyard like some kind of alien landing was transformed with the glow of white lights, flowers, and the smartly dressed tables beneath it. Flossy had been right: the all-white arrangement served as the perfect backdrop to the bluff and the ocean. It let the summer evening have center stage, in all its rosy-hued glory.

"Wow. Looks like a party is about to start." She turned to Sam. The setup was complete, and now only the servers remained, working on final details as the clink of pots and utensils from the kitchen played backdrop music to the scent of dinner cooking.

"Mom did a great job," Paige agreed.

Richard and Flossy were last to come down. Her father looked like a man of only sixty, Paige thought, as he strode across the yard, Flossy's arm tucked in his. He'd chosen a beige linen suit and pink dress shirt, neatly adorned with a checkered bowtie. The Merrill children clapped as their father held his arm out and spun Flossy around one time. She radiated in a flowy pale blue dress, and Paige could swear her mother giggled.

It was then Paige realized they were not the last family members to come down. She scoured the yard and the tent. "Have you seen Em?"

David shook his head. "She was getting ready up in her room, last I knew."

Paige handed him her champagne glass and headed for the house. She was halfway up the porch steps when out of the corner of her eye she spied a young woman in a white dress standing at the far edge of the yard. She realized with a start it was Emma. Paige watched her a moment, the arch of her neck, the strong posture. She swallowed hard.

"I was looking for you," she said, as she approached.

Emma turned, and Paige saw she'd put a little mascara and lipstick on. The lipstick was a shade too dark, and for a beat Paige was tempted to blend it with her thumb, but instead she shoved her hand behind her back. "You look beautiful, honey."

"Thanks, I guess."

Paige stood next to her, looking down at the beach. The waves were small, mere ripples moving slowly in and out across the sand. Across the dunes there was a pop of movement and color: it was the Weitzmans walking down the beach path on their way over. Paige watched Mrs. Weitzman bend to remove her shoes, and Fritz took her arm. Mr. Weitzman followed carrying what looked to be a bottle of wine.

"Guests are starting to arrive. You ready?" Paige asked.

Emma didn't answer. Just as Paige was about to turn back to the party, Emma leaned over and rested her head against Paige's shoulder. She was as tall as her mother, in her heeled sandals, so that she had to bend slightly. Paige turned and pressed her nose to Emma's hair. She recognized the scent of sun and sand, and something else: the scent of her daughter. Paige closed her eyes and inhaled. "Let's go."

Flossy

Peple were having fun. She was almost sure of it, but still she kept watch over the crowd, assessing everyone. The servers were passing plates of clams casino and gravlax and roasted fig crostini. The pink grapefruit gimlets were a hit, according to members of Flossy's book club, who, to her consternation, already seemed to be on their second round. Richard looked positively at home in the crowd, greeting guests and chatting animatedly among his university colleagues. She was thrilled! But there was still no sign of Judy Broadbent.

Flossy had confided in Sandy that a guest would be bringing the stuffed oysters. To which Sandy replied, "A guest?" Her composed expression did not crack, but Flossy was sure that an eyelid had twitched slightly. There, she was right! The whole notion *was* absurd— she had it on culinary authority! The party had started at six. By six-twenty when there was still no sign of Judy, a flash of triumph ran through her. But it was quickly trailed by dread: she'd hoped for those oysters. Who was she kidding? She'd hoped even more to watch Judy teeter in her heels as she carried a tray of them over-head to the serving table. No matter, Flossy would not give Judy or the shellfish any further thought. This was *her* party.

Drinks and conversation poured beneath the tent, and everyone commented on the open-air view of the water, the lovely summer evening. *She could not have ordered a more perfect night!* Flossy kept an eye on the children as she navigated the crowd and welcomed guests. Paige and David were chatting with the Weitzmans, whom she was delighted to see had arrived. The children were circling the food tables. Maddy was holding a dangerously red Shirley Temple drink close to her gingham dress. Emma was holding something pink; Flossy was not above giving it a sniff as she passed.

"Grammy!" Emma gasped when she did just that.

She winked at her granddaughter. "Don't you look lovely."

Sam and Evan were seated at a table with Fritz Weitzman and one of the Drake boys, all childhood summer friends. Oh, how it felt like yesterday that those boys were thin wisps of children, tugging at their swimsuits to keep them up as they raced from house to house and up and down the beach trails. Flossy shook her head. The memories were as thick and syrupy as dessert wine, tonight.

It was almost time for the toast, something she had asked Sam to do. All of her children were eloquent speakers, but she'd chosen Sam. However, he had not shared the contents of his speech, despite the many times she'd inquired over the week. She hoped he'd not forgotten. She decided that she better ask him now, before dinner was announced by Sandy at seven-thirty. Flossy made a beeline for his table, just as there was a flash of silver across the way on the porch.

Flossy paused. No. It could not be. But it was. Judy Broadbent had arrived with her husband, Percy. Judy stood on the back deck, surveying the crowd. Flossy recognized Sandy and two kitchen staffers behind her, each holding large silver trays. They were not the trays Flossy had asked them to be served on. But indeed, they appeared to be stuffed oysters. The woman had gone and done it.

Judy caught her in the crowd and her lips parted in a gruesome smile. "Flossy!"

Richard met her at the deck at the same time. He looked from Judy and her husband to the servers to Flossy. "My word."

Flossy struggled to regain composure. "Judy! Percy. Welcome."

Judy did not shake her extended hand, but turned instead to the women holding the large, and presumably heavy, trays behind her. "Ta da!"

Ta da, indeed, Flossy thought.

"What did you bring?" she asked.

Judy's face fell. "Stuffed oysters." Then, "My favorite recipe."

Flossy's eyes narrowed. Not Ci Ci's favorite, but Judy's. "I can see that. Thank you."

Richard shook their hands. "Is that my favorite stuffed oyster that I see?"

Judy fluttered her eyes. "None other!"

Richard was overjoyed. "What a wonderful treat. You shouldn't have!"

"No, you really shouldn't have," Flossy echoed. She tried to remind herself that Richard was thrilled. It was his party. And that was her goal. She directed Sandy and the girls to the appetizer table. "These smell amazing," Sandy said over her shoulder to Judy. "I'd love to know how you prepared them."

If she hadn't been wearing such clunky tacky shoes, Flossy was sure Judy would have floated a little. What Sandy didn't know was that Judy had likely not prepared them. Flossy hoped that she'd also delivered them in her own car. It gave her pleasure to think of the shellfish sliding across the trays on each turn of the road, the juices seeping into the fabric of the trunk. And the subsequent stench tomorrow, on what was predicted to be a ninety-degree day.

The oysters were tucked tightly against the clams casino, which Flossy was relieved to see were largely consumed by that point. Judy's gaze darted disapprovingly between the two trays. "You had clams, as well?"

It was Flossy's turn to beam. "Anything for Richard! You know, Judy, you really should try a gimlet. So tart." Then she sailed off into the crowd.

As if on cue, there was the clang of butter knife on glass. Evan stood at the opening of the tent and called the guests over. Everyone gathered in their summer finery, goblets flashing in the setting sun, laughter echoing. They crowded around him, eyes glistening. Sam got up to speak.

"I want to welcome you all this evening to celebrate my father, Richard Merrill, on his seventy-fifth birthday." The guests hushed.

"Many of you here tonight know Richard as a friend. As a summer neighbor who likes his Manhattans on ice, or as a colleague who stayed late in his office researching for his lectures, eating peanut butter sandwiches that my mother sent with him to work, like a schoolboy." There was a chorus of light laughter.

"But I want to share with you what it was like to grow up with him as a father. Here, where we spent our childhood summers, my father enjoyed lively summer gatherings with many of you. Just as much as he liked to sequester himself in his Adirondack chair with books and papers, as he did at Fairfield University. But no matter the setting or the company, I knew him best as an avid observer. My father would awaken us late on a summer night and call us down to the dining room window to peer through the telescope at Jupiter rising. He'd pile us into the car on weekend mornings, and ferry us down to Watch Hill to walk along the harbor wall. He knew the name of each boat moored there and its origin." Paige and Clem were nodding appreciatively in the crowd, as Sam spoke. Flossy watched their reactions echo the ones in her heart.

"Dad taught us to walk slowly along the water's edge, and to abandon the trails of footprints made by others and instead stray to the piles of seaweed left at the high tide mark. He showed us how to get down—close—on our hands and knees and sift through the tangled green stuff. It was slimy, and it smelled. But that's where the treasures were: the sand dollars, the sea urchins."

Maddy squealed in the crowd. "Urchins!"

"As I grew up, there were times I struggled, as we all do. I struggled to keep good grades. I struggled to make and then break my best times on cross country." Here his voice broke. "I struggled to fit in."

Flossy's throat went dry. She watched Sam, her eyes welling with love and hurt. She found Clem and Paige, Evan and David. At the edge of the crowd, dead center, was Richard. Tears were streaming down his cheeks.

"I sometimes wondered why my father was so reserved, why he lingered quietly in the background when he could have stepped forward. Why, at times, he remained silent instead of asking questions. We were different in that way. There were times I wondered if he could really see me." Sam cleared his throat and Flossy felt the guests' collective intake of breath.

"But I was mistaken. To this day, whenever I get lost, I think back to the nights he took me fishing down on Napatree Point. It was just us and the roaring sound of the ocean. We cast our lines, and we waited in the dark. Sometimes we caught stripers, sometimes we went home without. But it wasn't about the catch we brought back to the house (to clean, much to my mother's dismay)."

Flossy smiled, as those around her chuckled. Someone put a hand on her back.

"It was the art of going back out, night after night to cast. Listening to the water, watching the tide, and trying again. My father taught me that there is beauty in silence and there is love in patience. Casting is not a science: there is faith in sometimes letting the tide take your lure, just as, at other times, there is wisdom in keeping your lines taut. Fishing lines, like children, are fickle; they snag, they tangle, sometimes they even break away. But there is an art to casting.

The flick of your wrist, the arc of the line, the hissing spin of the reel. And in that, my father is an artist."

Flossy did not hear what else Sam said, because as he raised his glass, everyone burst into applause. "To Richard Merrill. Happy seventy-fifth!"

Paige appeared at her elbow, and hugged her tight. Then Clem. Beside her Cora Weitzman was just about weeping. And Judy—standing a few feet away—was outright blubbering. Flossy made her way to Sam, to Richard, to all of them. It didn't matter what else happened that night. She'd done it: she'd gotten them all here.

Sam

He'd written out his speech by hand the night before on the back deck. All week, he'd tried to think of things to say—eloquent things that the Fairfield University crowd would appreciate, or family things that his sisters and mother would get a kick out of. But he could not get the words down any more than he could peg down the character of his father. Richard Merrill was as elusive to him now as he'd ever been.

Sam wondered if he'd grasped the truest sense of his father as a child; if his innocent perspective had best focused the lens through which he viewed the man. After all, the very virtue of youth protected one from the outside world, a cottoned buffer from experience and wisdom. Sam was now certain that we did not grow and evolve as we grew older; rather, our truest selves and sense of the world around us came through the eyes of the innocent. And so when it came time to speak of his father, Sam turned to the most visceral and prominent things he could hold: his childhood memories at the summer house.

In doing so, a speech for a birthday party for a seventy-five-year-old gentleman had been written. But moreover, the early stories of the Merrill family had been offered up to the world once more, for each of the Merrills to hold in their hands and turn over in their palms, tracing the tactile memories with their fingers in the way a little girl traces the petals of a wild beach rose or the striation of a razor clam shell. As Richard had instructed, he spoke from the heart.

During dinner, Sam had barely been able to eat. His stomach swelled with both nerves and relief, and he sat at the table among his family satiated, if not with Flossy's carefully articulated menu, then with something else he had long craved: contentment.

Guests came to offer kind words on his speech, to inquire about work, to ask if they were enjoying their summer stay. Sam visited with them all, and after dessert, which he also did not taste, he mingled. There was music. By then, the sun had given way to dusk, casting a heavenly glow through the white tent and upon the faces that gathered and danced beneath it. Sam watched Richard lead Flossy into a small opening in the tables and dance as the strands of "Moon River" played. He saw David reach for Paige, and Paige accept his hand. At the far end of the tent, he saw Clem standing shoulder to shoulder with Fritz Weitzman, taking it all in.

And across his own table his eyes finally rested on Evan, who was also watching the small group of dancers join Flossy and Richard for a slow turn.

Sam had turned off his phone for the party. He reached in his pocket and felt the hard rectangular pull of the outside world, and he decided to leave it there. There had been no call from Mara when he last checked at four-thirty. But there had been one from the agency, from Malayka. She'd left a voice mail. He'd escaped to the front porch to best hear it.

"Sam, Evan—it's Malayka calling. I know you're still on vacation, but I received word today from Mara." Sam's chest had tightened, and he'd pressed the phone hard to his ear. "As you know, the baby is not due for another month, but Mara has come to a decision. She chose the two of you." Sam had raced upstairs to tell Evan, to replay the message, over and over as they danced around the bedroom. They knew nothing was a done deal. But there was possibility. And with that came hope.

Afterward, they lay on the bed catching their breath. Sam wasn't sure if he felt more relief over the fact that Mara had chosen them, or that he had not, in fact, ruined their chance of adoption with his clumsy slip in judgment. Now, he could look Evan in the eye again. To him, that was everything.

"So, this could really happen," Sam said, as they'd lain side by side processing the news.

"It could. And if it doesn't, we'll still be okay, right?"

"Promise."

There was something else Sam needed to know. Something that had haunted him since he'd found them on the morning of their arrival in Evan's duffel bag.

"Why did you bring the baby slippers here?"

Evan turned over, nose to nose with Sam. A more open face, Sam had never seen. He knew he would answer honestly. "I don't know. I guess I wanted to bring the hope of a baby here with us."

Sam contemplated that answer. It wasn't so much that Evan was carrying the tiny pink slippers, which Sam had mistakenly assumed was some kind of talisman. It was the destination to which he'd brought them. "You mean specifically here? As in the summer house?"

Evan reached for his hand. "Yes. We have good memories here. This is a place of family."

Sam kissed him and hopped up.

"Where are you going?" Evan asked.

"I can't tell you now, but I will." He paused in the doorway. "Do you trust me?"

Evan didn't hesitate. "Yes."

Sam had gone straight to Richard, who he'd found standing at the spot where the ravaged hedges used to be, watching the landscaper plant and mulch three new hydrangea bushes in their place.

"Well," Richard had said, indicating the decimated bed of shrubs. "I think Evan did me a favor."

Sam forced a smile. "Dad, there's something I want to ask you. Can we take a walk?"

They'd walked across the yard, down the beach path, and out onto the sand. Sam was finally taking that walk his father had been inviting him to take all week. Only they did not fish or hunt for shells. They made a deal.

Now, he nudged Evan gently under the table. Evan looked up.

Sam reached into his coat pocket and took out an envelope.

"What is it?"

Sam pushed it across the table toward him. "Go on," he said. "Open it."

Evan reached for the thin white envelope, and their fingers brushed. He opened it, withdrew the paper and unfolded it carefully. It was nothing more than lined legal pad paper with a handwritten note scrawled across it. Nothing typed, nothing printed. Two signatures and a date were at the bottom. Sam watched Evan's brown eyes travel over the note once, then again. He looked up at Sam, mouth open.

"Are you serious?"

Sam hesitated. He'd done this without consulting Evan first. It might not be taken the way he'd hoped.

"We can swing this?" Evan pressed.

Sam nodded, nervously. They could, but would Evan want to?

After a moment, Evan stood and circled the table and Sam rose to meet him. Evan grabbed him, hard, by both shoulders. "For us?"

Sam thought for the second time that night that his chest might break open and he would burst into a million starred pieces, sky-bound. "Yes. So we can nest."

Clem

She stood at the head of the stairs, weighed down by so many bags, she feared she might tumble down headfirst. "Kids!" she shouted, down the hall. "It's time."

When no one answered, Clem groaned and let the bags drop to the floor. "Don't make me come down that hall." There were anticipatory giggles coming from different directions across the second floor, and she laughed, too. "I'm going to get you!"

"Ten, nine, eight . . . " She passed her parents' room, the bed neatly made, the pillows plumped at the headboard. Clem poked her head in and did a quick sweep under the bed. No children there. Outside the window, the day was quintessential summer: sky, salt air, and sea. She headed back into the hallway. Paige and David were in their room, talking quietly. Their suitcases lay open like hungry mouths on the bed, and she stopped to watch them pack. "Almost done?"

"Why does it always seem like you go home with so much more stuff than you brought with you?"

Clem studied her sister from the doorway.

She looked more relaxed than she had since arriving, more like her old self. "Are we talking physical baggage or the emotional kind?" Without waiting for a reply, she winked, and continued down the hall. "Seven, six . . . " There was a scuffle in the hall closet to her right, and she tugged the door open.

Maddy screamed and sprang out.

"Gotcha!" Clem laughed, sweeping her up. "Now help me find your brother."

They passed Sam and Evan's room, which was already packed up and emptied out. Three seashells had been left on the dresser. Maddy picked one up. Clem wondered if they would keep this room—Sam's childhood room—or if they'd move into the master next summer. The thought filled her first with sadness, then relief. The summer home was staying in the family. That was all that mattered.

"Five, four, three . . . " She reached the end of the hall. Maddy danced behind her, nearly beside herself.

"Shhh!" Clem warned her.

Clem pushed the door open to the bunkroom. It had always been her favorite. Sunlight streamed in from every window, and the old sailing cloth Flossy had fashioned down the middle to divide the girls' half from the boys' held the faint smell of age and sun. She swept it aside. There, on Ned's top bunk, was a boy-shaped lump beneath a blue blanket. ". . . two, one!" she shouted.

The bunkroom exploded with commotion as George leaped up from under the blanket. To her right, Ned flew out from behind the door, so that Maddy screamed and flung herself at her mother. Emma rolled out from under her own bed, a tangle of red hair and laughter. They all hollered and ran about, and Clem rounded them up with tickles before setting them back to work. "Strip beds, empty dressers, grab bags!" she shouted. She left them there to pull themselves together. She had one thing left to do.

Downstairs, the house was calm. Gone were the servers, the dishes cleaned and put away, the food consumed, and all of Flossy's heirloom pieces returned to the dining room table in neatly polished rows. Only the towering hydrangea arrangements remained on the kitchen island. Clem breathed deeply as she passed them.

Flossy stood at the window with a cup of coffee, watching the event company workers take down the white tent. As the poles were removed, the taut top crumpled and sunk, like a sail without wind. Flossy sighed.

"It was a good party, Mom. You did it."

Flossy turned and smiled at her youngest. "We survived it, you mean."

"That we did." Clem glanced at her watch. It was almost nine o'clock.

Richard was outside on the deck with the morning paper in hand. "Good morning, birthday boy. You're officially an old man now." She stopped by his Adirondack chair. He looked tired, but happy.

"An old goat," he said thoughtfully, setting his newspaper down.

"A handsome old goat," Clem said. She leaned over and kissed his forehead.

"Where are you off to?" he asked her.

"To say goodbye to the beach."

"Ah." Richard nodded appreciatively. "Your mother already did."

"Have you?"

He shook his head. "You know the rule. I always go last."

It was a family tradition they adhered to each summer, each one at their own time and in their own way. Flossy never made it all the way down to the sand. Instead, she'd walk to the edge of the yard and look over the bluff. "I know what's down there," she told them impatiently. "I just need a moment with the view."

Paige would run down to the beach and back in less than a minute. Clem pictured her racing down to the sand and tagging it, like some kind of relay, before sprinting back up. She could be found packing up the kitchen or organizing the car moments later. Sam would head down the beach trail, and stand at the base, hands in his pockets. Clem knew, because she'd watched him do it from her bedroom window before. But for Clem, her goodbye was a longer one. She went all the way down to the water's edge, each time. There, she'd remove her shoes, if she had any, and roll up her pants and wade in. It was a sensory thing, as much as a visual thing. She needed to hear, to see, and to feel the ocean, in all its vast breathing glory. It was a feeling she tried to summon on winter days, to sustain her through all the seasons until the next summer.

Now, standing beside her father, Clem glanced at her watch again. It was exactly nine o'clock. It was time.

On her way down she could hear the waves before she could see them. The sun bounced off the white sand, and she shaded her eyes. Her chest caught. Fritz stood down by the water, right on time, as she hoped. She had told him last night that they were not leaving until tomorrow, a white lie she'd felt bad for telling. But it was better this way. She did not want him looking for her. She did not want him to alter his morning routine to come over and say goodbye. Too many things had changed that year, and this—*this moment*—was one she wanted to keep.

The beach was empty, save for a couple with a golden retriever making their way in the opposite direction. Gulls wheeled and cried overhead. Clem glanced up and down the beach.

So much life had been lived here: the early years shaded by sun bonnets and the making of sandcastles—the dribble kind that Flossy had taught them to create. Followed by a careless stretch of teenage and college summers spent around bonfires, with nothing but their lives before them, as vast and open as the ocean they took for granted beside them. And later, her life as a wife—now a widow—and as a mother with children of her own. There was still so much living here to be done.

Ahead, Fritz had waded into the surf, and she almost called his name. But she stopped herself. She would watch him dive in, one last time. That would be a worthy goodbye, she thought. But she would not get it. As if sensing her presence, he turned suddenly in her direction. Clem raised a hand in greeting, and he jogged over to her, smiling. How she would miss this smile.

"Where are the kids?" he asked. "You guys coming down to the beach this morning?"

When she didn't say anything he looked down at her capri pants, her blouse, and the driving moccasins in her hand. "You're leaving?"

Clem nodded, sadly. Last night, as they stood outside the white tent at her father's party, Fritz Weitzman had told her he thought he was falling in love with her. Clem had nearly cried. She did not remind him of how much older she was, or how inexperienced he was, by comparison, in the world. She did not mention the geographical logistics, or his ink-still-wet law degree, or the greatest grounds of all—her children. Because while she knew all of those preexisting facts, her heart had felt a similar tug. She took his face in her hands, and kissed him, wishing things were different.

"I know what you're thinking," he'd said in a rush. "You're thinking of the kids, of our age difference. And I get it."

She'd shaken her head. "You don't know me, Fritz. Not anymore."

"No," he'd said. "You're wrong. I've known you your whole life."

They were words that tumbled through her thoughts all night.

Now, she looked into his eyes, trying to memorize them.

"Can I see you? Can I at least call you back in Boston?" he asked.

"Fritz," she said softly. Clem did not love him any more than she knew he loved her, but she allowed that maybe, another time or simply with more time, she could have. Now, she saw in him sweet youth and chance, a gamble she was not foolish enough to make, lovely as it felt. He was right that he had known her his whole life; in that way, Fritz had given something back to her that week in the summer house, a piece of her past, a piece of herself. But there was more to her than what she brought to the summer house, a life that stretched inland to a home in Boston that she needed to return to. She had growing still to do.

Clem wrapped her arms around his neck and let Fritz kiss her. His lips were warm and full, and she pressed her own against them until she tasted salt. "I'll see you next summer," she said, pulling away.

He studied her, then let go. "Next summer."

Clem looked past Fritz, at the water. The glittering surf sparkled like fractured glass, reflections splintering across the sand and all around them. She shielded her eyes with one hand. "Good-bye, Fritz." She pressed her fingers to her mouth, then his, one last time. And then she turned and ran.

Clem ran through the dunes and up the beach path, back toward the summer house. She ran until her lungs ached and her heart pounded, and she wasn't sure if the roaring in her ears was from the beach or her body, but it did not matter because she felt alive. Up ahead, she could hear her children laughing. And Flossy's voice rising above the din in the driveway, as car doors slammed and goodbyes were being said. Clem ran back, as fast as her legs would carry her, to all of it.

Acknowledgments

Thanks must be given. To my editor, Emily Bestler, of Emily Bestler Books at Simon & Schuster, I am ever grateful for your remarkable attention to detail and perfectionism that translated through edits and into the characters who traverse these pages. Our working together was a joy. Your team at EBB is simply the best!

To my agent extraordinaire, MacKenzie Fraser Bub, who has been with me since the very first book and up to the very last draft, I would not be able to sit down and put the words on paper without your support, encouragement, and constant enthusiasm. When I send you a manuscript, you accept it like birthday cake.

To my keen publicists, Ariele Fredman (big baby congrats!) and Yona DesHomes, who came on board ready to set sail. And editorial assistant, Lara Jones, who cheerfully kept things on track and was a book fairy to my daughters. To Ciara Lemery, who saved me on copy edits and protected the purity of my metaphors.

To my friends, this year has been one of great

change, and I cannot think of a step I've taken forward or backward without each of you by my side: KA, AB, AC, CD, AR, JJ, BM, JR, JS, DV—you are the divine stuff of sisterhood. From chocolate pound cakes to mostly lady-like luncheons and crappy dinner parties, you showed up. Better yet, you stayed. And to JB: what a beautiful surprise. Then and now.

This novel is about family. To my own who has cheered me on through journeys big and small, there are not words of gratitude enough even from this writer. It all went noticed— and it will always be cherished. Mom, Dad, Jesse, Josh: I love you all. The Merrills have nothing on the Robertses. And to the Chicago clan and the Connecticut cousins, and family near and far who shared turkey dinners and Cape Cod summers—you helped shape the heart at the center of this story. Family is everything.

This year found me climbing a mountain and deciding to stay awhile. Proper thanks must be given to Catharine Cooke and Ian Gribble who not only invited me up and shared their breathtaking view, but who also welcomed my children, my rescue dogs, and all seven of our chickens with Yankee warmth and British cheer. A book was written and a new chapter begun: for that, I will be ever grateful. Chicken parties, forever.

For my own little family, for Finley and Grace:

I love you up and down and inside out. You are brave and clever and beautiful and good. And I thank those lucky stars over our mountain that I am your mama. Never forget how they sparkle.

Center Point Large Print
600 Brooks Road / PO Box 1
Thorndike, ME 04986-0001 USA

(207) 568-3717

US & Canada:
1 800 929-9108
www.centerpointlargeprint.com